LISA DIETRICH

In the Midst of Light

In the Midst of Light
Copyright © 2025 Lisa Dietrich
All rights reserved.

ISBN: (ebook) 978-1-964636-64-1
(print) 978-1-964636-65-8

Inkspell Publishing
207 Moonglow Circle #101
Murrells Inlet, SC 29576

Edited By Toni Kelley
Cover art By Emily's World By Design

DEDICATION

For Jen

LISA DIETRICH

Ju su k'u
Xe'aq'an chi kaj.
Jun k'u q'ij,
Jun nay pu ik' chike.

They ascended straight into the sky:
                    one arose as the sun,
                    the other as the moon.

The Popol Vuh translated from K'iche' by Michael Bazzett

LISA DIETRICH

CHAPTER ONE

The god of death inside me craved blood.

Blood was the price of life for the ancient Maya. The gods had sacrificed their own blood to shape humanity, and in return, humanity fed them with its blood. Life—Death—Life. A cycle sustained by sacrifice.

The scent of blood coiled through the air, a single drop igniting something primal in my veins. Heat slithered beneath my skin, pooling in my throat, in my fingertips. My tongue pressed against the roof of my mouth as I forced my body to remain still. The feverish compulsion clawed at me—to drink, to drown in the warm, coppery rush of it.

I closed my eyes. Breathed in slowly. Fought for control.

"There's a first aid kit in the staff break room," I said, my voice taut.

Stella, our new administrative assistant, frowned at the papercut on her finger. "Thanks." She turned and strode out the door, still nursing the tiny wound.

A dry, rustling laugh crackled through my skull.

"Weak," Hun-Came murmured. *"You deny what you are, but your body knows the truth."*

I exhaled slowly through my nose. Hun-Came, the

Mayan god of death who had haunted me since I'd awoken in a hospital in Guatemala, continued to snicker merrily. I inhaled again exhaling slowly, pressing my hands down on top of the manila folder in front of me as if I could crush his voice beneath legal paperwork. I could not give in to my possession-induced blood cravings. I had to focus.

This was my first real court case.

For two months, I had been working as an attorney for the Global Indigenous Advocacy Alliance, a nonprofit dedicated to defending Indigenous land rights. It had taken everything—student loans, years of study, my own relentless drive—to get here. I should have felt proud. Instead, I was barely holding myself together.

My clients were fighting to enforce a Conservation Easement—a legal agreement meant to protect their land from development. The owners had violated it, blocking access to sacred grounds. The case was a battle between preservation and profit, between those who saw the land as a living entity and those who saw it as real estate.

"They do not understand the weight of the dead," Hun-Came whispered. *"Their ancestors sleep beneath that soil, their bones woven into the roots. They cry for justice."*

I squeezed my eyes shut. "This is about land rights, not death," I muttered.

"Everything is about death, little vessel. All law, all civilization— it exists in defiance of mortality. You cannot escape me by hiding in legal documents."

I returned to my notes, but my hand trembled as I wrote.

My phone buzzed. A text from my boss.

Elena: *Telephone conference with clients moved up to 3 PM. Developer's lawyers pushing for early settlement.*

I checked my watch—barely an hour to prepare. The developer had been making aggressive moves to force a low settlement, hoping the Tribal council would take quick cash rather than fight a prolonged legal battle. They didn't know how stubborn I could be.

"How stubborn 'we' can be," corrected Hun-Came.

The office door opened and Stella walked in, a band-aid wrapped around her finger. "Sorry about that. Are you feeling okay, Niki? You look pale."

"I'm fine," I lied, gathering my papers. "Just need some fresh air before the client meeting."

I made my way to the second-floor balcony and stepped outside to a picture-perfect Southern California afternoon. The cloudless blue sky and bright sunshine did nothing to dispel the exhaustion and anxiety gnawing at me. Slumping tiredly against an exterior wall, I pulled a small obsidian jaguar from my pocket. I had received it as a gift in the Guatemalan jungle and had begun carrying it with me as a talisman against the blackouts I'd been experiencing.

The blackouts were becoming more frequent. Three days ago, I'd found myself standing in my kitchen at 3 A.M., with no memory of how I'd gotten there. The week before that, I lost two hours in the middle of the day.

The smooth stone felt cool against my palm. I'd researched obsidian after I returned to California—volcanic glass, formed when lava cools too quickly for crystals to grow. A material caught between states, neither fully solid nor liquid in its atomic structure. Like me—caught between human and divine, alive yet housing death.

I slipped the obsidian jaguar back into my pocket, rubbing my thumb against the smooth cold surface, grounding myself in the weight of it.

My phone buzzed again, another text from my boss.

Elena: *I'll meet you in the conference room.*

I inhaled, straightened my blazer, and headed back inside. I had clients to meet. A case to win.

Whatever was happening to me—whatever presence had taken root in my skull, haunting my steps—none of it changed the fact that I had work to do.

But as I rode the elevator up to the conference room, the feeling gnawed at me. This tightrope I'd been walking between worlds couldn't last forever. I was going to have to choose.

The doors opened. I squared my shoulders, pushing Hun-Came's whispers to the back of my mind.

I was still Niki Balam, attorney at law.

For now.

CHAPTER TWO

I woke with a jolt, the cold concrete of the sidewalk seeping through the thin fabric of my pajama pants. My bare feet were numb, dirty, and scraped raw at the heels. A car rumbled past, its headlights momentarily blinding me as I tried to orient myself.

Where was I? How had I gotten here?

A sickly-sweet smell of rot and decay filled my nostrils despite the cool night air. I gagged, recognizing the scent—death. It clung to me like perfume, as if I'd been bathing in it.

"What did you do?" I whispered into the darkness. "What did you make me do?"

"Nothing you didn't want to do." Hun-Cames voice slithered through my mind, amused and cryptic. *"You should be thanking me. I let you sleep through the messy parts."*

"Where am I?" I demanded, looking around frantically. I recognized the neighborhood now—I was about six blocks from my apartment, standing in front of the old cemetery. Of course. Where else would the god of death take me?

"Home is that way," Hun-Came said lazily, as if directing a

lost tourist. *"Unless you would prefer to continue our explorations?"*

I wrapped my arms around my middle to ward off the chill and began walking back toward my apartment. This was the third blackout in two weeks, and by far the worst. Before, I'd woken up in my kitchen or my living room, confused but safe. Now, I was wandering the streets of Oceanside at—I checked my wrist only to realize I wasn't wearing my watch—God knows what hour it was—with no memory of how I'd gotten here.

Since I was a child, I'd been able to control my dreams. My father had taught me strategies to help me manage the night terrors I'd suffered. I could shape the dreamscape, decide where to go, what to do, but now my dreams were controlling me, or rather, he—the Mayan god of death—was controlling them.

The worst part was, I had no memory of what happened during these blackouts. In Guatemala, I'd discovered I could dream-walk—my wahy, my shadow soul, was able to infiltrate other people's subconscious minds through my dreams. It was both terrifying and exhilarating to discover this power.

But now I was afraid of what my wahy might be doing during these blackouts. Was Hun-Came, the Mayan god of death, using my dreaming ability to...do what exactly?

"Such a limited imagination for someone so gifted," he taunted. *"Dream-walking is merely the surface. Think deeper, darker, beyond the veil that separates the living from the dead."*

A chill that had nothing to do with the night air ran through me. "Are you using me to reach the dead?"

"The dead are already mine," he responded with a hint of impatience. *"It's the ones balanced on the edge that interest me. The not-quite-dead, not-quite-alive. The in-between spaces where transformation is possible."*

I quickened my pace, desperate to get back to the relative safety of my apartment. When I finally reached my building, I fumbled with the security code, my fingers trembling so badly I had to try three times before the door unlocked.

Inside my apartment, I leaned against the closed door and slid down until I was sitting on the floor. I reached for my phone on the side table where I always left it, but it wasn't there. Of course not—I wouldn't have brought it with me on whatever midnight excursion Hun-Came had taken me on.

I found it eventually, charging on my nightstand. It was 3:47 AM. I had to be at work in five hours. I couldn't go on like this.

I needed help, but the one person I thought I could count on to understand had vanished like smoke in the wind. Zen Cazares—the man who'd held me through trembling nights in Guatemala, who had promised he'd never leave me to face the darkness alone. The man who'd traced my scars with reverent fingers and whispered that we'd survived the worst together.

Until we hadn't.

He'd left his job with the DEA, returned to Guatemala, and disappeared from my life without so much as a goodbye. In my darkest moments, I missed Zen so desperately it felt like drowning—missed his steady presence, the way he'd understood the supernatural world that had claimed me, the heat of his skin against mine when the nightmares came. Had he seen what I was becoming and fled in horror? Or had he left to protect me from something worse—something he'd never had the chance to explain? The question tormented me for months.

Until I decided it no longer mattered why he left, because there was no way in hell I was ever going to ask him.

My thumb hovered over my mother's photo on my phone's contact list, but even she didn't know the full truth. I'd told her I was having nightmares, that I was struggling to readjust to normal life after Guatemala. But I hadn't told her about the blackouts, about Hun-Came's voice scraping against the inside of my skull, about the strange cravings for blood and death that made me question if I was still human.

Perhaps now it was time.

"She cannot help you," Hun-Came whispered. *"No one can. You and I are bound by blood and sacrifice. Until death do us part."*

"Shut up," I muttered, and pressed Call before I could change my mind.

It rang four times before she answered, her voice thick with sleep. "Niki? What's wrong?"

"Mom," I said, and to my horror, I began to cry. "Something's happening to me. I think... I think I'm losing myself."

There was a long pause, and when she spoke again, her voice was clear, as if she'd been expecting this call for a long time. "Tell me everything," she said. "Start from the beginning."

It's not easy confessing to your mother that a Mayan god has co-opted your soul, but then not everyone's mother is a Celtic wise woman well versed in the world of magic and demons.

"You're saying he takes control when you sleep?" My mother's voice remained calm on the speakerphone as I paced my small living room, the sky outside gradually lightening from black to deep blue.

"Not just when I sleep. I think it's happening during the day, too. Last week, I lost two hours in the middle of an afternoon. One minute I was reviewing documents for the case, the next I was sitting in my car in the parking garage with no memory of how I got there." I rubbed my temples, fighting the exhaustion that threatened to pull me under. "Mom, I'm scared. What if I hurt someone during one of these blackouts?"

She was quiet for a moment, and I could picture her sitting at her kitchen table, surrounded by the herbs and crystals that had been fixtures of my childhood. Finally, she sighed.

"The binding of a deity to a human vessel is... complicated, Niki. In the old traditions, it was never meant to be permanent. Druids would channel gods for specific rituals, then release them. Your situation is different."

"Because I wasn't trained for this," I said.

"Because you sacrificed yourself," she corrected gently. "You offered yourself willingly, with no conditions or boundaries. That creates a different kind of bond."

"Listen to the wise one," Hun-Came murmured. *"She understands the nature of sacrifice better than you do."*

"Can it be broken?" I asked, ignoring him.

Another long pause. "Not without great risk. Gods don't relinquish their vessels easily, especially gods of death. They're... possessive by nature."

"Possessive? How uncharitable. I prefer deeply invested."

"Then how do I control him? Because I can't keep waking up in cemeteries."

"You don't control gods, Niki." There was a weight to her words that made me stop pacing. "You negotiate with them. You establish boundaries. You find common ground."

I laughed bitterly. "What common ground could I possibly have with a death god?"

"More than you think. Death isn't just about ending, Nikita. It's about transition, transformation. Death is a doorway, not a wall." I heard her moving around, opening drawers. "You've always straddled two worlds—your father's and mine. That's not a weakness; it's a unique strength."

"It doesn't feel like a strength right now."

"The triskele—are you wearing it?"

I touched the pendant that hung at my throat. "Yes."

"Good. It won't block him completely, but it creates a barrier, a delineation between his consciousness and yours. It's important you maintain that barrier. Very important. The next step is communication."

"I talk to him all the time," I said. "Usually telling him to shut up."

"That's not communication, that's resistance. And resistance only makes a god push harder. You need to create a situation where you can co-exist. A truce that is mutually beneficial to both of you. You need to establish a council ground."

"A what?"

"A neutral space in your mind where you can meet as equals. The druids used sacred groves. The Maya had cenotes. You will need to create your own."

I sank onto my couch, suddenly exhausted. "How exactly am I supposed to do that?"

"Through ritual. Through meditation." I heard the familiar sound of pages turning—her grimoire, the thick leather-bound book that had been passed down through generations of women in her family. "I can guide you, but..." I heard the underlying tension in her voice.

"Mom?" I asked, my stomach churning. "What aren't you telling me?"

She paused, choosing her words carefully. "When a supernatural entity inhabits a mortal, there is always a risk to the mortal."

My heart stuttered. "What do you mean 'a risk' to the mortal?"

There was a long pause. When she spoke again her voice was clinical, like a doctor giving a patient unpleasant news. "When there are two entities occupying the same physical space, it is difficult to maintain equilibrium. One entity will usually try to overpower the other."

"What do you mean? Are you saying he will eventually overpower me?" I asked, unable to keep the panic out of my voice.

"No. That is *not* what I am saying," she replied, her voice sharp. I heard her exhale forcefully, regaining her composure. "Nikita, I want you to listen to me. You are unique. Your bond with Hun-Came is unique. Conflict between the entities can happen, but that doesn't need to be the path you take."

"She speaks wisdom," Hun-Came said, his voice unusually respectful. *"The old ways remember what the modern world has*

forgotten."

"He respects you," I told her, surprised.

"Death respects those who understand its purpose," she replied. "Now listen carefully. Tonight, before you sleep, you need to perform a boundary ritual. I'll text you the specific ingredients, but you'll need salt, water from a natural source if possible, and something that represents both life and death."

"Like what?"

"A seed. A bone. Something that speaks to the cycle."

The image of Zen's jaguar tooth pendant flashed in my mind. "I have something."

"Good. Create a circle with the salt, place water at the cardinal points, and the token in the center. Sit within this circle and invite Hun-Came to council. Not to fight, not to surrender, but to negotiate."

"Interesting," he mused. *"Traditional, yet innovative. Your mother adapts ancient practices well."*

"And what do I negotiate for?" I asked, ignoring his commentary.

"Control. Consciousness. Boundaries." Her voice softened. "Niki, you cannot expel him, not without consequences neither of you want. But you can establish terms for coexistence."

"Coexistence," I repeated flatly. "With a death god."

"With a part of yourself now," she corrected. "That's what you need to understand. Since the ritual in Guatemala, Hun-Came isn't simply possessing you. You've merged. The boundaries between vessel and deity are blurring."

Cold dread settled in my stomach. "Are you saying I'm becoming him?"

"I'm saying you're becoming something new. Neither fully human nor fully divine. It's a transformation as old as humanity itself—the apotheosis of the willing sacrifice."

"She understands more than I expected," Hun-Came said, sounding impressed. *"Few modern practitioners grasp the true nature of divine bonding."*

"I don't want to transform," I whispered. "I just want my life back."

"Oh, Niki," she said, her voice filled with love and compassion. "That's not how sacrifice works. You gave yourself freely. Now you must find a way forward in this new reality."

The sky outside had lightened to pale gray. Soon my alarm would go off, demanding I prepare for court.

"I have to go," I said. "I have a meeting this morning."

"Be careful, Niki. Strong emotions can weaken the boundaries. If you feel him pressing forward, ground yourself. Touch something natural—wood, stone. Breathe deeply. Remember who you are."

"And who am I now?" I couldn't keep the bitterness from my voice.

"You are my daughter," she said firmly. "A protector. A bridge between worlds. You always have been."

After we hung up, I sat in silence, watching the sunrise paint my apartment walls gold.

"Your mother is wise in the old ways," Hun-Came said quietly. *"She understands what you do not yet accept."*

"And what's that?" I asked aloud, too tired to care I was speaking to the voice in my head.

"That death is not your enemy. It is your inheritance."

I had no response to that. Instead, I rose and began preparing for my meeting, trying to focus on the mundane task of defending indigenous land rights while ignoring the god of death whispering in my ear and the phantom scent of decay that clung to my skin like a memory.

CHAPTER THREE

"Did I hear you on the phone last night or was I dreaming?" Sierra asked, shaking her cropped fucshia-colored hair as she blinked at me bleary-eyed across our small kitchen.

She poured herself a cup of coffee. Morning sunlight streamed through our apartment windows, making the metal on her multiple ear and nose piercings glint.

"Sorry. Did I wake you? I was talking to my mom," I said, focusing on buttering my toast to avoid her curious gaze.

"Everything, okay?"

"Yeah," I replied with a nod. My life was too complicated to try and explain to my roommate of two months.

When I was hired for a full-time position in the legal department with Global Advocacy, I had visions of living in my own apartment by the beach. Unfortunately, my meager non-profit salary wasn't enough to cover renting my own place—not in Southern California with its astronomical housing costs.

So, job offer in hand, I'd answered an ad on

roomies.com that had made me laugh:

Looking for a roommate to share 2 bed apartment who is not psychotic and will wash their own dishes. Female preferred. Do not apply if you have a drug-addicted douchebag for a boyfriend/girlfriend.

When we met, Sierra told me I was the only person who'd contacted her who seemed normal. Everyone else had some kind of red flag, plus I was single she'd explained. *"I wasn't interested in going another round with a douchebag ex."*

I rinsed my coffee cup and left it on the drainboard, grabbing my briefcase from the counter. "I have a meeting I need to get to. My first big case."

Sierra raised her cup in a toast. "Good luck."

"You'll need it," Hun-Came whispered. *"The greedy care nothing for sacred ground. They will build their houses on bones without a second thought."*

I shook my head slightly, trying to dislodge his voice as I headed out the door.

***

I pulled into our office parking lot and made my way to the conference room where Elena was already waiting. Her dark hair was pulled back in a perfect chignon, her suit crisp and immaculate. I felt rumpled by comparison—my midnight foray to the cemetery had left me exhausted, and the coffee I'd gulped down had only made me jittery, not alert.

"How are you feeling?" Elena asked, eyes narrowing as she assessed me. "You look tired."

"I'm fine," I lied. "Just nervous about the hearing."

"Why not tell her the truth," Hun-Came suggested. *"I'm sure she'll understand."*

I smiled wanly at my boss, ignoring Hun-Came's self-satisfied laughter reverberating inside my head.

As Elena and I reviewed my notes, my stomach churned with anxiety. Not just about the case, but about the blackouts, about what might happen if Hun-Came decided to make an appearance during the meeting. The triskele pendant I wore felt heavy against my chest, a constant reminder of the precarious balance I was trying to maintain.

At the time of our appointment, the developer—a large, heavy man—and his equally large attorney showed up fifteen minutes late, another one of their bullying tactics. Every interaction I'd had with them followed the same pattern they'd used to desecrate the sacred grounds of our clients: bulldoze first and ask forgiveness afterward.

They greeted us with toothy smiles, all false bonhomie. "Let's be reasonable here," the developer, Mr. Harrington, said as he settled his bulk into one of our conference room chairs. "What's done is done. We need to find a way to move forward. We're happy to compensate your clients monetarily."

"This man has no respect for the dead," Hun-Came whispered in my ear. *"Look at him. He is not healthy. He will die soon. I could kill him now if you like. Just reach out and stop his heart."*

"Stop it," I hissed out loud.

Three pairs of eyes turned to me, widening in surprise.

"Um—" I stammered, feeling heat rise to my face. "You dumped thousands of yards of construction debris and dirt on a burial site. We expect you to mitigate the damage—removing debris, restoring the site, and establishing a contribution to the preservation fund to ensure this doesn't happen again."

The meeting continued, tense and difficult. Harrington and his attorney pushed for mediation rather than litigation, offering settlements that were insultingly low. Elena remained firm, and I presented our evidence methodically, despite the constant commentary from Hun-Came about the various ways he could end Harrington's life.

By the time we finished, I had a pounding headache and a sick feeling in the pit of my stomach. Harrington and his attorney refused to meet our demands, but we held our ground. The hearing date was set, so the fight was far from over.

"You did well," Elena said as we walked back to our offices. "Don't let them intimidate you."

"I won't," I promised, though intimidation from the developers was the least of my worries.

Back at the office, Stella, our administrative assistant, was tapping her lacquered nails excitedly on her desk as I passed.

"They found another one," she said, her eyes gleaming.

"Another what?" I paused, briefcase still in hand.

Her eyes shone with ghoulish excitement. "Another mauled corpse. That's two now. They're saying there's a man-eating mountain lion stalking people. They're going to call in a bunch of authorities—state wildlife people, hunters, the works."

My stomach lurched, and I suddenly felt nauseous. Hun-Came chortled deep in my mind. *"Should we tell them the truth, my little vessel? What do you think?"*

"Some people are saying it's not a mountain lion but a serial killer," Stella continued, clearly relishing the gossip. "The bodies were found completely drained of blood."

"Is that the best she can come up with?" Hun-Came's laughter echoed through my skull, gleeful and terrifying.

I smiled weakly and excused myself, fumbling for my phone. I texted Elena.

Niki: *Not feeling well. Taking the rest of the day off if that's okay.*

Her response came quickly.

Elena: *Get some rest.*

As I drove home, my hands shaking on the steering wheel, I couldn't stop thinking about those bodies. Mauled. Drained of blood. Found during the same nights I'd experienced blackouts.

"You're catching on," Hun-Came said. *"Clever, little vessel."*

16

"What did you do?" I whispered, gripping the wheel so tightly my knuckles turned white. "What did you make me do?"

"I did not make you do anything," he replied, his voice silky with satisfaction. *"I simply unleashed what was already inside you. Your wahy is very strong. The hunger. The power. Your co-essence is jaguar. You are a predator by birth. You are more like me than you care to admit."*

"I'm nothing like you," I hissed, pulling into my apartment complex parking lot.

"No? Then why is there blood under your fingernails?"

I looked down at my hands in horror. There, crusted in the creases around my nails, was something dark red. Something I'd missed in my hasty shower that morning.

"We make quite the team," Hun-Came said. *'You and I. The lawyer who fights for justice by day and exacts it by night."*

I stumbled out of my car and barely made it to the bushes before I vomited, my entire body shaking with revulsion and fear.

Two bodies. Two blackouts.

I needed to perform that ritual my mother had described. Tonight. Before whatever it was that was happening to me happened again.

Before I killed someone else.

CHAPTER FOUR

The ingredients spilled across my kitchen counter like evidence from some bizarre crime scene—bottles of Lake Arrowhead water, bundles of dried herbs, small pouches of salt and ash, a jar of honey, and four silver bowls that had cost more than I wanted to admit. I traced my fingers over the triskele necklace my mother had given me, its triple spiral catching the afternoon light filtering through my kitchen window.

I reached into my pocket and my fingers found the obsidian jaguar figurine—a reminder of Fire Jaguar the ancient god who'd protected me in Guatemala and a talisman against—Death. I couldn't help but wonder if she had left me because I had reluctantly become the personal assistant to the Maya god of death, Hun-Came, her nemesis. The thought left me feeling bereft at the loss and angry and resentful at Hun-Came's role in my life.

Hun-Came huffed angrily, accompanied by a testy jangling of bells, making his opinion of my current thoughts quite clear.

"Don't you dare say anything. I don't want to hear it," I said to the empty kitchen. For once, he complied, though not without a final shaking of bells ensuring he had the last word.

I checked my phone—4:36 PM. The sun wouldn't set for hours, and this ritual needed moonlight. Celtic magic like this wasn't something to rush through in the harsh light of day.

I reviewed the text my mother had sent once more, scanning through her meticulous instructions for the boundary ritual. She'd included notes about the best timing—a waning moon for banishing and containment work. Tonight would be perfect; we'd just passed the first quarter.

Mom: *For a proper Celtic boundary ritual, you'll need to be barefoot, with nothing between you and the earth. And don't forget something to represent the cycle of life and death.*

With a resigned sigh, I headed to my bedroom closet. Tucked in the back corner was an old shoebox. I pulled it down, sat cross-legged on my bedroom floor, and removed the lid.

The jaguar tooth and its simple leather cord lay at the bottom, where I'd angrily tossed it months ago. I'd nearly thrown it in the trash when I found his note, but something had stopped me. Zen Cazares. The man who had rocked my world then disappeared from it, leaving me with only a hastily scribbled note and a memento meant to represent our intertwined fates. I'd been so furious I'd stuffed both the note and the tooth into this box of accumulated junk and emotional debris, burying them and my feelings for Zen under a collection of concert tickets and old birthday cards.

I ran my thumb over the jaguar tooth's smooth surface. How fitting that I now needed something from the man who had saved my life only to leave me at the mercy of a Mayan death god. The universe had a sick sense of humor.

"Balam," I murmured, thinking of my last name—my father's name. Jaguar. That was who I was. I was both a daughter of the moon and a daughter of the jaguar.

My father had been more than just the brilliant lawyer and activist I'd grown up admiring—the man who'd specialized in indigenous land rights and taught my twin sister, Nayla, and me to stand up for justice. After he died, I'd discovered he had also been a Mayan day keeper, a spiritual guide who used his skills to help others navigate the supernatural world alongside the natural one.

He'd raised me on the stories and myths of his Mayan ancestors. I'd believed that was all they were—stories and myths. That was before Guatemala. Before the Mayan god of death himself began hitching a ride on my wahy, my shadow soul, using me as a conduit to travel from the supernatural realm into this one. Now I knew the myths my father had raised me with weren't myths at all.

Slipping the leather cord around my neck, I rubbed my fingers across the smooth surface of the jaguar tooth. The unfamiliar weight of Zen's necklace settled against my sternum beside the triskele pendant my mother had given me. My recent past and my heritage, colliding in the most uncomfortable way.

I was born under the sign of I'x. My shadow soul took the form of a jaguar. Something Zen and I had in common. We were both hunters, only now I had also become prey, stalked relentlessly by Hun-Came.

Sighing, I caught sight of my reflection in the mirror—the two pendants lay side by side against my skin. And apparently, that complicated heritage is exactly what is going to help me create boundaries and protect myself from Hun-Came.

"*You do not need protection from me. You need only to embrace your true nature and accept who you are meant to be.*" Hun-Came's voice thrummed along my nerves like a plucked guitar string.

I ignored his comment and focused my attention on gathering the ingredients I needed into a basket. The silver bowls, the herbs, the salt and ash. The obsidian jaguar figurine. Each item a connection to a different part of myself.

"This should be interesting," I murmured, watching the sun begin its descent through my window. I needed to find a way to conduct this ritual, negotiate with the god of death, and hide everything from my roommate Sierra.

From the shadows in the corner of my kitchen, I swore I heard Hun-Came laugh.

I waited until almost midnight before quietly making my way to the grassy common area of our apartment complex. I hoped the other residents would be happily tucked into their beds getting their eight hours of hard-earned rest on a Monday night allowing me to conduct my ritual undisturbed.

The grass was wet and cold beneath my bare feet. As my mother had instructed, I created a circle with the salt, placed the silver bowls at the cardinal points, and poured the bottled water into them. The moonlight caught the ripples in each bowl, sending ghostly reflections dancing across the ground.

"First, connect with the earth and center yourself," my mother's text had read.

I took a deep breath, feeling the damp grass between my toes, rooting me to the ground. The night air was heavy with the scent of wet earth and the distant tang of the ocean. Moonlight bathed the common area in silvery light, transforming the mundane space into something otherworldly. The jaguar tooth and triskele pendants felt warm against my skin, as if responding to my intentions.

I placed a sprig of rosemary in the eastern bowl. "For clarity of mind," I whispered.

In the southern bowl, I dropped a bundle of dried sage. "For strength of will."

The western bowl received a pinch of ash. "For transformation and change."

And finally, in the northern bowl, I drizzled honey. "For binding and holding fast."

The night seemed to hold its breath as I stood in the center of my circle. The ritual was simple in execution but complex in meaning—a perfect melding of my mother's pragmatic approach to magic and my father's reverence for the sacred. I closed my eyes and began the chant my mother had taught me over the phone, the ancient Celtic words feeling strange yet familiar on my tongue.

"Teorainn idir dá shaol, críoch idir dá fhód..."

Boundary between two worlds, limit between two realms.

As I repeated the words, I felt a shift in the air, a density gathering around me like an electrical storm building. The jaguar tooth pendant grew hot against my chest, and I heard the unmistakable sound of tiny bells jingling in the darkness beyond my circle.

"Hun-Came," I called, my voice steadier than I felt. "I summon you to this council ground."

The air thickened and folded in on itself at the edge of my circle. The jingle of bells became louder, more insistent, like the warning rattles of a serpent. A cold wind swept through the common area, carrying with it the unmistakable scent of copal incense and something deeper, earthier—the scent of open graves, freshly turned soil, and decay.

And then he was there.

Hun-Came materialized at the edge of my circle, towering and terrible. In this world, he chose to appear much as the ancient Maya had depicted him—a skeletal figure draped in a cloak of darkest night, studded with stars that seemed to move and shift as he did. His skull-like face was painted with intricate patterns in what looked like blood and ash. Around his neck and wrists hung strings of tiny golden bells that jangled with his slightest movement. His eye sockets were empty and yet held pinpoints of cold fire that fixed on me with predatory focus.

"Daughter of Balam," he said, his voice like stone grinding against stone. *"You play with forces beyond your understanding."* His gaze moved around the circle, taking in the silver bowls

and the herbs with a dismissive glance. "*Celtic magic. What use is this power to one with the blood of jaguar in her veins?*"

I squared my shoulders. "I am both Celtic and Maya. Both are my birthright. Both are my power."

Hun-Came tilted his head, bells chiming softly. "*And yet it was your Maya heritage that allowed me passage through your wahy. It is the jaguar soul that serves me.*"

"Which is why we need to establish boundaries," I said firmly. "You can't keep using my wahy to hunt in Oceanside. People are noticing. Questions are being asked."

Hun-Came laughed, a sound like the rustling and crackling of dry leaves. "*I am Hun-Came. One-Death. Lord of Xibalba. I take what pleases me. I hunt where I wish.*" He stepped closer to the edge of my circle, and I could feel the salt barrier straining under his presence. "*And it pleases me to walk this world through you, Niki Balam.*"

"You don't have my permission," I insisted, grasping both pendants in my fist.

"*Permission?*" He seemed genuinely amused. "*Gods do not ask permission from mortals.*"

"Maybe that's why the old gods are forgotten," I shot back. "Because they never bothered to respect those who kept their memory alive."

The air around Hun-Came darkened, as if absorbing the ambient moonlight. "*Watch your tongue, child. I have been patient with you. That patience has limits.*"

I felt sweat beading on my forehead despite the cool night air. This wasn't working. Hun-Came was too powerful, too ancient to be intimidated by my makeshift ritual. I needed something more, something that would speak to him in terms he understood.

That's when I saw it—a flicker of gold at the edge of my vision. A glimmer of something bright and fast, circling high above the common area. My heart stuttered in my chest. I knew that shape, that particular shimmer of wings. I'd seen it before, in a cave in Guatemala. My sister's wahy—the golden quetzal.

My dead twin sister Nayla was here. Or at least, some part of her was.

The quetzal dove suddenly, a streak of green-gold light that spiraled down into my circle, landing beside me in a burst of radiance that momentarily blinded me. I felt a surge of power unlike anything I'd experienced before—the combined strength of quetzal and jaguar, of sun and moon, of life and death, of this world and the next.

"Nayla?" I whispered. A golden light shimmered next to me rippling in the dark night air like moonlight on water.

Hun-Came had gone utterly still, his bells silent. "The Hero Twins," he murmured, and for the first time, I heard uncertainty in his voice.

Of course. The Hero Twins of the ancient Mayan text the Popol Vuh—Hunahpu and Xbalanque. The Hero Twins who had gone into the Mayan underworld and defeated the Lords of Death through cunning and sacrifice. My father had told us those stories countless times as children. Nayla and I had even acted them out, taking turns being the brave twins tricking the death gods.

"Not quite," I said, understanding dawning; Death was a doorway, not a wall. "But we are twins. And we are here to negotiate."

Hun-Cames fiery eyes narrowed. *"There is nothing you can offer me, daughters of Balam, that I cannot claim as my own. I am Hun-Came. I am One-Death. And death cannot be tamed."*

"We can offer you recognition," I said firmly. "I can offer you a place in this world. My father was a day keeper— I can learn those ways. I can honor you properly, as he would have. In exchange," I continued. "You will respect my boundaries. You will not hunt without my consent. You will not use my wahy without my permission."

I touched the jaguar tooth hanging beside the triskele. "Then we work together. As equals. As the Popol Vuh tells us, even the Lords of Death can be transformed through understanding."

Hun-Came's laughter rang out, a discordant rattle of

bells and bones. *"A covenant that would give a mortal dominion over the god of death? I reject your proposition, daughters of Balam. I will hunt as I choose."*

Hun-Came raised his hand, and from his palm bloomed a small flame, dark as obsidian but glowing with inner light. *"Blood of the living, breath of the dead, witnessed by the moon. I am One-Death. I walk in the world of the living and rule the world of the dead. I will not be bound by one such as yourself."*

With that, he seemed to fold in on himself, collapsing into shadow and sound until nothing remained but the faint jingling of bells that faded slowly into the night.

I reached a hand toward the golden light shimmering beside me. Nayla's wahy fluttered across the palm of my hand, impossibly soft like the kiss of butterfly wings, before slowly fading and merging with the surrounding darkness.

I stood alone in my circle, the silver bowls reflecting moonlight, the scent of herbs and honey hanging in the night air. I would not concede defeat to Hun-Came. The god of death could not disguise his fear when Nayla had joined me in the circle. I understood now what my father had been preparing Nayla and me for all along. The quetzal and the jaguar, his hija del sol and hija de la luna, the twins of legend reborn. The hero twins had defeated the Lords of Death. Nayla and I would find a way to do so also.

I carefully closed my ritual, thanking each direction and element, then gathered my bowls and remaining materials. As I walked back toward my apartment, I felt different—stronger, more certain. The pendants against my skin no longer felt like conflicting heritages but complementary powers.

From the shadows, from somewhere high above, I heard the faint cry of a quetzal bird—impossible in California, yet undeniably there.

CHAPTER FIVE

So much blood. I awoke with the scent of blood in my nostrils and the sharp metallic taste of it in my mouth. As the warm liquid slid down my throat, I groaned with pleasure.

The corpse lay at my feet. Judging by the haircut, he was a young marine out for an early morning run. He'd been ambushed, his jugular vein pierced by dagger-like teeth before being dragged into the underbrush by the neck.

Hun-Came's voice sounded inside my head. "*You cannot deny what you are, my little vessel. You hunger for his blood. Your jaguar wahy craves flesh and blood.*"

"No!" I shouted angrily. Sobbing, I thrust my hands over the marines wound to try and staunch the blood flow, but it was no use. There would be no saving him.

Hun-Came had co-opted my wahy, releasing me at the precise moment of the kill to demonstrate he was in control of our relationship. He was using my shadow soul to hunt and kill for sport.

"*This is what happens when mortals presume to negotiate with gods,*" Hun-Came whispered through my mind, his voice like obsidian blades wrapped in velvet. "*Your boundaries mean nothing. Your rituals are like children's games to me. I can collapse the boundaries between the supernatural realm and this one at my choosing."*

I scrambled away from the body, my hands leaving bloody prints on the dry earth. The sun was just beginning to rise, casting long shadows through the trees along the jogging path. This was Hun-Came's message—delivered in blood and death at dawn after my midnight ritual. A divine temper tantrum.

"He was innocent," I choked out, bile rising in my throat as I looked at the young man's face. His eyes were still open, frozen in terror. What had he seen in his final moments? My face? Or the jaguar-form of my wahy with Hun-Came's death mask superimposed over it?

"Innocence is meaningless to death," Hun-Came replied. The taste of blood was overwhelming in my mouth. *"All mortals come to me eventually. Some sooner than others."*

I could feel him there, not just in my head but in my very cells, a cold presence twining through my nerves and muscles, demonstrating his power in the most horrific way possible.

"You are a vessel," he continued, the faint jangling of bells accompanying his words. *"A particularly useful one because of your heritage, but still a vessel. Do not forget your place, daughter of Balam."*

I struggled to my feet, wiping my bloodied hands on my thighs. Dawn light filtered through the trees, revealing just how much blood covered me—my hands, my chest, even spattered across my face. My triskele and jaguar tooth pendants were both stained crimson.

Even as I was repulsed by the mauled corpse at my feet, part of me craved the warm blood pooling on the ground. Its coppery scent triggered a savage hunger deep within me, leaving me thirsting for more.

"I will find a way to stop you," I promised, voice shaking.

Hun-Came's laughter echoed in my skull. *"You will try.*

And I will enjoy watching you fail." The presence retreated slightly, like a predator stepping back after making its kill. *"Clean yourself, little vessel. The sun rises, and the world of the living awakes."*

I stumbled away from the scene, keeping to the underbrush and shadows. I couldn't be seen like this. I couldn't explain this. The young marine would be discovered soon enough, another mysterious animal attack in Oceanside. The third this month.

By the time I reached my apartment complex, the sun had fully risen. I hoped to slip in unnoticed, shower, and figure out what the hell I was going to do next.

Unable to sleep after the ritual, I had opted for an early morning run, hoping it would help settle the turbulent thoughts roiling around inside my head. I hadn't counted on Hun-Came. He had made his point. The ritual had failed. I needed something stronger, something he couldn't simply ignore or overwhelm.

I slipped my key into the lock and pushed the door open, already planning my dash to the bathroom.

"What the actual fuck, Niki?"

I froze. Sierra stood in our small living room, coffee cup in hand, eyes wide with equal parts fear and disgust as she stared at me.

I glanced down at my blood-spattered running clothes. There was no hiding it. I looked like I just walked off the set of a horror movie. I stammered, trying to hide behind the door. "I…I can explain—It's not what you think," I began, knowing how pathetic that sounded. "I—I stopped, realizing there was no explanation I could give that wouldn't sound insane. I couldn't tell her the truth—that a Mayan death god had possessed my shadow soul while I was jogging and used it to kill a marine just to prove a point to me.

"Is that…oh my god! Is that actual blood?" Her eyes raked me up and down searching for an injury.

"The blood's not mine," I hastened to assure her.

29

"If it's not yours then whose is it?"

"I...I don't know."

"You don't know." Sierra stared at me; arms crossed over her chest. "Is that supposed to make me feel better? Because what I am thinking right now is that my roommate is part of some fucked-up Satanic cult." Her voice rose with each word. "I saw you last night, you know. In the common area, dancing around and chanting. And now you show up at 6 AM covered in blood?"

"It wasn't Satanic," I protested weakly. "It was a Celtic protection ritual. From my mother."

"Then how the fuck do you explain that!" She pointed to my bloodstained clothes.

"I...I...went for a run this morning and...there was an accident. I...I stopped to help." The half-lie flowed out of my mouth without any conscious input from my brain.

She stared at me incredulously.

"Look. I've got to shower and..." I held out my hands helplessly as I stepped forward. "I'm sorry. I'll clean up the mess."

"Don't come near me!" She held up her hands. "Just... just take a shower. You're dripping blood on the carpet."

I sidled past her, head down, and made my way to the bathroom, leaving a trail of red footprints on the beige rug.

"I've got to go to work, but we need to talk tonight," Sierra called after me. "My name is on the lease. I don't plan on being evicted because my roommate is someone who comes home covered in blood after performing weird rituals in the common area where everyone can see her."

Inside the bathroom, I locked the door and finally looked at myself in the mirror.

A stranger stared back at me—wild-eyed, dark hair tangled with leaves and twigs, pale face streaked with drying blood. The pendants at my neck were caked with it. I looked feral, dangerous—exactly what Hun-Came wanted me to see.

The hot water of the shower turned pink, then red, then

finally ran clear as I scrubbed myself raw. I could still taste blood, no matter how many times I brushed my teeth and used mouthwash. Hun-Came's message had been received, loud and clear.

After drying off and changing into clean clothes, I sat on the edge of my bed and pulled out my phone.

I dialed my mother.

"Niki?" Her voice was warm and slightly concerned. "It's early. Is everything alright?"

"No," I whispered, my voice cracking. "The ritual didn't work. Hun-Came... he's stronger than we thought. I...I'm in trouble. I might need a place to stay. I think my roommate is going to kick me out."

There was a moment of silence on the other end. Then my mother sighed, a sound so familiar it made my chest ache with homesickness.

"I was afraid of this," she said. "The Celtic ways can only do so much against a power like his." A pause. "Come home, Niki. We'll figure this out. I have some ideas—older rituals, stronger boundaries."

"I can't just leave," I protested, though the thought of home—of safety and my mother's wisdom—was desperately appealing. "I have a job. I can't just walk away from that."

"You can't stop him alone," my mother said firmly. "Not like this. Not unprepared." I heard rustling papers in the background.

I glanced at the jaguar tooth pendant, now clean but still carrying the memory of blood before stuffing it and my triskele pendant into my pocket. I was no longer willing to wear them around my neck. "Nayla appeared last night," I said softly. "During the ritual. Her wahy—she was there, Mom. I felt her."

My mother's breath caught. "Twins," she murmured. "Just like your father predicted." Another pause. "This settles it. You need to come home. Pack what you can and start driving today. We'll figure this out together."

Maybe a few days at home wouldn't be a bad idea. I could regroup and give Sierra a little space.

"Okay," I said finally. "I've got a few things I need to take care of first, but I'll leave today."

"Good," my mother said, relief evident in her voice. "Call me when you're on the road. And, Niki?"

"Yes?"

"Be careful."

I felt a chill pass through the room, the faintest jingling of tiny bells.

CHAPTER SIX

The work emails blurred together—another eviction case, a draft response to Harrington Developments ludicrous settlement offer. I popped into Elena's office, keeping my voice casual. "I've got a family thing this weekend. I'll be driving home. Do you mind if I take off a little early to beat traffic?"

She nodded. "Of course, not. Feel free to leave when you need to. By the way, I liked your response to Harrington. It was well written."

"Thanks." I returned to my office to pack up my laptop.

There was a light rap on my door. Stella stuck her head into my office, her gold hoop earrings jangling with excitement. "Did you hear?"

"Hear what?" I asked, already feeling the knot forming in my stomach.

"Another one!" Her eyes gleamed with morbid excitement. "A marine from Camp Pendleton. They think it's a mountain lion—the teeth and claw marks were brutal. The image is all over the internet. The thing practically took the guy's head off."

Hun-Came's voice slithered through my mind, dripping

with contempt. "*Humans. So limited in their perception.*"

"A mountain lion?" I managed, my voice sounding distant even to my own ears. The memory of blood on my hands—hands I couldn't control—threatened to overwhelm me. I dug my fingernails into my palms, using the sharp pain to anchor myself to reality.

Stella nodded vigorously. "No way it's a mountain lion. My money's on a serial killer. Or..." She leaned in conspiratorially. "Maybe a chupacabra."

Hun-Came laughed, ice scraping against my skull. "*A vampire who sucks the blood from goats? I am insulted. This one is too stupid to live.*"

"Stop," I whispered under my breath, a flash of protective anger cutting through my fear. Stella might be annoying sometimes, but she was innocent. She didn't deserve to die for a throwaway comment.

"Why not?" Stella continued, pouting a little. "Why couldn't it be a chupacabra. We don't know everything that's out there. I mean, people believe in aliens and astrology, why couldn't it be a chupacabra?"

"You're right. We don't know everything." I forced a smile. "I'm almost finished here. I'm leaving a little early today. Driving up to visit my mom."

"Good for you. Have a good weekend."

"You, too. And Stella—be careful."

She laughed. "Yeah, wouldn't want the chupacabra to get me."

After she left, I closed my office door and hissed, "You are not going to kill Stella!"

"*I do what pleases me.*"

"You just can't keep killing people." My voice cracked with desperation and rage. I was tired of being powerless, tired of waking up with blood on my hands and no memory of how it got there.

"*I am the god of death,*" Hun-Came replied. "*That is precisely what I do. Mortals do not have dominion over me.*"

"No. But they do over me," I hissed as the reality of my

situation crashed over me. I'd touched the body when I tried to staunch the blood. My DNA was on the dead marine. What if the police connected me with the murders? I began to shake, trembling so hard I could barely stand.

"I'm the one who is going to get caught not you!" I whispered.

"You are under my protection. Nothing will happen to you, my little vessel, until I decide."

I wasn't sure if that was a comfort or a threat.

"Protection?" I muttered. "You call this protection? You're using me to kill innocent people."

"Innocent?" The gods voice dripped with disdain. *"No mortal is truly innocent. Each breath they take is borrowed time. I merely collect what was always meant to be mine. Though with your help, it has become a more entertaining and enjoyable experience."*

I shuddered. "I won't be your weapon."

"You already are," Hun-Came replied, the sound of distant bells accompanying his words. *"And you will continue to be, until I decide otherwise."*

Bile, sour and salty, rose at the back of my throat as I choked on his words.

As soon as I arrived at my apartment, I texted my mother to let her know I'd be on the road in an hour, then messaged Sierra about heading home for the weekend. As I packed, my mind raced. Hun-Came wouldn't kill me—I was his vessel, his conduit to this world. When I'd severed his connection to his previous host, I had unknowingly bound myself to him. The bitter irony wasn't lost on me—I'd sacrificed myself to stop an evil shaman from binding himself to Hun-Came, only to become the Mayan death god's instrument of death.

I stuffed my overnight bag into the back of my car and climbed into the driver's seat. My phone buzzed.

Zen: *We need to meet in Cobán. As soon as possible. When can you arrive?*

Zen.

After months of silence. After disappearing without a word. After leaving me to deal with Hun-Came alone, he was finally texting me? Not just texting me, but telling me I needed to drop everything and jump on a plane to meet him in Guatemala?

I stared at the message, a confusing storm of emotions swirling inside me—relief that he was alive, fury at his presumption, and beneath it all, a treacherous longing that I couldn't seem to extinguish. The last time I'd seen Zen, he'd held me through the night as I'd trembled with fear, and shame, weeping as I confessed that Hun-Came had bound himself to my wahy. Then I'd woken to an empty bed and a hastily scrawled note.

It's safer this way.

Safer for whom? I'd wondered thousands of times since. For him? For me? Had he known what Hun-Came would do, what I would become?

Niki: *WTF?*

I typed, jabbing the keyboard display angrily. Then stopped, my thumb hovering over the screen. Instead of hitting reply, I dropped my phone into my bag and started the car. Zen had made me wait for months, now it was his turn to wait.

As I drove north to Ventura, my traitorous heart filled my mind with images of Zen—amber eyes, tawny skin, thick dark curls, faint white scars spilling down the smooth, hard muscles of his back like rivers of moonlight. He earned those scars saving my life in Guatemala. But they were also a reminder of how much he'd kept from me—a story he'd never shared, a piece of his past that he'd locked away.

"Alejandro Lorenzo Rafael Ignacio Cazares y Mendoza," I whispered the syllables of his full name like a spell on my tongue—each one a memory, a caress, a prayer

I'd whispered against his skin.

"Ah," Hun-Came's voice materialized, sharp as obsidian. *"You remember his full name."*

I gripped the steering wheel tighter, my knuckles white. "What do you know about Zen?"

A low chuckle echoed through my head, making my bones ache. *"More than you, little vessel. Far more."*

A cold finger of dread traced my spine, but beneath it burned something hotter—the memory of Zen's hands tangled in my hair, his voice rough with desire. "What does that mean?"

"He understands the power that death commands," Hun-Came said, his voice silky with malice. *"He recognized what you had become before you did. Why do you think he ran?"*

I flinched as if struck. The same thought had haunted me for months—that Zen had looked at me after I'd confessed about my connection to Hun-Came and seen only a monster, a vessel for death.

"He looked into your eyes that last morning and saw death staring back," Hun-Came continued, relentless. *"Saw the blood that would stain your hands. Saw me."*

Tears blurred my vision, and I had to pull over, my whole body shaking with the force of suppressed sobs. The memory of our last night together—tender, desperate, like he was trying to memorize me—now felt like a funeral rite. Had he been saying goodbye to the woman I used to be? Had he already mourned me while I slept in his arms?

Part of me had hoped his message meant he'd found a way to free me, that love could conquer even a death god's claim. But a larger, more broken part of me feared what he would see when he looked at me now—not the woman who'd fought beside him in the jungle, but a killer with innocent blood on her hands and darkness pooling in her eyes.

Eventually, I eased myself back onto the road, tension coiling in my muscles. By the time I turned onto the familiar street of my childhood home, my neck and shoulders were stiff with fatigue and stress. The afternoon light was fading, casting long shadows across the weathered wooden fence and my mother's herb garden.

My mother stood waiting on the porch. Even from a distance, I could see the worry etched into her face. She looked older than I remembered—her auburn hair now streaked with more silver, lines of concern bracketing her eyes.

I parked and stepped out of the car. Before I could take two steps, she was walking toward me, her movements a mix of urgency and caution.

"Niki," she said, not quite a greeting, not quite a question.

I dropped my bag and walked into her arms. For a moment, I was a child again, safe, protected. Then the weight of Hun-Came, the marine's death, Zen's mysterious message—all of it crashed back.

"He killed again," I whispered into her shoulder.

Her arms tightened around me. "I know," she said softly. "We'll figure this out."

Somewhere in the shadows, I felt Hun-Came watching, waiting, his presence a cold whisper just beyond perception.

My mom had prepared dinner—a simple meal of tomato soup and grilled cheese sandwiches on her fresh-baked bread, comfort food from my childhood. We sat at the kitchen table as the savory scent filled the warm kitchen.

"Tell me about Nayla," she said suddenly, setting down her spoon.

She closed her eyes and breathed deeply. Guilt pricked my heart as I told her what I had seen— Nayla's shadow soul taking the form of a golden quetzal bird, soaring through realms I could barely comprehend. My mother's expression grew sad but not surprised. She understood better than most the fluidity between supernatural and natural realms, having merged her druid traditions with my father's Mayan ones when they married. But understanding didn't ease the loss of her daughter.

"Some bonds can survive death. It gives me a great deal of comfort to know Nayla is still part of the universe. Still supporting her sister." She took a deep breath. "Tisane?"

I nodded, grateful for the familiar ritual.

"Lavender or chamomile?" she asked, already reaching for the canister of dried lavender buds.

"Lavender." Old remedies from my childhood to promote sweet dreams—though I doubted anything could ward off the nightmares Hun-Came brought, the ones I was powerless to stop myself.

I cleared the dishes and loaded the dishwasher while my mother heated water in the battered copper kettle that had been in our family for generations. We sat at the table as she poured the steaming water over the herbs, releasing their soothing fragrance.

"What does the spirit call himself?" she asked, her voice casual but her eyes sharp.

"Hun-Came."

"Is that his true name?"

I shrugged. "He calls himself One-Death—Hun-Came, but I think he goes by many names."

"Most demons and spirits do." She stirred honey into her tea.

"Demon? Spirit?" Hun-Came's voice huffed indignantly. *"I am a god, not a demon."*

"He says he's a god, not a demon," I relayed.

The corners of my mother's mouth lifted into a small knowing smile. "Of course. Modesty and humbleness are not common traits among supernatural beings."

"I am the god of death!" Hun-Came's voice thundered imperiously inside my head. *"I am One-Death! I am Kisin! I am Yum Cimil! I am Ah Puch! I am the ruler of Xibalba! I have no need for modesty."*

I pressed my palms against my temples, trying to quiet his outraged voice.

My mother paused, studying me. "I take it Hun-Came is unhappy with my characterization of him?"

I nodded, the pressure in my head building.

"If you could find out his true name, that would help... balance your relationship." Her fingers traced the rim of her mug, a gesture I recognized from childhood—she was choosing her words carefully.

"Good idea," I said weakly. "Which one is your real name?" I asked aloud.

Hun-Came remained mulishly silent, his presence a cold shadow against my thoughts.

I raised my eyes to meet my mother's gaze. "I don't think he's going to share that."

"Well, it was worth asking." She sighed, reaching across the table to squeeze my hand. "I'm still researching how to..." She paused, aware that Hun-Came could hear everything she said. "Lessen his influence. Right now, what we can do is prevent you from dream-walking. He won't be able to roam if you don't."

She handed me a small sachet tied with a purple ribbon embroidered with silver runes.

I sniffed the fabric bag. "What's in this?"

"Betony root to expel evil spirits and nightmares."

"I am not an evil spirit," Hun-Came retorted, his voice scraping against the inside of my skull.

My mother held up her hand and ticked off the other ingredients on her fingers. "Henbane, mandrake, myrrh, and frankincense for protection, healing, and exorcism." She reached into the pocket of her sweater. "I also brought this for you from the store."

She pulled out a simple iron bangle etched with ancient Celtic runes. "Iron to help ward off evil spirits and bind you to the earth. It won't expel him, but it might help you maintain control."

"Thanks." I slipped the bangle on my wrist before taking another sip of my tea, feeling the cool metal against my skin. For a moment, Hun-Came's presence seemed to recede, like a tide pulling back from shore. I knew it wouldn't last, but for now, in my mother's kitchen with the scent of lavender between us, I could breathe.

The buzz of my phone broke the momentary peace. I pulled it from my pocket and stared at Zen's name on the screen, a second message beneath the first.

Zen: *It's about Hun-Came. There's a way to break the connection without killing you. But we need to do it soon.*

My heart lurched, hope and suspicion warring inside me. After months of silence, why now?

"Is everything okay?" my mother asked, watching my face.

I hesitated, then handed her the phone. "It's Zen."

She read the messages, her expression unreadable. "Do you trust him?" she asked, returning my phone to me.

The question hung between us, heavy with implications. Did I? The man who'd saved my life, then abandoned me. The man who'd held me through nightmares and whispered Mayan legends against my skin. The man who'd disappeared without explanation, leaving me to navigate this horror of Hun-Came alone.

"I don't know," I admitted finally, staring at Zen's message. "But if there's even a chance..."

I looked up to find my mother watching me intently. She reached across the table to clasp my hands. The iron bangle slid against my wrist, cool and reassuring.

For the first time in months, I felt something like hope stirring beneath the fear and guilt—fragile, but real. If there was a way to be free of Hun-Came without dying, I wanted to find it. And if Zen was the key to that freedom, I would deal with my complicated feelings for him later.

Right now, survival was enough.

LISA DIETRICH

CHAPTER SEVEN

I lay in my childhood bedroom, the iron bracelet cold against my wrist. My mother had reinforced its protective symbols before we'd parted for the night, tracing each Celtic rune with oil of cedar and sage. The room smelled of herbs and memory—a comforting scent that carried me toward sleep despite Hun-Came's restless presence within me.

"You think this trinket can hold me?" he whispered as consciousness began to slip away. *"Iron and symbols are nothing to a god."*

"They've worked so far," I mumbled, already half-dreaming.

His laughter followed me into darkness.

***

I stood at the edge of a cenote, its waters impossibly blue. The jungle around me hummed with life, vines creeping across ancient stone. This was Guatemala, but not as I remembered it. Everything was sharper, more vibrant, saturated with impossible color.

Niki.

I turned. Zen stood several yards away, his silhouette backlit by streaming sunlight. He looked thinner than I remembered, his cheekbones more pronounced, dark circles shadowing his eyes. In the past, he'd always appeared in my dreams in the form of a jaguar, his shadow soul. I couldn't understand how it was that he had entered my dream space. My mother's spells should have kept me from dream-walking.

"How are you here?" I asked. "This shouldn't be happening."

Zen took a step forward. "You are not dream-walking. I am."

Something cold stirred within me. Hun-Came, listening, watching.

"I thought only trained shamans could dream-walk."

"I've learned a lot since I left." Zen's amber eyes were serious, scanning my face as if searching for something. "That's why I'm in Cobán."

The water of the cenote began to darken, turning from blue to inky black. The jungle sounds quieted, replaced by the soft jingling of tiny bells.

"He's here," I whispered. "Hun-Came can hear us."

Zen stepped closer, urgency in his movements. "Listen carefully. I found someone—who knows how to sever your connection to Hun-Came without creating another vessel."

The ground beneath us trembled.

"How?" I demanded. "I've tried everything—"

"Not everything," Zen insisted. "There's a ritual, but we need to—"

The cenote erupted, black water shooting upward like a geyser. The droplets hung suspended in the air, each one reflecting not the jungle around us but Hun-Came's empty eye sockets and his grinning death mask.

"Foolish child," Hun-Came's voice boomed, no longer inside my head but all around us. "You think I cannot reach you here?"

The water droplets began to coalesce, forming a figure of shadow and mist—a skeletal being, tall and crowned with obsidian knives.

Zen grabbed my shoulders. "Guatemala. Cobán. Hurry." His eyes flickered to something behind me. "I have to go. You're not safe."

"This vessel is mine," Hun-Came hissed, his skeletal hand closing around my throat.

I gasped, struggling against his grip. "Zen!"

44

"Iron keeps your shadow soul bound while you sleep," Hun-Came whispered in my ear. *"But it cannot stop me, daughter of Balam. Nothing can."*

The world dissolved into darkness.

***

I awoke gasping, sheets twisted around my legs, sweat soaking my nightshirt. Pale morning light filtered through the curtains. My hand flew to my throat—where the pain and the memory of Hun-Came's grip lingered.

The iron bracelet was still securely fastened around my wrist. It had kept my shadow soul from wandering, prevented Hun-Came from using my body while I slept— but it hadn't kept him from my dreams.

"Zen," I whispered. Zen had learned to dream-walk.

"A parlor trick." Hun-Came's voice was faint in the morning light but edged with something I hadn't heard before. Concern? *"The boy plays with forces he cannot comprehend."*

I swung my legs over the side of the bed. "He's found a way to free me from you."

"Nothing but delusions of power," Hun-Came scoffed, but there was tension beneath his words. *"He will lead you both to destruction."*

I stood, stretching muscles stiff from the tension of my dreams. "You're afraid."

Silence. Then, *"Gods do not fear mortals."*

But I could feel it now—a ripple of unease in his usually cold presence. Whatever Zen had found in Cobán had disturbed Hun-Came enough to break his veneer of indifference.

I showered quickly and dressed, the memory of the dream still vivid. Zen looked worn, haunted even. Whatever he'd been doing in Guatemala these past months had taken a toll on him. But he'd found something or someone who might help.

My mother was already gone when I went downstairs, a note on the kitchen counter directing me to meet her at the shop when I woke. Gaia's Embrace had been her sanctuary since before I was born, an apothecary store that walked the line between modern herbalism and ancient Celtic knowledge.

The morning was cool and misty as I walked the familiar route to downtown Ventura. Hun-Came remained silent, withdrawing into whatever dark corner of my consciousness he occupied when not tormenting me. His unease was a balm to my own fear. If he was worried about what Zen had found, then maybe there was hope after all.

The bell above the door jingled as I entered Gaia's Embrace. The shop smelled of dried herbs, essential oils, and the faint sweetness of beeswax candles. My mother looked up from behind the counter where she was wrapping a package for an elderly woman I recognized as Mrs. Petrovich, a regular customer.

"Niki," she said, her smile warming her eyes. "You're just in time. I could use help with the new shipment."

I waited while she finished with Mrs. Petrovich, making small talk about arthritis remedies and the unseasonably cool weather. When the door closed behind her customer, my mother's smile faded.

"You look like you haven't slept," she said, coming around the counter to examine my face. "Was it him?"

"Yes and no." I followed her to the back room where boxes of supplies waited to be unpacked. "I had a dream. Zen was there."

My mother stilled, her hand hovering over a box cutter. "A visitation dream ?" I nodded, recounting the cenote, Zen's message, Hun-Came's appearance. As I spoke, she began methodically unpacking dried herbs into glass jars, her movements precise but her attention entirely on me.

"Zen said he had learned to dream-walk." I touched the iron band around my wrist. "My soul was tethered, so he found a way to me, but I didn't think someone could learn to dream-walk."

"It is a skill that must be developed, so it is possible to learn," she said when I'd finished. Her brow furrowed. "Though most often it is a gift passed through a person's bloodline."

"It's not a gift," I said. "It's a curse."

"Oh, Niki." She shook her head, her disappointment obvious. "You know better than that. The universe craves balance. For every gift, the universe exacts a price, but that does not make the gift a curse." She sealed a jar of dried lavender with more force than necessary.

I leaned against the worktable. "Right now, it's nothing but a curse unless I can learn to protect myself from Hun-Came when I dream-walk."

"Your father worried about you when you began to show signs of dream-walking. When a dream-walker's consciousness travels, the body they leave behind is very vulnerable. There are ways to navigate the dream realm more safely. Ways that wouldn't leave you as vulnerable to Hun-Came's influence. Your father used to use obsidian mirrors as anchors."

"Obsidian mirrors?" The image of dark, reflective stone flashed in my mind.

"Yes. They create a tether to your physical body while allowing your consciousness to travel." She sighed. "But I don't have one here. And I don't really know how they work. We'd need to find someone who specializes in Mayan artifacts. Someone who knows the old ways."

My mother pulled a book from the shelf behind her—old, leather-bound, the pages yellowed. "Your father's first journal," she said, placing it before me. "The one he kept before you and Nayla were born, when he was studying with his teacher in Guatemala."

I opened it carefully. The pages were filled with my father's neat handwriting, diagrams, pressed plants, and sketches. My throat tightened at the sight of it.

"Page ninety-three," my mother said.

I turned to the page. There was a detailed drawing of a cenote, the very one from my dream with a phrase underlined twice: *Boca de Xilbaba.*

"The mouth of Hell," I translated under my breath. I looked up at my mother.

"Your father saw it in a dream. It's the portal to the Mayan underworld."

"Hun-Came's realm."

My mother nodded. "He never spoke about it until after you and Nayla were born. He said the two of you needed to be aware of your heritage. That it would protect you." She pulled a second book from the shelf. "Your father's teacher lived near Cobán. If she's still alive..."

"I think she is!" I said excitedly. "Zen said he'd found someone who can help me in Cobán. Hun-Came was afraid when Zen mentioned her, I could feel it. Zen must have found her."

"Good." My mother's eyes glinted with something fierce. "I think it's time we read your father's journals together."

We spent the morning going through my father's journals, looking for anything else that might help. By noon, I'd made my decision.

"I need to go to Guatemala," I said, closing the last journal. "To Cobán. To find Zen and Pápa's teacher."

My mother didn't argue. Instead, she went to the safe hidden behind a painting of the Irish coastline, entered the combination, and removed a small wooden box.

"Your father left this for you," she said. "He told me I would know when it was time."

Inside lay two identical amulets—jade carved into the shape of a jaguar, so detailed I could see individual whiskers and the pattern of spots. It hung on a cord woven from what looked like human hair.

"Is that—"

"His hair," my mother confirmed. "And mine. And yours and Nayla's, from when you were babies. Blood ties, woven together."

As I lifted one of the amulets, Hun-Came stirred, his presence suddenly alert and watchful.

"Pretty trinket," he said, but there was strain in his voice.

I slipped the cord over my head. The jade jaguar settled against my chest, inexplicably warm.

For a moment, my mother's eyes filled with sorrow and loss as she stared at the second necklace, the one I knew had been created for Nayla.

Grief wrapped its fingers around my heart and squeezed. Nayla's death had ripped a hole in our carefully constructed universe, just like my father's had done years earlier. I had no idea how to repair the void left behind by their deaths. I laid my hand on top of my mother's, heartache lodging in my throat like a boulder, unable to voice the words I wanted to say.

My mother's jaw tightened, her expression changing to one of focused determination. She closed the box firmly. "Book your flight. I'll prepare what you'll need to take with you."

"He'll try to stop me," I said quietly.

She squeezed my hand. "We won't let him."

The jade jaguar seemed to pulse against my skin, a counterpoint to the chill of Hun-Came's presence. For the first time since the death god had taken residence in my shadow soul, I felt something like hope stirring.

Guatemala. Cobán.

And possibly, freedom.

LISA DIETRICH

CHAPTER EIGHT

I slipped into my apartment well after midnight, praying Sierra would be asleep. I was in luck. She was. I couldn't blame her for being upset. No one wants to have a roommate who arrives home covered in blood, I just wasn't sure how I was going to convince her I wasn't part of some Satanic cult.

Unfortunately, luck wasn't on my side the next morning. Sierra ambushed me as I stumbled bleary-eyed toward the kitchen, desperate for coffee.

"There you are," she said, perched on a barstool, already dressed for her shift at Starbucks. "The cops came by yesterday."

My mug slipped, clattering against the counter. "Cops?"

"Yeah. They're canvassing the neighborhood for witnesses to that latest mountain lion attack." She tilted her head, studying me. "You, okay? You don't look so good."

My heart hammered against my ribs. "I'm fine. Just... didn't sleep well."

"Anyway, I mentioned you might have seen something." Sierra took a sip of her coffee. "Since you were out late and came home—covered in blood."

Ice flooded my veins. "You did what?"

"I told them about you," she said, her voice deceptively casual. "You said you witnessed an accident. No big deal, right?"

"Right," I managed, forcing a shaky smile. "No big deal."

I skipped my morning run and drove to work in a daze, imagining police cars following me, wondering if every ping on my phone was a detective calling to question me about mutilated bodies. By the time I reached the office, my shirt was damp with cold sweat.

I'd barely settled at my desk when Stella appeared in my doorway, vibrating with excitement. She waved bright blue lacquered nails in my direction.

"Police are here asking for you," she stage-whispered. "In Elena's office. They look serious."

My heart plummeted to the soles of my feet. This was it. They knew. Somehow, they'd connected me to the deaths. I stood on wooden legs, my file folders slipping from nerveless fingers.

"Did they say why?" I heard myself ask.

Stella shook her head, eyes bright with morbid curiosity. "Nope."

The walk to Elena's office felt like a death march. Hun-Came remained suspiciously silent, offering neither mockery nor reassurance. When I pushed open the frosted glass door, three sets of eyes turned toward me—Elena's sharp and assessing, flanked by two uniformed officers whose expressions gave nothing away.

"Ms. Balam," the taller officer said, rising from his chair. "I'm Officer Rodriguez, this is Officer Chen. Thank you for taking the time to speak with us."

Elena nodded toward the empty chair beside her. "Niki, the officers are canvassing the neighborhood about the recent animal attacks."

Animal attacks. Not murders. I felt a flicker of relief, quickly extinguished by the next question.

"We understand from your roommate that you were present at the site of one of the earlier incidents?" Officer Chen leaned forward, pen poised above his notepad.

I swallowed hard. "I—I don't think so."

"Sierra Williams informed us that you returned home last Friday covered in blood," Officer Rodriguez said. "She said you claimed to have witnessed an accident."

"Oh. That." My mind raced. "Yes, I... I came across someone who had been hurt. I tried to help, but they were already... someone else arrived and I left."

"And you didn't report this to the authorities?"

"I panicked," I admitted, the truth slipping out before I could stop it. "I mean, the other person said they were going to help. I just... went home."

Their expressions remained professionally neutral, but I could sense their suspicion. My palms began to sweat.

"We'll need a description of the people involved and the exact location of the accident."

"I'm not sure I can help you. It was dark. I was out jogging. I can tell you the person who was hurt was a man. The other person who stopped to help was also a man, but that's all," I replied, mixing a partial truth with the lie.

"Would you be willing to provide a DNA sample? For elimination purposes?" Officer Rodriguez asked. "We've found trace evidence at several scenes that doesn't match the victims."

My blood turned to ice water.

"No," Elena cut in before I could respond. "As her attorney, I'm advising you to return with a warrant if you want a sample. Is my client under suspicion for something, officers?"

"Not at all," Officer Chen said smoothly. "Just routine investigation."

"Then routine can wait for proper paperwork," Elena replied with a tight smile. "Now, if there's nothing else?"

After they left, Elena fixed me with a look far more disapproving than anything the police had managed.

"Is there something you need to tell me, Niki?"

I shook my head, a shaky feeling settling into the pit of my stomach. "No. Nothing."

"Good." She stood, straightening her immaculate blazer. "Because we have the Harrington meeting in twenty minutes, and I need you focused."

The meeting with the developer and his attorney went south almost immediately. Once again, Mr. Harrington dismissed my evidence of his company's transgressions and counteroffered with a wave of his hand.

"This is ridiculous," he drawled, his eyes narrowing as he focused on me. "Do you know how much this is costing me in time and money? I suggest you accept my very generous offer or your clients will get nothing. We all know how this is going to end. My lawyer has documentation of permits allowing us to grade and develop the property as I see fit. If you can't read basic documentation, that's hardly our problem."

Something hot and electric stirred beneath my skin as anger flooded me. How dare this man dismiss the destruction of an entire burial ground? The buzzing sensation beneath my skin grew stronger, crawling up my arms like static electricity.

"The permits are fraudulent," I said, my voice sounding strange even to my own ears. "If you have documents, they were forged. You know it, we know it, and soon enough, the judge will know it."

Harrington's face reddened. "Who do you think you are? Accusing me of forgery? Because I can end your career right now with one phone call, you little—"

The buzzing reached its crescendo, a storm of power surging through my veins. Hun-Came's presence, dormant all morning, suddenly expanded within me, cold and gleeful.

"You will end nothing," I heard myself say, though the words weren't entirely mine.

Harrington clutched at his chest, his eyes widening with shock. For a frozen moment, our gazes locked—his panicked, mine horrified as I realized what was happening. Then he toppled forward, face smacking the conference table with a sickening thud.

Elena rushed to his side while Harrington's lawyer dialed 9-1-1. I stood paralyzed, watching as they turned him over and Elena began CPR. Paramedics arrived minutes later with a crash cart and grim expressions.

They went through the motions of reviving him, but I already knew. I could feel it—the hollow space where Harrington's life force had been, the satisfied hum of Hun-Came's power receding back through my body.

"Clear!" a paramedic shouted, pressing the defibrillator paddles to Harrington's chest.

His body jerked. Nothing.

"Clear!"

Again. Still nothing.

"Time of death, 10:47 AM."

"*Ah, my little vessel,*" Hun-Came whispered seductively as the paramedics covered Harrington's face with a sheet. "*See what we can do together? The power I bestow can be yours for the taking.*"

I stumbled from the room, barely making it to the bathroom before vomiting. When I could stand again, I called my mother with trembling fingers.

"Mom," I choked out when she answered. "I killed someone. Me. Me. I did it. I…He…killed someone."

"Slow down," she said, her voice steady. "Tell me what happened."

I spilled the story in fragments, tears streaming down my face. "He just—his heart just stopped. I was angry, and I felt this power, and then he—"

"Listen to me," she interrupted, her voice stern. "You did not kill that man. It was just a coincidence."

"No," I whispered. "Hun-Came is toying with me. He wanted me to see what he could do."

"Niki—"

"I felt it, Mom. I felt his life just... stop."

A long silence stretched between us, filled only by my ragged breathing.

"Don't do anything. Don't say anything to anyone. The only thing you need to do is to keep telling yourself that you are not to blame," she finally said, her voice brooking no argument. "Let me hear you say it."

"I'm not to blame," I whispered.

"Right. You keep telling yourself that." I could hear her relieved exhalation. "That's right. Niki, you just keep repeating that. Okay, sweetheart. Just keep repeating that. Don't worry. We'll figure this out."

After we hung up, I splashed cold water on my face and tried to compose myself. Hun-Came remained uncharacteristically quiet, as if sated by the morning's events. When he finally spoke again, his voice was almost bored.

"*These fat Americans offer no challenge,*" he said dismissively. "*I am ready to return to Guatemala.*"

I gripped the edge of the sink, staring at my reflection— pale face, haunted eyes, the shadow of something ancient and terrible lurking just beneath the surface.

"I'm not sure I am," I whispered.

But deep down, I knew I had no choice. If there was any chance of freeing myself from Hun-Came, I would have to return to where it all began. Back to the jungle. Back to the ruins. Back to Zen.

And pray I didn't kill everyone around me before I found answers.

CHAPTER NINE

It took a week to make the arrangements. Elena had been surprisingly understanding when I explained I needed personal leave for a family emergency in Guatemala. She'd even offered to arrange for another associate to cover my cases while I was gone. Whether her generosity stemmed from genuine concern or from the fact that she'd watched me fall apart after a man died in our conference room, I couldn't say.

The airport was crowded with spring break travelers, families with overtired children, and businesspeople hunched over laptops. I'd just settled into the uncomfortable plastic seat at the gate when a familiar voice, with a hint of an Irish brogue, jolted me upright.

"Fancy meeting you here."

I froze, then slowly turned to face the voice I hadn't heard in over two years. Aedan O'Kearney stood at the head of the row of seats, an unusually long backpack slung over one shoulder, and a knowing smirk on his face. He was as handsome as ever—what my mother called "black Irish," with thick raven hair that curled slightly at the ends, startling blue eyes rimmed with impossibly long dark lashes, and skin that tanned golden despite his Celtic heritage. The sleeve of his black t-shirt rode up, revealing the edge of the intricate tattoos that covered his arms—a mixture of Celtic knotwork and druidic symbols.

Around both wrists he wore iron bracelets covered in ancient Ogham script—wards against dark magic that he never removed. I'd once joked they were the only thing he wouldn't take off in bed. He hadn't laughed.

"What are you doing here?" I demanded, ignoring the flash of irritation that rippled through me. "And don't tell me it's a coincidence."

A nagging thought struck me. "Did my mother call you?"

My mother had always had a thing for Aedan—a druid warrior with powers that exceeded her own. She'd never said as much, but her eyes lit up whenever he visited, and she always seemed to have his favorite honey cakes freshly baked.

"What makes you think that?" Aedan asked, sapphire eyes wide with fake innocence.

"Oh, I don't know. Maybe because you just happened to show up at my gate when I'm traveling to Guatemala." I crossed my arms.

"It's good to see you haven't changed a bit." He leaned closer, the scent of sage and cedar wood washing over me. "Always suspicious. Can't a lad go on vacation without you seeing some deep, dark, nefarious plot?"

"No." I glared at him. "Since when do you travel to Guatemala?"

"There you go again." He shook his head sorrowfully. "Tsk Tsk. So suspicious."

"I'm suspicious because I know you have a problem with the truth—not to mention fidelity."

The barb hit its mark; a flicker of discomfort crossed his face before the charming mask slipped back into place.

"Fine. Your mother called in a favor," he said with a careless shrug. "Or rather, I owe her several, and she's collecting on one of them. I'm to accompany you on your... adventure."

My mother was definitely going to hear from me. "I don't need a babysitter," I retorted archly.

Aedan's face turned serious for a moment, the playboy facade dropping away to reveal something older, more dangerous. It was the part of him that had first drawn me in before I discovered his wandering eye—that glimpse of something ancient and powerful beneath the charm.

"Your mother's worried about you," he said quietly. "Think of me as your bodyguard and personal warrior. I'm here to protect you from your Mayan...friend."

"*An Irish faerie is no match for the god of death*," Hun-Came thundered inside my skull, making me wince.

"My Mayan friend is not impressed," I relayed.

Aedan's dimple appeared as he grinned, his natural charm radiating like sunshine. "Tell him the feeling's mutual." He leaned back, appraising me. "Honestly, Niki— couldn't you have picked a better-looking god?" He wrinkled his nose dramatically. "Not to mention one that doesn't stink. I can smell him from here."

"What?" I took a quick, panicked sniff of my armpits. Did I reek of death? Was that why people on the subway had been giving me space?

Hun-Came growled menacingly, the sound of his discordant bells jangling inside my head. I winced.

Aedan winked. "Don't worry—most people don't have my superior senses, so they won't be able to catch a whiff of that lovely eau de death and putrefaction you seem to be sporting."

I gritted my teeth, torn between embarrassment and irritation. "*Shall we kill him?*" Hun-Came suggested, a little too eagerly.

"No," I muttered. Not that I didn't want to, at least a little, but death seemed a bit extreme even for someone as irritating as Aedan.

When boarding was called, Aedan settled into the seat

next to mine—of course, he'd somehow managed to book the seat that would most annoy me. Instead of the aisle seat I thought I booked, I was now sandwiched in the middle seat, with Aedan sitting next to me. I watched as he charmed the flight attendant into allowing him to keep his extra-large, oddly-shaped backpack, stuffing it into the overhead bin with practiced ease.

"What do you have in that thing?" I asked, nodding toward the bulging pack.

"This and that," he replied vaguely, tucking a strand of dark hair behind his ear. I noticed a new tattoo curling around his earlobe—a small spiral that hadn't been there when we were together.

"You brought Sky-Splitter, didn't you?" I asked, eyeing the suspiciously sword-shaped pack.

His eyes widened in mock surprise. "How on earth would I get a magical three-foot iron blade through airport security?"

"The same way you get everything—charm and a bit of druid magic."

His grin confirmed my suspicion.

Aedan was more than just charming; he was a druid warrior as well as a healer. He could call fire with a whisper and calm storms with a gesture. Hun-Came wasn't far off when he called him a fairy—Aedan had powers and abilities far beyond those of my mother. My mother had warned me when I first started dating him that he was different, more connected to the old ways than most modern druids.

"My mother thinks you and Sky-Splitter can protect me from Hun-Came," I said as the plane began taxiing. It wasn't a question.

"Among other things." He reached for my hand, his fingers brushing over the iron bangle my mother had given me. "This is good work, but basic. The death god's influence runs deeper than iron can reach."

I pulled my hand away. "And you think you can do better?"

His blue eyes met mine, all traces of humor gone. "I know I can. I've faced death gods before."

"When?" I challenged.

Before he could answer, the plane accelerated, pressing us back into our seats as it lifted into the air. Through the small window, the city of San Diego receded, becoming a maze of lights and roads, then a smudge on the horizon.

"So, what's the plan?" I asked when we reached cruising altitude. "You wave your magic druid hands and exorcise Hun-Came?"

Aedan's expression darkened. "It's not that simple. Your mother said he's bound to you in ways she and I haven't seen before. The connection is... unusual."

"That's not reassuring."

"It wasn't meant to be." He leaned closer, his voice dropping to ensure our conversation remained private. Something flashed in Aedan's eyes—recognition? Concern? "And the killing? Is that new, or has Hun-Came always been bloodthirsty?"

"He's the god of death," I said. "What do you think?"

"I think," Aedan said carefully, "that not all death gods crave violent deaths. Some are shepherds, guiding souls peacefully to the afterlife. Others feed on suffering and terror." He studied my face. "Hun-Came seems to prefer the latter."

"*Lies,*" Hun-Came hissed. "*The druid spreads lies.*"

"He doesn't like what you're saying," I translated.

Aedan's smile was cold. "Good. That means I'm onto something." He reached up to rub his jaw, his expression thoughtful. "The thing is, Niki, I think our Mayan friend is a bit theatrical. His...antics are designed to impress you. To make you believe he's more powerful than he is."

Hun-Came's anger blazed through me like wildfire. "*You dare?*" The voice roared inside my skull, so loud I gasped. Several passengers turned to look at us.

"Indoor voice," Aedan murmured, gently touching my wrist where the iron bangle sat. A cool sensation spread from his fingers, dampening Hun-Came's rage to a manageable simmer.

"How did you do that?" I whispered.

"Iron and intent," he replied. "The basics work; they just need a bit of power behind them."

I stared at him, really looking at Aedan for the first time since our paths had crossed. Beyond the charming exterior I'd dated—there was something dark and dangerous in his eyes. Something that made me wonder if I'd ever known him at all.

"What do you know about jungle survival, anyway?" I asked, trying to regain some control of the situation. "Your power comes from Celtic forests and Irish hills, not Central American rainforests."

He looked mildly offended. "Nature is nature, love. The trees may have different names, but they speak the same language." He paused, a cocky grin spreading across his face.

"Why did you really come?" I asked.

His playful mask slipped back into place. "Maybe I missed you," he suggested, dimples flashing.

"Try again." I rolled my eyes.

Aedan sighed, running a hand through his dark hair. "Your mother called, yes. But I would have come anyway." His gaze shifted to the window. "There are forces at work in Guatemala that haven't stirred in centuries. The old gods are awakening, not just your death-scented friend."

"And you know this how?"

His eyes met mine, for a moment, serious and unfathomable, before changing once again to the flippant expression I knew so well. "You doubt my superior senses?" He grinned. "Besides, what self-respecting druid turns down the chance for a good fight with malevolent ancient powers?"

A chill ran through me as the plane carried us closer to Guatemala, to Zen, to whatever waited in the jungle. Hun-Came retreated to a distant corner of my consciousness, watchful and wary. Beside me, Aedan leaned back and closed his eyes. As I glanced at his smug profile, I wondered if having Aedan as a sidekick might prove to be its own kind of curse.

LISA DIETRICH

CHAPTER TEN

The shuttle ride from Guatemala City stretched into a grueling five-hour ordeal. Aedan and I were packed into a white van like sardines alongside an American couple with their teenage son and two young German women. With no air conditioning, the van was stifling. Sweat trickled between my breasts and the back of my shirt stuck to the upholstery like wet glue. We were all red-faced and miserable with the exception of Aedan who somehow managed to find humor in our situation.

The misery of our ride was compounded by our driver who seemed to have a death wish—accelerating around blind curves to overtake slower vehicles on the narrow mountain roads. After the first near-miss with an oncoming truck, I made sure my seatbelt was securely fastened.

"You know, you could have listened to me about taking one of the chicken buses," Aedan murmured, looking thoroughly entertained by our harrowing journey.

I shot him a glare. "Camionetas," I corrected him. "And no way was I riding on a retired school bus packed with people, cargo, and actual chickens. They're called chicken buses for a reason."

Aedan grinned.

I rolled my eyes and turned to look out the window. Big mistake. The winding road hugged the mountainside so closely that one wrong move would send us plummeting into the lush valleys below. My stomach clenched with anxiety as I resolutely turned my gaze forward, wondering if the chicken buses might have been the safer option, after all.

While the rest of our fellow passengers looked as stricken as I felt, Aedan treated the death-defying ride as a lark. At one point, as we swerved around a particularly sharp bend with yet another sheer drop to our right, he grinned and turned to our small, terrified audience.

"Has anyone heard the one about the pastor and the bus driver?" he asked.

Five pairs of eyes turned to stare in mute astonishment at him.

"I'll take that as a no." His eyes lit up with merriment as he told his joke. "A pastor and bus driver arrive at the gates of heaven," he began. "God gives the pastor a nice house. Then he gives the bus driver a gigantic villa with a pool and everything he could ever want. The pastor turns to God and asks, 'I have dedicated my life to you. Why does the bus driver get such a grand reward?'"

Aedan paused, and grinned widely, displaying his dimples. "God replies, 'Well, people fell asleep during your sermons, but everyone on the driver's bus was always praying.'"

No one in the van laughed. The American father tightened his grip on the overhead handle, while his wife closed her eyes, lips moving in what I suspected was an actual prayer.

"Shut up," I huffed angrily, jabbing an elbow into his side. Aedan laughed.

By the time our driver finally deposited us at the Cobán bus depot, my legs were wobbly and my nerves frayed. I offered up my own prayer, thankful to have arrived in one piece.

The terminal buzzed with activity—local vendors hawking colorful textiles and street food, passengers rushing to catch connections, and taxi drivers competing for fares. The air was thick with diesel fumes. The German women quickly grabbed their backpacks and disappeared into the crowd, while the American family waited for the driver to unload their luggage.

I stood on the hot asphalt, breathing in the exhaust from dozens of idling buses, scanning the crowd for a pair of familiar amber eyes.

Instead of Zen, an unknown woman strode purposefully toward us. Wearing black thigh-high boots, form-fitting jeans, and a cream-colored silk shirt that clung to her lush figure, she fixed her heavily made-up eyes on our little group. The teenage boy from our shuttle stared at her, eyes wide, mouth agape as if he couldn't believe this living, breathing vision of a video game fantasy was coming his way.

With full red lips and yards of shiny black hair cascading down her back, she looked like a cross between a Barbie doll and a dominatrix. She stopped directly in front of us, the teenage boy sighing audibly before being pulled away by his parents into a waiting taxi.

Her eyes found mine without hesitation. "Hello." Her English was perfect, her voice low with just the slightest Spanish accent softening her vowels. She smiled, though she couldn't quite mask the faint moue of distaste that flitted across her perfect face. "You are Nikita Balam." Not quite a question.

Beside me, I felt Aedan straighten with lively curiosity. "Yes," I answered, suddenly very self-conscious of my appearance. After flying all night and spending hours in a van without air conditioning, I looked and smelled about as fresh as week-old gym socks.

She offered me another flawless smile, but the eyes she focused on me were cold. I revised my assessment of her.

Forget Barbie. I put this woman in the category of someone who definitely enjoyed wielding a whip.

"My name is Isadora Gonzalez Montoya. Zen asked me to collect you from the terminal."

"Zen. Asked you? To meet us?" My brain was having a hard time connecting this woman with Zen. Everything about this felt wrong. Zen was supposed to be here. He'd practically summoned me to Cobán. Where was he? And who was this woman? I felt my stomach twist with a mixture of confusion and something that felt uncomfortably like jealousy.

Beside me, Aedan hefted his backpack onto his shoulders. "Aedan O'Kearney," he introduced himself, laying on a brogue as thick as clotted cream. "And what might your relationship be to our mutual friend?"

Her eyes flicked to Aedan, taking his measure in that brief look and dismissing him just as quickly, addressing her reply to me instead. "Zen and I are old friends. When he realized he would not be able to meet you, he called and asked me to escort you to your hotel."

Not quite able to get the image of her with a whip out of my head—or worse, the image of her with a whip in her hand and Zen—I wasn't ready to go anywhere with this woman.

"Um—thank you but I'm sure we can find our own way."

She smiled, revealing perfect white teeth. "That is quite out of the question. Zen would be most disappointed if I did not escort you."

"*Witch*," Hun-Came's voice slithered into my head. He'd been uncharacteristically quiet ever since Aedan had touched the iron bracelet I wore, but I could feel his antipathy toward this woman pulsing through me. The Mayan god of death didn't like her? Was this a good thing or a bad thing? I couldn't decide, but the fact that Hun-Came was disturbed by her presence only added to my growing sense of unease.

At least Aedan had the presence of mind to ask what I was desperately wondering. "Perhaps you'd be so kind as to tell us where Zen is or how we might contact him?"

She smiled. "He is, unfortunately, unable to speak with you at the moment."

"Is he hurt?" I asked, my heart constricting.

"No. He is detained."

Detained? What the hell did that mean? Was he in trouble? Or just busy with something—or someone—he considered more important than meeting me?

I glanced over at Aedan.

She gestured toward a large SUV idling nearby. "Shall we?"

Aedan hefted our bags, making the decision for me. "Lead the way then, my fair cailín."

"My name is Isadora. You may call me Isadora or Izzy," she corrected.

Izzy's gaze shifted back to me, waiting for my response. I nodded reluctantly. I hadn't been thrilled to have Aedan accompanying me on this trip, but now I found myself grateful for his presence—and Sky-Splitter's—as we followed this mysterious woman through the crowded terminal.

She led us to a gleaming black SUV with tinted windows parked in a reserved spot near the entrance. We climbed into the air-conditioned interior. The leather seats were cool against my skin but did nothing to soothe the hot knot of tension forming in my stomach.

As we pulled away from the depot, Izzie turned in her seat to face me. "The hotel is about thirty minutes from here. Zen has arranged everything for your stay."

"When will we see him?" I asked, trying to keep the edge from my voice and failing miserably.

Something that might have been amusement flickered across her face. "Soon. He had some... business to conclude before your arrival."

Business. The word hung in the air between us, heavy with

implication.

"Business," Aedan repeated, one dark eyebrow raised in question.

Izzy ignored him, her attention focused entirely on me. "Zen speaks very highly of you, Nikita Balam." The way she said my name made it sound like she was tasting it, assessing its flavor and finding it lacking. There was something possessive in the way she talked about him, something that made my skin prickle with irritation.

"Does he?" I replied, aiming for nonchalance. "Funny. He hasn't mentioned you. How exactly do you know Zen?"

Her smile widened a fraction. "We are old friends. We have history together," she said simply, the words landing like small stones in the pit of my stomach.

We arrived at the hotel—a colonial-style building with a central courtyard and elaborate fountain—and followed Izzie to the reception desk. The lobby was cool and serene, with whitewashed walls, dark wooden beams, and colorful local textiles.

"Zen reserved one room," she informed me as the clerk tapped at his computer. "I do not believe he was expecting you to arrive with a,"— she paused, her eyes raking over Aedan, — "friend."

"That won't be a problem," Aedan said smoothly. "I'm sure they can accommodate both of us."

Izzy's perfect lips curved into a smile that didn't reach her eyes. "Of course. Then I will leave you to make the arrangements with the hotel."

As I watched her leave, Hun-Came stirred restlessly in my mind. "*Be wary of this witch,*" he warned, his voice like dry leaves scraping against stone.

For once, I was inclined to agree with him.

CHAPTER ELEVEN

The hotel clerk offered me a polite smile. "Will you be requiring one bed or two?"

Before I could answer, Aedan leaned forward, resting his forearm on the counter. "One will be fine," he said with a lazy grin.

I elbowed him sharply in the ribs. "Two beds," I said firmly, ignoring Aedan's theatrical wince. "Definitely two."

"As you wish, señorita." The clerk made a note in the system, his expression professionally neutral. "Room two-fourteen, second floor." He handed me the key to the room.

As we walked up the staircase with its polished wooden banisters, Aedan leaned in close enough that I could feel his breath on my ear.

"You realize I can't properly protect you if I'm sleeping across the room," he murmured, amusement threading through his words.

"I've managed to survive this long without you sleeping next to me," I replied, keeping my voice low. "I think I'll take my chances."

He chuckled. "As you wish. But don't come crying to me if the gruagach and the bobodha come for you in the night."

"I'm not afraid of goblins and bogey-men." I opened the door to reveal a spacious room with terra cotta tile floors, whitewashed walls, and heavy wooden furniture. True to the clerk's word, two queen-sized beds dominated the space, each covered with intricately woven Mayan textiles in vibrant blues and reds.

I sank down onto the edge of one bed, my mind spinning. I'd come to Cobán to meet Zen. Where the hell was he? And who the hell was Izzy? His girlfriend? Ex-lover?

"I was expecting to explain my presence to your feral boyfriend. I have to admit, Izzy was quite the lovely surprise," Aedan said, dropping his backpack onto the other bed. He began unpacking his belongings with methodical precision.

"Lovely is not the word I would choose to describe her," I muttered.

Aedan paused, a neatly folded shirt in his hands. "Ah. Do I by chance detect a wee bit of the green-eyed monster?"

"I'm not jealous," I protested, too quickly.

He gave me a knowing look. "Of course, not. And I'm not Irish."

I shot an annoyed look his way as I grabbed my toiletry bag. "I need a shower."

"Want me to scrub your back?" he called after me.

I slammed the bathroom door in response to his laughter.

Under the hot spray of water, I tried to wash away not just the grime of travel but the tangle of emotions knotting my insides. The water pressure was surprisingly good, pummeling my tense shoulders as steam filled the small bathroom. I shampooed my hair twice, determined to rid myself of the shuttle van stench.

As I stood there, eyes closed against the cascade of water, Zen's face materialized in my mind—those amber eyes that seemed to look straight through to my soul, the full lips that had once pressed against mine with such hunger. And now there was Izzy, with her perfect body and knowing smile, claiming they had "history."

"This was a mistake," I muttered to myself, rinsing conditioner from my hair. "I should never have come."

"*You had no choice,*" Hun-Came whispered in my mind, his voice like silk sliding over stone. "*The pull of destiny is not so easily ignored.*"

Great. Just what I needed—commentary from the Mayan god of death.

"Stay out of my shower," I grumbled.

I thought I heard a dry chuckle in response before his presence receded to that familiar corner of my mind where he lurked.

My eyes felt like sandpaper after the long flight and dusty shuttle ride, but the hot water was doing wonders to rejuvenate my body, if not my spirits. I was just working up a lather with a bar of hotel soap when there was a sharp rap on the bathroom door.

"Almost finished," I called, assuming it was Aedan getting impatient.

"Take your time," Aedan's hollered, slightly muffled through the door—and tinged with what sounded suspiciously like smugness.

Something in his tone made me pause. I quickly rinsed off, shut off the water, and reached for a towel, wrapping it securely around my body. I realized too late that I'd forgotten to bring clean clothes into the bathroom with me.

With a sigh, I opened the door a crack. "I forgot my—"

The words died in my throat as I saw who was standing in the hotel room with Aedan.

Zen.

He stood near the window, sunlight streaming in behind him, creating a golden halo around his silhouette. He wore a simple white linen shirt and khaki pants. He had lost weight and his hair was longer. He wore it pulled back into a small, neat ponytail which emphasized the sharp angles of his face.

His eyes locked with mine, and for a moment, the world seemed to stop.

Beside him, Aedan lounged against the wall, arms crossed over his chest, looking entirely too pleased with himself.

Zen's gaze traveled slowly from my face down to where I clutched the towel at my chest, then back up again, his expression unreadable. "Niki," he said my name like honey on his tongue.

I tightened my grip on the towel, acutely aware of my near-nakedness and dripping hair. "You left without saying goodbye," I said, the words leaving my mouth before I was able to stop them.

A shadow crossed his face. "I know. I'm sorry. Can we talk?" His eyes flicked toward Aedan. "Alone."

"Don't mind me you two. Just pretend I'm a part of the furniture."

I glared at Aedan. "Aedan, you need to leave."

He crossed his arms in front of his chest. "Sorry, Niki. No can do. I'm under the strictest of orders to keep you safe." His expression suddenly serious, he raked Zen with his eyes. "Leaving you alone with a shape-shifting ex-boyfriend with a drug problem, is not my definition of safe."

"There are so many things wrong with that statement, I don't even know where to start!" I retorted, my voice tight with anger.

Aedan shrugged but remained where he was, unmoved by my outburst.

I turned toward Zen, and the sight of him knocked the breath from my lungs. The confident, mysterious man I remembered had vanished. In his place stood someone haunted, hollow-eyed, with shadows cutting deep beneath his amber gaze. A muscle worked in his jaw as he tried to maintain his composure. Every line of his face spoke of exhaustion and something worse—guilt, perhaps, or a bone-deep fear that made my stomach twist into knots.

For one traitorous heartbeat, my fingers ached to trace the sharp angles of his face, to soothe away whatever demons had carved those new lines around his eyes. But beneath that impulse surged months of hurt and abandonment, a tide of anger that swept away any softness. This man had left me alone with a death god whispering in my mind.

"I'm getting dressed," I said, each word clipped and precise. I jabbed a finger toward Aedan, the gesture sharp enough to cut glass. "When I come out, you will be gone." My gaze swung back to Zen, and despite my best efforts, my voice wavered. "And you... you had better have one hell of an explanation ready."

I snatched the first clothes I could find from my suitcase—a faded blue t-shirt and worn jeans—and retreated to the bathroom. My hands trembled as I dressed, a storm of emotions churning beneath my skin. Through the door came the low rumble of their voices, the words indistinct but the tension unmistakable.

Bracing myself against the sink, I confronted my reflection. A stranger stared back—pale, haunted, with dark eyes that seemed older than the rest of my face. Water dripped from my hair onto my shoulders, each cold droplet a reminder of how exposed I felt.

"What am I doing here?" I whispered to myself.

"They are obstacles," Hun-Came's voice slithered through my mind, not with his usual rage but with something far more dangerous—reason. *"The shapeshifter seeks to use you. The druid seeks to control you. Neither understands what we could become together."*

A chill traced my spine despite the steam-filled bathroom. Hun-Came had been changing, his voice growing clearer, his suggestions more... persuasive. That terrified me more than his fury ever had.

"You need neither of them," he continued, his voice like obsidian—dark, smooth, and cutting. *"Embrace what you are becoming, and their petty conflicts will mean nothing. I can give you*

power beyond imagining, Nikita Balam."

My knuckles whitened as I gripped the edge of the sink. "Get out of my head," I hissed through clenched teeth.

"I am not in your head," he replied with cold amusement. *"I am in your soul. And I have waited centuries for someone like you."*

I closed my eyes and touched the iron bracelet at my wrist. The metal was cool against my fevered skin, a tangible anchor to reality. Focusing on my breathing—in for four counts, hold for seven, out for eight—I pushed against Hun-Came's presence until he receded to that familiar dark corner of my consciousness where he lurked, watching, waiting.

When I opened my eyes again, some composure had returned to my face, though the shadows beneath my eyes told their own story. I drew in one final steadying breath and reached for the doorknob, armor in place.

I emerged from the bathroom fully dressed, my wet hair dripping onto my shoulders. The tension in the room was thick enough to cut with a knife. Zen stood by the window, his eyes fixed on me, while Aedan remained lounging against the wall, his casual posture betrayed by the alert watchfulness in his eyes.

"Aedan," I said firmly. "Out."

He pushed himself off the wall, hands raised in mock surrender. "Fine, fine. I'll be right outside the door." He shot Zen a look that was somewhere between a warning and a threat. "Shouting distance."

"We won't be shouting," Zen said quietly.

Aedan paused at the door. "That remains to be seen." With a final glance at me that managed to be both concerned and smug, he slipped out, closing the door behind him.

The silence that followed felt like a physical presence in the room. I crossed my arms over my chest, waiting.

Zen took a step toward me, then stopped himself. *"You look good, Niki."* His voice slipping inside my thoughts.

"Don't." I shook my head. "Don't do small talk. And

don't get in my head like that. You lost that right months ago. You disappeared without a word, then summoned me here only to send someone else to meet me. Someone who made it very clear you have 'history." I made air quotes around the word. "So, start explaining."

Zen ran a hand over his face. He looked exhausted up close, dark circles under his eyes contrasting sharply with the amber irises.

"Izzy is an archaeologist," he said. "Specializing in Mayan hieroglyphics and codices. She's an old friend and also a student of Mayan religious practices."

My mind zeroed in on the word *student*. So, Izzy wasn't the teacher Zen had found.

"She's been helping me do some research. Connecting me with some local day-keepers and spiritual guides."

"Research? About Hun-Came?" I asked, feeling the god stir restlessly at the mention of his name.

"Yes." Zen's gaze was direct now.

Something twisted in my chest—hope, fear, I couldn't tell which. "Do you really think you've found a way to get him out of me?"

"Yes." Zen moved to sit on the edge of the bed—Aedan's bed, I noted with faint amusement.

"Lies," Hun-Came hissed in my mind. *"Do not trust him. He seeks to destroy us both."*

I ignored the god's voice, focusing on Zen. "How?"

"Basically, we need to find the entrance to Xilbaba. Then we need to convince Hun-Came to return to his realm or find another vessel."

I stared at Zen, disbelief warring with anger and disappointment. "Let me get this straight. Your plan is to find the entrance to the Mayan underworld and then nicely ask Hun-Came to go home. That's not a plan! That's a fantasy!"

"Not exactly." Zen stood again, restless energy radiating from him. "I've found something ..." He stopped abruptly. "The important thing is that we need to get Hun-Came out of you before—"

"Before what?" I demanded.

Zen's eyes met mine, and the intensity in them made me shiver. "Before Hun-Came becomes too powerful."

"He wants to kill you," Hun-Came whispered. *"Without me, you are nothing. Without me, you die."*

"Is that true?" I asked, unsure if I was addressing Zen or the god inside me. "If we separate, will I die?"

Zen's face registered surprise, then understanding. "He's talking to you right now, isn't he?" When I nodded, he continued. "It's a lie, Niki. The texts are clear on this. A vessel can survive separation if the ritual is performed correctly."

"And has he performed such a ritual before? Does he know the price?" Hun-Came's voice was silky, dangerous.

I relayed the question to Zen, whose expression darkened.

"No," he admitted. "But I've been...working with someone who has experience with these kinds of things."

"My father's old teacher."

Zen's eyes clouded with confusion. "Your father's teacher?"

"Yes. You found her, right?"

"No," Zen admitted, his fingers working nervously at the hem of his sleeve. "But I've been... learning from someone who understands these forces better than anyone."

Something in his hesitation made my blood run cold. "Who?" I demanded.

Zen's eyes met mine, then darted away. In that moment of silence, dread snaked up my backbone.

"Li Xul." The name crashed between us like a boulder, smashing our mental connection.

The reaction was immediate. A tidal wave of rage surged through me, so violent that my vision blurred crimson at the edges. My knees buckled, and I clutched at my temples as white-hot pain lanced through my skull.

"Do not trust the wahy b'alam!" Hun-Came's voice thundered, no longer a whisper but a roar that threatened to split my head in two. *"Betrayer! Liar! Death comes for him!"*

I could barely breathe through the fury that wasn't mine, yet burned in my veins as if it were. When I managed to lift my head, I found Zen watching me with alarm, his hands half-raised as if to catch me.

"It's not what you think," he said quickly.

My laugh was bitter, scraping my throat raw. "Not what I think?" Each word trembled with the effort of containing Hun-Came's rage alongside my own. "Li Xul murdered my sister and tried to kill me. And you're 'studying' with him." I spat each word like poison, my voice rising with fury. "What. The. Fuck!?"

The door crashed open, and Aedan stood framed in the entrance, Sky-Splitter gleaming in his hand. "Everything alright in here?" His casual tone belied the battle-ready tension in his stance.

"Fine," Zen and I answered in unison, then glared at each other across the chasm that had opened between us.

Aedan's gaze fixed on my face, his expression sharpening. "Your eyes are glowing, love," he said quietly. "And not in the metaphorical sense."

I closed my eyes and pressed my fingertips against the iron bracelet, its cool weight grounding me as I fought to push Hun-Came back. The god resisted, clawing at the edges of my consciousness like a beast at the bars of its cage.

Zen crossed the room in two quick strides, his hands settling on my shoulders. "Niki, I need you to listen to me," he said, his voice urgent. "It's not what you think."

I jerked away from his touch as if burned. "Then explain it to me!" My voice cracked with the strain of keeping Hun-Came contained. "Make it simple enough for me to understand why you're working with the man who wanted me dead!"

"Li Xul is dangerous," Zen acknowledged, his eyes never leaving mine. "But he knows things, Niki. He understands

Hun-Came in ways no one else does. There was no one else who could help you." His voice softened. "No one else who could help us."

"Us?" The word tasted like ash on my tongue. "There is no 'us' right now, Zen. You left. You disappeared when I needed you most, and now you're spending time with the man who tried to kill me."

"To save you," Zen insisted, desperation bleeding into his voice. "Everything I've done—every compromise, every risk—has been to find a way to free you from him. From Hun-Came."

"Free her?" Aedan interjected, moving further into the room with predatory grace. "Or claim the power for yourself?"

Zen's eyes flashed, the pupils elongating briefly into vertical slits—a glimpse of the jaguar spirit that shared his soul. "Stay out of this," he growled. "You know nothing about me or my intentions."

"I know enough," Aedan replied, his casual tone belied by the cold calculation in his eyes. "I know shapeshifters have their own agendas. I know Hun-Came's power would be quite the prize for someone willing to pay the price to claim it."

"If I wanted power," Zen snarled, his voice dropping to a dangerous register, "I wouldn't be trying to separate them."

I held up my hands. "Stop it, both of you." To my surprise, they fell silent. I turned to Zen. "You should leave," I told him tiredly.

"Niki, please?" His voice had a desperate edge to it. "Let me explain."

Aedan raised Sky-splitter threateningly, though his voice was calm. "The lass asked you to leave. I think it's best you do so."

"This is between Niki and me. You stay out of it!" Zen snarled at him. "Niki, you have to listen to me!"

"No. I don't." I turned away, my shoulders rigid with the

effort of containing both my own anger and Hun-Came's rage.

Zen's fingers closed around my arm, his grip desperate but not painful. "Niki, please—"

The contact shifted his sleeve, exposing the inner flesh of his forearm. My eyes caught on the marks there—a constellation of small punctures, some fresh, others fading to yellow-green bruises.

My breath caught in my throat. The room seemed to tilt beneath my feet as I stared at the evidence of what Aedan had already claimed. Needle marks. Track marks. The telltale signs of someone who had been injecting... something.

My gaze snapped up to Zen's face, searching for denial, for explanation, for anything that might make sense of what I was seeing. His eyes met mine for a heartbeat before sliding away, his expression a complex mix of shame and defiance.

"You'd best let go of her," Aedan warned, his voice deceptively soft. The edge of Sky-Splitter caught the light, a subtle reminder of his readiness to intervene.

Zen released my arm as if it burned him, self-consciously tugging his sleeve down to cover the marks. The simple gesture—so full of shame and habit—made my chest ache despite everything.

Aedan's gaze remained fixed on Zen like a predator tracking wounded prey. "I told you your shapeshifter boyfriend was an addict," he said to me, though his eyes never left Zen. "I smelled it on him the moment he walked into the room."

"Zen?" My voice emerged smaller than I intended, the single syllable laden with questions I wasn't sure I wanted answered.

"It's not what you think." Zen shot Aedan a venomous look before turning back to me, his eyes pleading for understanding. "I'm not an addict. I have everything under control." His voice dropped, urgent and intimate. "I made a deal with Li Xul, to help him in exchange for his knowledge. I can't dream-walk unless I'm in an altered state. So, I have to..."

"How often?" I cut him off, unable to bear his justifications.

Zen's jaw worked as he struggled with the answer, or perhaps with whether to give one at all.

"How often are you dream-walking to help Li Xul?" I reached for his arm again, pushing up his sleeve with trembling fingers. The marks were worse than I'd first thought—at least half a dozen injection sites in various stages of healing, telling a story of regular, frequent use.

Still holding his arm, I turned to Aedan. "Can you heal him?" My voice was steady despite the turmoil inside me.

Aedan's expression shifted, the mocking smile replaced by something more complex—pity, perhaps, or reluctant understanding. He shrugged one shoulder, neither committing nor refusing.

"Your druid cannot help him." Hun-Came's voice slithered through my mind, seductive and knowing. *"But we can."*

"How?" I whispered, not realizing I'd spoken aloud until Zen's eyes widened.

Hun-Came's response was immediate, his voice almost gleeful. *"If you want to heal your shifter, you must feed his jaguar soul. We can help him if we hunt together, my little vessel, and allow the wahy b'alam to feast with us."*

The offer hung in my mind, terrible and tempting—a bargain with the god of death himself.

CHAPTER TWELVE

I couldn't tear my eyes away from Zen. He lay curled on the bed in a fetal position, his body wracked with violent tremors. Sweat soaked through his thin t-shirt, plastering it to his skin. His face was ashen, eyes sunken into dark hollows, his lips cracked and bleeding where he'd bitten them to keep from crying out. Every few minutes, a spasm would seize him, twisting his features into a mask of agony.

More than seventy-two hours into withdrawal, and he looked like he was dying.

"Like my Nan used to say," Aedan remarked from where he leaned against the doorframe, arms crossed over his chest, "if you lie down with dogs, you wake up with fleas."

I shot him a withering glare. "That's incredibly helpful, thank you."

Aedan shrugged, unperturbed by my sarcasm. "Just making an observation."

"Well, observe silently," I snapped, turning back to Zen. I dipped a cloth into the bowl of cool water on the nightstand and gently wiped his forehead. He flinched at my touch, eyes flying open. For a moment, they were wild, unfocused—then recognition dawned.

"Niki," he rasped, his voice sandpaper rough. "You're still here."

"I'm still here," I confirmed softly.

A tremor rippled through him, stronger than the others. He curled tighter into himself, a low moan escaping through clenched teeth. I felt utterly helpless watching him suffer.

"There's no need for this barbaric cold turkey approach," Aedan said, pushing away from the doorframe to enter the room fully. "I could ease his symptoms, at least enough to make this bearable."

"No," Zen managed between gasps. "No magic. No... intervention. Need to... purge it all."

Our earlier argument echoed in my mind. We'd gone around in circles for hours before Zen had finally relented to detox, but only under two conditions—neither of which I'd liked, but both of which I'd ultimately accepted. No hunting with Hun-Came to feed his jaguar soul, and we would call Izzy.

The first condition I understood. Hunting with Hun-Came would mean surrendering more control to the death god, potentially accelerating our bond. One that, if Zen was correct, could be dangerously close to becoming permanent. But the second condition—bringing Izzy deeper into our mess—had felt like a knife twisting in my gut.

"I can't believe he agreed to help Li Xul."

"He wanted to protect you," Aedan said. "I'll give him credit for that."

I sighed, pressing the heels of my hands against my tired eyes. "I know."

Zen had explained, in between bouts of vomiting and chills, that he'd been trying to shield me all along. Li Xul had been tracking me since our last encounter, determined to either harness Hun-Came's power for himself or destroy us both. Zen had made contact with the sorcerer not out of betrayal but desperation—a calculated risk to learn what Li Xul knew while simultaneously diverting his attention away from me.

It was noble, foolish, and exactly the kind of reckless self-sacrifice that made me want to simultaneously hug him and strangle him.

Another violent spasm gripped Zen. His back arched off the bed, muscles rigid with pain. I grabbed his hand, letting him squeeze mine until I feared my bones would crack.

"Muscle cramps, cold sweats, vomiting, diarrhea, insomnia," Aedan listed clinically. "Classic opioid withdrawal. It's going to get worse before it gets better."

"How much worse?" I whispered, unable to imagine what "worse" would look like.

Aedan's expression softened slightly. "The acute phase typically peaks around day three or four. After that, the physical symptoms should begin to subside, though the psychological withdrawal can last much longer."

As if on cue, the door opened to reveal Izzy, carrying a tray laden with various supplies. Her long dark hair was pulled back in a messy bun, and she wore no makeup, yet somehow managed to look effortlessly beautiful. I tried not to hate her for it.

"How is he?" she asked, setting the tray down on the dresser.

"About as well as can be expected," Aedan replied before I could speak.

Izzy nodded grimly, then began unpacking the tray—bottles of water, electrolyte drinks, more clean cloths, a digital thermometer, and several small containers of what looked like herbal remedies.

"These will help with the nausea," she said, holding up one of the containers. "No opioids, no sedatives—just traditional Mayan herbs. My grandmother's recipe."

I wanted to refuse her help out of pure spite, but Zen's suffering overrode my petty jealousy. "Thank you," I said stiffly.

She met my eyes briefly, something unspoken passing between us. Not quite understanding, not quite alliance—but a temporary truce centered around the man shivering on the bed.

We had arrived at Izzy's family compound three days ago—a sprawling estate nestled in the lush hills outside Cobán. The main house was an imposing structure of stone and dark wood, surrounded by meticulously maintained gardens and smaller outbuildings. The entire complex was ringed by a high wall and patrolled by men with the watchful eyes and sturdy builds of professional security.

I had been too focused on getting Zen settled to fully process our surroundings, but in the harsh light of day, the implications were impossible to ignore. This wasn't just wealth—it was the kind of fortress only built by those with serious enemies.

Izzy had been forthcoming about her family's connections once we were safely inside. Not only had she facilitated Zen's ability to connect with Li Xul through her relatives—once heavily involved in Guatemala's less savory trades—her family had provided additional layers of protection. She was indeed a legitimate archaeologist specializing in Mayan hieroglyphics, but the family business had funded her education and continued to provide resources for her research.

Aedan had spent hours reinforcing the compound's existing security with druidic binding spells, creating a shield against magical detection. He was particularly concerned about Li Xul retaliating against Zen for breaking contact and fleeing.

"His fever's rising again," Izzy said, pressing the back of her hand to Zen's forehead. The casual intimacy of the gesture made my stomach clench.

I reached for the thermometer. "I'll check."

Izzy hesitated for a fraction of a second before surrendering the device, her fingers brushing mine as she passed it over. Our eyes met again, a silent acknowledgment of the tension between us.

"I'll go prepare more of the herbal tea," she said, rising gracefully to her feet. "It should help bring the fever down."

After she left, Aedan settled into a chair by the window, his gaze alternating between the view outside and Zen's trembling form.

"You know," he said conversationally, "I can only do so much for him. The physical symptoms I can somewhat alleviate, but the addiction—the craving for whatever power or vision that substance gave him—that's beyond my abilities."

"I know," I said, gently coaxing Zen to open his mouth for the thermometer. "But Zen is strong. He has more self-control than anyone I know. He'll beat this. All of it."

Zen's eyes fluttered open, focusing on me with effort. "Don't listen to Hun-Came," he rasped.

His comment startled me. I hadn't spoken aloud about Hun-Came's constant whispering in my mind; his alternating offers of power and threats of retribution.

"Nothing to listen to." I pasted a smile on my face. "He's been unnaturally quiet," I lied, wiping his face with the cool cloth again.

"*Do not lie to the wahy b'alam.*" Hun-Came's voice slithered through my consciousness. "*Tell him I offered you both power beyond imagining. Tell him what you're denying him by your weakness.*"

I ignored the god's prodding, focusing instead on the thermometer as it beeped. "103.6," I read, concern tightening my chest. "That's higher than before."

Zen managed a weak smile that looked more like a grimace. "Runs hot...jaguar thing." Another spasm wracked his body, and he curled tighter, a low moan escaping his lips.

"*The shifter is weak,*" Hun-Came whispered now. "*He cannot protect himself from Li Xul in this state. Nor can he protect you or the others. The witch and druid's powers are limited. You need me, little vessel. You need my strength.*"

"Shut up," I muttered under my breath.

Aedan raised an eyebrow. "Our divine houseguest making himself known?"

Before I could answer, Zen suddenly lurched upright, his

eyes wild and unfocused. "He's coming," he gasped, his voice thick with terror. "He's found us. Li Xul—he's coming!"

I exchanged alarmed glances with Aedan, who was already on his feet, his hand moving to where Sky-Splitter rested between his shoulder blades.

"It's the withdrawal," Aedan said, his voice low and urgent. "Hallucinations, paranoia—they're common symptoms."

"No," Zen insisted, his fingers digging into my arm with surprising strength. "Not hallucinating. I can feel him—searching, probing. He's dream-walking. The barriers you've put up—they're holding for now, but he's persistent. He knows where I am. He knows I am with you."

Aedan's expression hardened. "I need to check on a few things." He strode toward the door, pausing to look back at me. "Stay with him. If anything changes—anything at all—call for me immediately."

The door had barely closed behind him when Izzy reappeared, carrying a steaming mug. Her eyes darted from Zen's panicked face to my worried one.

"What happened?" she demanded, setting the mug down with a sharp click.

"He thinks Li Xul is searching for us," I said. "Aedan's gone to check the protective barriers."

Izzy's face paled slightly, but her voice remained steady. "This property has its own protections, even beyond what your Irish friend has added."

She approached the bed, her movements careful and practiced as she helped Zen lie back against the pillows. There was an easy familiarity between them that spoke of shared intimacy—exactly the kind of "history" she had alluded to when we first met.

"Try to drink some of this," she urged, holding the mug to his lips. "It will help with the fever and calm your mind."

Zen took a few obedient sips before turning his face away. "Can't," he mumbled. "Will come back up."

"Just a little more," she insisted with a gentleness that made my chest ache. "For me?"

He managed a few more sips before slumping back, exhausted by even this small effort. Izzy set the mug aside and brushed his sweat-soaked hair from his forehead with a tenderness that felt intimate enough to make me look away.

"Oh, Zen. What were you thinking?" I whispered, my heart breaking at the sight of him suffering.

"He was thinking of you." Izzy's eyes flicked to mine, unable to mask the accusation behind the words. "He took the risk because of you. He wanted to find answers. To save someone he cares about." Her expression softened slightly. "He's always been willing to sacrifice himself for others. It's his greatest strength and his most dangerous weakness."

A familiar guilt twisted in my gut. How many people had been hurt—would continue to be hurt—or die because of Hun-Came's presence in my life? Had I stopped Li Xul from merging with Hun-Came, only to become the very agent of death and destruction I'd been trying to prevent?

"He speaks of you often," Izzy said abruptly, her tone carefully controlled. "He told me what you did to keep Li Xul from merging with Hun-Came."

I didn't know how to respond to that, so I remained silent, watching Zen's fitful sleep.

"I thought he was exaggerating," she continued, a hint of bitter amusement coloring her words. "But I've watched Zen destroy himself trying to save you. To protect you from Li Xul." She paused, her expression unreadable. "So yes, now I believe that he believes you are in danger."

The door opened again, admitting Aedan, his expression grave. "The spells are holding," he reported, "but Zen was right. Something—or someone—is probing at them."

"Li Xul," I said, feeling Hun-Came stir restlessly at the name.

"Most likely," Aedan agreed, moving to the window to peer out at the darkening sky. "The question is, how did he find us so quickly?"

"He didn't find us," Izzy said, rising to her feet with fluid grace. "He found Zen." She looked down at him, her expression a complex mixture of tenderness and resignation. "Li Xul is a powerful shaman. Zen has been working with him for months. Now that Zen is no longer working for him, Li Xul will try to destroy him. Zen's shared experiences with Li Xul have strengthened the connection and extended the range of contact. He will strike when Zen is least able to fight back." She glanced down at Zen who lay still as death, eyes closed. "Like now."

I shivered, remembering the connection I'd forged with Li Xul when I'd dream-walked into his consciousness and how much effort it had taken to block him from my dreams. "He's vulnerable while he's hallucinating. It creates an opportunity for Li Xul to dream-walk into his consciousness," I said, horrified understanding dawning. "If Li Xul can find him, he can kill him."

Izzy nodded grimly.

A soft moan from Zen drew our attention back to the bed. His eyes fluttered open, focusing on me with difficulty. "Niki," he whispered, his voice thick with pain and need.

I hesitated, feeling Hun-Came's eager anticipation flare within me. The god had been waiting for precisely this moment—

"*Yes,*" Hun-Came hissed, his voice like silk sliding over stone. "*One hunt. One small surrender. To save the shifter you care for. He needs to feed his wahy. Only you can do this for him.*"

"We need to help Zen so he can protect himself from Li Xul."

"Absolutely not," Aedan said firmly, moving to stand beside me.

Izzy looked between us, confusion evident on her face. "What are you talking about?"

I gazed at Zen, understanding the terrible choice before me. To hunt of my own volition with Hun-Came would strengthen the god's hold on me, potentially accelerating the very bond we were trying to break. But it might also help

Zen heal faster and he needed every advantage we could give him.

"I can dream-walk, too."

Izzy arched her eyebrows in mild surprise. "Another dream-walker. How fortunate. And you are planning to…"

"To dream-walk. With Zen," I explained to her, my voice tight. "Right now, he's weak. In this state, he's unable to protect himself from Li Xul. I am going to dream-walk with Zen. To heal him from this." I gestured toward where Zen lay shaking on the bed.

"At what cost?" Aedan demanded.

I closed my eyes briefly, feeling the weight of all their gazes. When I opened them again, I had made my decision.

"It doesn't matter. I have to do it," I said, my voice stronger than I felt. "*Yes, I will hunt but only animals, as we agreed.*" I directed this last part inward, to Hun-Came himself.

The death god's satisfaction curled through me like smoke. "*As we agreed,*" he echoed, his voice rich with dark promise. "*Let us begin the hunt.*"

CHAPTER THIRTEEN

I lay in the twin bed next to Zen's, hoping proximity would make it easier for me to weave him into my dreamscape. I'd done this before but now—given that Hun-Came had commandeered space in my shadow soul—I was no longer certain it would work.

"You're making a mistake," Aedan said from where he stood by the window, his voice tight with barely contained anger. "There are other ways to help him."

"Name one that would work as quickly," I challenged, meeting his gaze directly.

Aedan's jaw clenched, but he offered no alternatives. We both knew there weren't any—not with Li Xul closing in and Zen too weak to defend himself.

"If this goes sideways," he warned. "If Hun-Came takes more control than you've bargained for—"

"You'll do whatever's necessary," I finished for him. "I know."

Izzy entered looking between us with wary confusion.

I inhaled deeply trying to settle my nerves. "You wouldn't happen to know anything about obsidian mirrors, would you?" I asked Aedan, only half-joking.

Aedan shook his head. "Sorry. I'm Irish, love." His expression turned thoughtful. "Though my Nan would talk about using sacred pools and reflective surfaces to anchor her to this world when she was 'walking between.' Perhaps we should wait and think this through a bit?"

I looked over at where Zen lay, pale and shivering with fever. "We don't have time to wait." My voice sounded far calmer than I felt.

"I should have guessed you were a dream-walker. And what happens to you in this process if you dream-walk with Hun-Came?" Izzy asked, her dark eyes shrewd.

"Nothing good," Aedan muttered.

I ignored him. "I'll be fine."

That was a lie, of course. By surrendering control to Hun-Came, I allowed him to dig his claws in deeper, make himself more at home in my soul. This deliberate invitation—this willing partnership—would accelerate our bond in ways I could only guess. But I saw no other choice. Not with Zen suffering and vulnerable, and Li Xul circling like a vulture.

Izzy studied me for a moment, her expression carefully blank, though I had the feeling she wouldn't shed any tears if something happened to me.

I closed my eyes, my hand straying to touch the jade pendant around my neck once more. "You should leave," I said, already feeling Hun-Came stirring eagerly within me. "This isn't something you want to watch."

Izzy hesitated, then bent to press a gentle kiss to Zen's forehead before rising. "I'll be in the next room if you need anything," she said, her eyes lingering on his face before she slipped out the door.

Aedan remained; arms crossed over his chest. "I'm not leaving you alone with him," he said firmly.

I didn't have the energy to argue, and part of me was relieved. If things went wrong—if Hun-Came tried to take more than I was offering—I would need Aedan there to stop me.

"Fine," I conceded. "But stay back. And no matter what you see or hear, don't interfere unless I tell you to."

His eyes darkened. "Unless you're no longer in a position to tell me anything."

I nodded, understanding his meaning. If Hun-Came took over completely, Aedan would do what needed to be done. The thought should have terrified me, but instead, it brought a strange comfort.

"Keep Sky-Splitter close," I advised, settling more comfortably on the bed.

I took several deep breaths, deliberately slowing my heartbeat as I prepared to surrender myself to sleep—and to Hun-Came. My father had helped me develop this technique when I was a child to control the night terrors I suffered, a symptom of my dream-walking ability. I closed my eyes and began to build my dream.

As my consciousness began to drift, I felt Hun-Came's presence growing stronger, his essence expanding from that dark corner of my mind where he normally resided.

"*At last,*" he whispered, his voice rich with anticipation. "*You finally see reason, little vessel.*"

I felt him spreading through me slowly, like ink dropped in water, inhabiting space inside me. With the seductive power of a lover, he moved through me, caressing my consciousness, spreading along my shoulders, my breasts, flowing down my arms and fingertips then winding his way along my torso and my hips. He stroked my inner thighs with the sensation of phantom hands leaving the pleasant sensation of heat in their wake. It was pleasant at first, but as he progressed the heat intensified into a burning hunger that consumed my every cell. A craving urgent and demanding. A need for death. A need for blood.

"*Yes,*" Hun-Came purred in my mind. "*Feel it. Embrace it. This is what I offer you—the primal joy of the hunt, the sacred power of taking life.*"

I surrendered completely, letting myself fall into the dream realm where Hun-Came's power was greatest.

***

I am in the jungle. My ears twitch, listening to the drone of insects and the chirring of cicadas that fill the air. The night wraps around me like a living thing, but darkness is no impediment. I see everything with supernatural clarity—each leaf, each insect, the tiny mammals scurrying through the underbrush. The air is thick with scents—decaying vegetation, damp earth, the musk of animals, the tang of fear.

I look down at my hands, but they are no longer hands. Powerful paws tipped with razor-sharp claws flex against the soft earth. My body is sleek and powerful, covered in a pale golden fur marked with distinctive dark rosettes. I am jaguar—the embodiment of my shadow soul, the physical manifestation of my Mayan name.

Hun-Came's presence is no longer separate from mine. We move as one consciousness in this magnificent predator's body. I feel his satisfaction as I prowl through the jungle, my padded feet silent on the forest floor.

"You were born under the sign of I'x." Hun-Came's voice whispers through me, no longer confined to my mind but resonating through every muscle and sinew. "Jaguar is your spirit guide, your shadow self. This is your birthright."

I drop into a crouch, instinct taking over as I detect movement ahead. My nostrils flare, drawing in the scent of warm blood and fear. A peccary, small and plump, rooting among fallen fruit a few yards away. Unaware of the death that watches from the shadows.

I stalk forward, each movement precise and measured. The jungle seems to part for me, branches bending away, vines retreating. I am death incarnate, moving through the night like a shadow given form.

The peccary raises its head suddenly, sensing danger. Too late.

I launch myself in a powerful surge of muscle. The prey squeals once, a high, terrified sound cut short as my jaws close around its throat. I feel the soft flesh give way as the taste of blood explodes across my tongue, hot and metallic. The peccary struggles briefly, then goes still.

My teeth rip into the soft flesh, tearing away chunks of meat. Warm blood trickles down my throat, quenching the burning need that had been searing me from the inside. The relief is immediate and exquisite—a pleasure so intense it borders on pain.

"More," Hun-Came urges, his voice thick with satisfaction. "We need more."

The hunger rises again, insatiable and demanding. I want to hunt again, to feel the rush of the kill, to bathe in the sacred moment when life becomes death. But I force myself to stop, to remember why we're here.

I throw my head back and roar, the sound echoing through the jungle like thunder. It is both an invitation and a command, summoning Zen into my dream-walk.

For a moment, nothing happens. The jungle holds its breath around me; time suspended between heartbeats. Then the air shimmers, reality folding in on itself as another presence enters the dream.

A second jaguar appears, moving slowly and cautiously from between the trees. This one is emaciated, bones visible beneath the dull coat that has lost its sheen. His amber eyes—Zen's eyes—regard me warily, hunger and exhaustion evident in every line of his body.

I step back from my kill, watching as he approaches. Every instinct within me—both human and jaguar—screams to protect my prey, to drive away this intruder. Hun-Came's influence surges, urging me to attack, to demonstrate dominance.

"He is weak," the god whispers. "Together we could destroy him, take his power for our own."

But that is not why we are here. I resist Hun-Came's urgings, forcing myself to remain still as Zen's jaguar form cautiously approaches the kill.

He feeds slowly at first, then with increasing desperation, tearing into the carcass with renewed strength as the nourishment begins to flow through him. I watch, quivering with the desire to join him, to reclaim my prey, to take everything.

"This is sacred sharing," Hun-Came whispers, his fury at being denied gradually subsiding into something like grudging respect. "As it was in the old days, when wahy b'alam and death hunted together."

Zen raises his blood-smeared muzzle, his amber eyes meeting mine. Something passes between us—understanding, gratitude, a connection that transcends our human forms. In this moment, we are simply predator spirits sharing the night, bound by ancient magic.

He lowers his head to feed again, his movements already more fluid, strength visibly returning to his limbs. The transformation is remarkable to witness—like watching a withered plant revive under rainfall.

When he has taken his fill, Zen steps back from the remains, his coat already beginning to regain some of its luster. He approaches me slowly.

The touch of his muzzle against mine sends a jolt of electricity through my entire being. Not Hun-Came's power, but something different—something that belongs solely to Zen and me. For a brief, dazzling moment, I feel our spirits connect directly, bypassing Hun-Came's influence entirely.

In that connection, I glimpse fragments of Zen's experiences—the pain of withdrawal, but also his determination, his unwavering resolve to free me from Hun-Came. His fear not for himself, but for what I might become if the god's possession becomes permanent.

Then Hun-Came's jealousy flares, shattering the connection with a surge of possessive rage.

"Enough," the god snarls within me. "He has taken what he needs. The bargain is fulfilled."

Zen seems to sense the shift. He backs away, his golden eyes still fixed on mine, as he turns and melts into the jungle shadows, his form gradually fading as he withdraws from the dream.

I remain, still locked in jaguar form, still bound to Hun-Came in this realm of his power. The hunger returns, redoubled now, demanding satisfaction.

"We hunt again," Hun-Came declares, not a question but a command. "The night is young, and there is more power to be gained."

I try to resist, to remember our agreement—one hunt, one kill. But in this form, with Hun-Came's essence mingled so completely with mine, my human will seems distant and unimportant. The jaguar wants to hunt. Hun-Came wants to kill. And I... I am losing the distinction between myself and them.

From above, I hear the unmistakable cry of a quetzal. Nayla! I look up to see a flash of gold feathers circling overhead. Then Nayla folds her wings and dives toward me.

***

I woke with a violent jerk, gasping for air as if I'd been underwater. My body felt strange—too small, too weak, too human. For several disorienting seconds, I couldn't remember who or what I was.

"Welcome back," Aedan said grimly from where he sat beside the bed, Sky-Splitter laid across his knees. "Had a nice hunt, did we?"

Memory crashed back—the dream, the jaguar form, the kill. The raw, primal pleasure of it. The way Hun-Came had moved through me, the lines between us blurring until I couldn't tell where the god ended and I began.

I sat up shakily, touching the jade pendant around my neck as a wave of dizziness made the room spin. Nayla. Once again, my sister was there when I needed her.

"How long was I out?" My voice sounded rough, unfamiliar to my own ears. I breathed through the nausea that roiled through me, my fingers brushing the iron bracelet as I clasped it once again around my left wrist. It felt surprisingly warm, the way a battery does when it's being used.

"Almost four hours," Aedan replied. "And before you ask—yes, you were moving. Twitching, making sounds." His expression was carefully neutral. "Hunting sounds."

Shame washed through me. "Did I... did I hurt anyone?"

"No. You stayed put, physically at least." He nodded toward the other bed. "And it seems your little experiment worked."

My head had begun to throb; I carefully turned to look at Zen and gasped in surprise. The change was dramatic. Gone was the pallid, sweat-soaked wraith of just hours before. His color had returned, his breathing deep and even. Though still thin, the hollow, skull-like appearance of his face had filled out, and his sleep seemed peaceful rather than tortured.

"The fever broke about an hour ago," Aedan continued.

"His pulse is steady, breathing normal. Whatever you did in there," he gestured vaguely at my head, "it appears to have accelerated his healing considerably."

Relief flooded through me, followed immediately by unease. The cost had been high—higher than I'd anticipated. Hun-Came's presence felt more firmly entrenched than ever, his essence woven more thoroughly through mine. As I closed my mind to him, the pain at the base of my skull began to intensify.

"I killed a peccary," I said softly, the memory vivid and unsettling in its clarity. "In the dream. But it felt... real."

Aedan's expression darkened. "It was real, in its way. Dream-hunting with a death god isn't just symbolic. Something died tonight to feed that power."

Before I could respond, Zen stirred, his eyes opening slowly. They were clear now, alert, the fevered glaze gone. He looked directly at me with an intensity that made my breath catch.

"You shouldn't have done that," he said, his voice stronger than it had been in days. "But thank you."

I managed a weak smile. "You're welcome."

CHAPTER FOURTEEN

My dream-walk with Hun-Came left me with a terrible migraine—not just pain, but nausea, dizziness, and strange sensations burning and tingling through my arms and legs. The aftermath rendered me weak and blind as a newborn kitten. Unable to eat or drink, I lay in the darkened room, breathing through waves of agony.

"*With resistance comes pain.*" Hun-Came's voice crashed and boomed through the electrical storm raging inside my head, each syllable a thunderclap against my skull. "*Join with me. Embrace your destiny.*"

A fierce primal hunger knifed through me—sharp, urgent, demanding. My body convulsed with the need of it, my spine arching off the bed as something ancient and terrible clawed at my insides.

"*We were magnificent tonight,*" Hun-Came whispered, his voice clearer than ever despite the iron's protective influence. "*Now let us hunt something worthy of our power.*"

My hand crept to the jade jaguar talisman around my neck, grasping for something to help protect me from the death god's onslaught. I moaned, desperate to end the pain, terrified that I was losing the battle against the death god residing within me. Something had changed during our dream-walk—a boundary crossed, a barrier weakened. I could feel him more distinctly now, a separate consciousness pressing against my own, no longer just whispers but a presence with weight and substance.

It was Aedan, with his healing powers, who kept me from shattering completely. He sat beside my bed, his fingers on the iron bracelet encircling my wrist. The cool sensation spread from his touch through the metal and into my skin, dulling the hunger, diminishing Hun-Came's presence until the pain in my head slowly receded. "Go to sleep, Niki. Close your eyes and your mind to him," Aedan whispered.

As his touch eased the worst of my pain, I caught a flicker of worry in his eyes—something deeper than mere concern for my comfort. It was fear, quickly masked, but unmistakable. I wanted to ask what he wasn't telling me, but exhaustion pulled at me like gravity, making it impossible to keep my eyes open.

As I drifted into darkness, Hun-Came's voice echoed through my mind, intimate and knowing. *"Oh, my little vessel. Now that you've tasted true hunting, you will crave it again. And when you do, I will be waiting."*

***

When I awoke, I was in a different room. Sunlight streamed through wooden window shutters, illuminating dust motes that danced in golden shafts of light. The walls were a warm terracotta, adorned with woven textiles in vibrant patterns of red and gold. I had no recollection of being moved here, but someone—Aedan? —had carried me from the guest room where Zen had been sleeping.

Without any conscious thought, my fingertips sought the jaguar pendant at my neck and the iron bracelet around my wrist. The pain in my head was gone, but a vague, unsettling hunger still echoed through me. I could feel Hun-

102

Came lurking close, watching, waiting, but he remained silent—a predator conserving energy before the next hunt.

I carefully pushed myself up to sitting, noticing with unease how my senses seemed unnaturally heightened. The dust motes in the sunlight appeared individually distinct, the textured pattern of the blanket beneath my fingers felt almost three-dimensional, and I could detect the faint scent of copal incense lingering from what must have been a ritual performed hours earlier.

Someone had thoughtfully left a pitcher of water and a glass on the nightstand. Hands trembling, I poured myself a glass of cool water, letting it soothe my parched throat.

There was a light rap on my door, and Zen entered. Looking pale and thin, the contours of his face sharper than before, he carried himself with the cautious movements of someone still healing. The shadows beneath his amber eyes spoke of a night without sleep, but his gaze was alert as he studied my face with concern.

"How do you feel?" he asked, keeping his distance.

"I'm fine," I lied. In truth, I felt hollowed out, as if something essential had been scraped from inside me and replaced with something darker, hungrier—a void that whispered of insatiable appetites.

"Liar," Zen said softly. His amber eyes saw too much, as always. "I felt what happened in the dream. I know what it cost you."

A flicker of shame warmed my cheeks. He had witnessed it all—the hunt, the kill, the terrifying fusion of myself with Hun-Came. More disturbing was the memory of how natural it had felt, how right, in those moments of perfect predatory union.

"It was worth it." I breathed in the heady scent of him before shifting my gaze toward the window, avoiding his penetrating gaze. "Can you feel him? Li Xul? Is he out there?"

"Yes," Zen said grimly. "The tether is weaker now that I'm healing, but it's still there. He knows where to find us."

He reached for me, his eyes filled with tenderness, his fingers brushing mine in a gesture of comfort.

The contact sent a jolt through me, reminiscent of that moment in the dream when our jaguar forms had touched. A connection that felt powerful and raw, both ancient and new—like lightning finding the path of least resistance between sky and earth.

Zen abruptly jerked back as if he'd been scorched, his expression shifting from tenderness to alarm. Something dark flickered behind his eyes, a shadow passing over his face. He curled his fingers into a tight fist.

"What was that?" I whispered, still feeling the electric buzz of our connection lingering in my fingertips.

Zen's expression was guarded, a mix of longing and concern. "Something has changed. The boundaries between you and Hun-Came—they're less defined now."

"Is that... bad?" The question sounded naïve.

He hesitated, and in that moment of silence, I knew there was more he wasn't telling me. "It's probably best that we minimize any contact between us," he finally said. "It's safer for you."

I nodded, my heart heavy with understanding. For the first time, I truly comprehended the cryptic note he'd left me months ago. For a shapeshifter, contact with Hun-Came posed its own risks. And now? Any contact between Zen and myself risked joining the shaman Li Xul and Hun-Came—a connection with the potential to undo the forces that held the universe in balance.

"Do you want me to bring you something to eat?" he asked, carefully maintaining space between us.

"No. I'll get up." The thought of food awakened the strange hunger that had been simmering beneath my skin. It wasn't just ordinary hunger—something primal stirred at the prospect of sustenance.

"Are you sure? What you did... it takes a toll. Hun-Came fed on your energy as much as on the kill."

He was wrong. Hun-Came hadn't fed on my energy; I

had feasted on his. An energy I still felt thrumming below my skin like a faint aching hunger. It frightened me that I wanted more of it—that strange power, that exhilarating release. I pushed off the covers and swung my legs over the bed. "Let's go."

Zen led me to the dining room. I was surprised to find it was afternoon. Izzy and Aedan sat at a long mahogany table, poring over papers spread across its dark polished surface. Old maps, the paper curled and yellowed with age, and photocopies of what appeared to be Mayan codices covered half the table. Aedan rose to his feet as we entered, his face lighting with relief.

"There she is, back among the living," he said, his Irish lilt warming the words. His eyes, however, remained concerned as they swept over me. "Had us worried, love. How's the head?"

"Better," I said, avoiding Zen's knowing gaze. "Thanks for... whatever you did last night."

Aedan shrugged. "Just a wee bit of energy work. Nothing special."

"Don't be modest," Izzy said without looking up from the document she was studying. "It doesn't suit you." She finally lifted her head to acknowledge me with a crisp nod. "Niki. You appear... recovered." Her tone suggested clinical observation rather than genuine concern.

I slid into a chair across from her, eyeing the scattered papers. "What's all this?"

"Research," Zen said, taking the seat beside Aedan rather than next to me. The deliberate distance stung more than it should have.

"Now that Niki has joined us, shall we eat?" Izzy asked, pushing aside the papers and reaching for a small silver bell positioned at her elbow. "You must be famished after your... adventure." Her dark eyes studied me with an intensity that felt invasive, as if she could see the remnants of Hun-Came still swirling beneath my skin. "Though perhaps you have already eaten your fill?"

I was still feeling disoriented from the dream-walking, my body heavy and sluggish as if I'd run miles rather than merely slept. The boundaries between Hun-Came's consciousness and my own felt blurred, raw at the edges. I fought to center myself in the present moment, to meet Izzy's challenge.

One eyebrow arched involuntarily. "A bell? You ring for service? How very Downton Abbey of you." The words came out sharper than I'd intended, Hun-Came's irritation bleeding into my own.

Izzy's lips twitched, though whether from amusement or irritation was hard to tell. "My family maintains certain traditions."

She rang the bell with a practiced flick of her wrist. Within moments, uniformed staff entered carrying trays laden with food. They moved with the silent efficiency of those who'd been trained to be invisible. They set before us steaming plates of pepián, a rich stew of chicken and vegetables in a spiced sauce, accompanied by fresh tortillas, black beans, and sliced avocados.

The hunger that had been lurking beneath my skin surged violently at the overpowering scent of food. It wasn't just ordinary hunger it was ravenous, primal, almost painful in its intensity. My hands trembled slightly as I reached for my fork, and I could feel a cold sweat breaking out along my hairline. Something predatory stirred within me, and I had to fight the urge to abandon utensils entirely.

"Slowly," Aedan cautioned quietly, his hand hovering near mine without touching. "Your body's been through a shock."

I nodded, forcing myself to take measured bites despite the primal urge to devour everything in sight. Hun-Came's influence, I realized with a chill that had nothing to do with the room's temperature. The death god's appetite wasn't limited to spiritual hunting. The food tasted impossibly good, each flavor magnified to an almost overwhelming degree. I closed my eyes briefly, struggling to maintain composure.

"You are feeling well?" Izzy asked, her dark eyes fixed on me with unsettling intensity. There was something calculating in her gaze, like a scientist observing a particularly fascinating specimen.

I swallowed my bite of food, feeling it travel down my throat. "Yes," I lied, meeting her gaze steadily. A little voice inside me—my voice, not Hun-Came's—wondered if there were dark circles under my eyes, if my skin looked as pale and clammy as it felt.

"I imagine it must be... challenging... to share consciousness with an entity like Hun-Came," Izzy remarked, her tone deceptively casual as she delicately cut a piece of chicken. "The ancient texts describe him as authoritative, ruthless, easily offended and vengeful. Not exactly someone I'd choose for a soulmate."

I tensed, sensing the direction of her probing. "It's complicated."

"I'm sure." Her eyes flicked briefly to Zen. "Complicated seems to be a recurring theme for you."

The subtle dig wasn't lost on me. I felt a flicker of jealousy, quickly followed by a surge of something colder, darker—Hun-Came's presence stirring at my emotional response.

"I find it very interesting from an academic point of view," she continued, observing my reaction. "The texts speak of a gradual merging—psychological and physiological changes, heightened senses, unusual physical appetites." Her gaze dropped pointedly to my plate, where I'd been unconsciously tearing a tortilla into small pieces. "Are you experiencing those symptoms?"

"Izzy," Zen warned, his posture deceptively relaxed but his muscles visibly tensed beneath his shirt.

She smiled thinly. "Zen, you know better than most. Knowledge is power, especially in her... situation." Her eyes returned to me. "Tell me, how much control do you have? When he speaks to you, when he…joins with you?"

"That's enough," Aedan interjected, his usually friendly face hardening. "Niki isn't one of your research projects."

Something in Izzy's expression shifted, a brief flash of genuine emotion breaking through her composed exterior. Was it concern? Jealousy? Whatever it was, it vanished quickly, replaced by her usual cool detachment.

"My apologies," she said, though her tone held little remorse. "Professional curiosity. Since we may not have much time, I can't help myself."

"What do you mean by that? Not much time?" I asked, my gaze shifting between Izzy, Zen, and Aedan.

A heavy silence fell over the table. Izzy glanced between Zen and Aedan, surprise evident in her expression. "You haven't told her?" When neither man responded, she laughed softly, the sound lacking any warmth. "How very protective of you both."

"Told me what?" I demanded, my heart beginning to pound. The food suddenly tasted like ash in my mouth.

Aedan shot Izzy a warning look, but she ignored him, leaning forward with the eager intensity of someone delivering long-awaited news.

"The mortal vessel doesn't survive the joining," she said simply. "Not in any form recognizable as human."

The room seemed to tilt sideways. "What do you mean?" My voice sounded distant, as if it was coming from someone else.

"What she means,"— Zen said slowly, his eyes fixed on me with quiet intensity, — "is that without intervention, the process can be... fatal."

"Fatal." The word fell from my lips like a stone. Hun-Came's presence suddenly felt heavier within me, more ominous. "I'm dying."

"Dying isn't quite accurate," Izzy corrected, her academic tone at odds with the gravity of her words. "It's more of a transformation. A consumption. Existential erasure. The human consciousness gradually gives way to the deity's."

My hands began to tremble. I pressed them flat against the cool mahogany of the table to hide their shaking. "And you waited until now to mention this?"

"I assumed you understood the need for expediency." Her eyebrow arched in genuine curiosity before shifting her gaze to Zen and Aedan. "You didn't tell her?"

They looked down at their plates. Blood thundered in my ears. "You knew? All of you knew this? My mother, too?"

Aedan answered with a brusque nod of his head.

"When were you going to tell me?" I asked, my voice low but steady, surprising myself with my control when inside I was screaming.

Zen met my eyes, his expression solemn. "We were looking for solutions first. We didn't want to—"

"Scare me?" I finished for him, a bitter taste flooding my mouth that had nothing to do with the food. "That wasn't your decision to make. This is my life—what's left of it."

"It's not that simple," Aedan said gently. "There are ways to slow the process, maybe even halt it."

"The iron helps," Zen added, nodding toward my bracelet. "It buys us time."

"Time for what?" I demanded.

Izzy's cool voice cut through the tension. "Time to find a way to separate you from Hun-Came. Or to negotiate terms that allow you both to... coexist."

I stared at her, trying to process her words through the shock. "Negotiate? With a death god?"

"Gods have rules," Aedan said simply. "Even death gods."

"And you know these rules?" I asked, skepticism evident in my tone.

"Some of them," Izzy replied. She pulled a weathered document toward her. "That's what this research is about. Finding the entrance to Hun-Came's domain—the Boca de Xibalba."

"The Mouth of the Underworld," I translated softly, the

words sending a chill down my spine.

"Yes," Zen confirmed. "If we can reach Xibalba—the real Xibalba, not just the dream version—there are ways to... renegotiate terms."

I looked between them, absorbing the gravity of what they were saying. The blackouts and the persistent hunger for blood suddenly made terrible sense—it wasn't just Hun-Came's influence I had to worry about, it was my own humanity being slowly consumed. From the moment we first joined together, Hun-Came had been laying claim to me, replacing my human soul with something else.

"How long?" I forced myself to ask, my voice steadier than I felt. "How long before I'm... gone?"

Izzy considered me for a long moment. "I don't know. No one knows." She glanced meaningfully at the iron bracelet. "That helps, but it's only delaying the inevitable, unless we find another solution."

"And there is one," Zen said, his voice forged in steel. "There is a solution."

"Potentially," Izzy countered, lazily. "First, we need to locate the entrance to Xilbaba. Not a simple task but I believe I've located several options that could be the entrance," she continued, her tone shifting to something more businesslike. "Caves that align with ancient Mayan descriptions of paths to Xibalba."

"So that's the plan?" I asked, trying to focus on action rather than the terrifying revelation that I was being slowly erased. "We just... walk into the Underworld?"

"Not exactly," Izzy replied. "There will be guardians, tests. The way to Xibalba is never straightforward."

"*You may travel to my kingdom, my little vessel.*" Hun-Came's voice whispered inside my head, no longer muted by the iron at my wrist. "*But be warned. I have chosen, and what I have chosen I will not relinquish.*"

A chill ran down my spine, raising goosebumps along my arms. Across the table, Izzy's eyes narrowed, as if she could sense the conversation happening inside my head.

"He's speaking to you now, isn't he?" she asked.

I met her gaze, refusing to flinch. "Yes. He says we can travel to his kingdom."

"Good." She smiled, and for the first time, it reached her eyes. "Then we're all in agreement about what comes next."

LISA DIETRICH

CHAPTER FIFTEEN

We weren't in agreement. Not even close.

"You're going to have to help me a bit here," Aedan said, rubbing his temples. "Boca de Xilbaba? Literally 'mouth of hell'? Have I got that right?"

The dining room was transformed into a makeshift war room, with maps spread across the mahogany table, each corner weighted down with artifacts and books. The remains of our meal had been cleared away, replaced by notebooks, pencils, and ancient texts.

Aedan leaned forward, letting his fingers fall on the maps laid out before us. "I'm seeing a lot of caves here. Lots of mouths to choose from."

Izzy nodded, uncapping a red pen. With practiced precision, she circled three locations on the largest map.

"These are the most likely locations," she said. "The Chiquibul cave system in Belize, Chichen Itza on the Yucatan peninsula in Mexico, and somewhere near Dzibanché, also in Mexico."

She looked at me, her eyes knowing. "The Popol Vuh isn't just an origin myth—it's a map. We know that caves are portals to the underworld. We are looking for a cave system with rivers, thorns, and the 'dark houses'—the House of Razors, House of Jaguars, House of Bats, and so on. A site associated with disease, death, and ritual sacrifice, where the temples or caves are aligned with celestial events."

Zen frowned. "Why not Choja Q'eq? It has water. The cavern Li Xul was using has a cenote. It was obviously a ceremonial site."

"Yes," Izzy replied, "but it's a stand-alone site. We need a cave system with a subterranean river. Choja Q'eq was a ritual site where priests provided human sacrifices to appease the gods of the underworld, but it's not an entrance." She tapped the worn pages of a book beside her. "The Popol Vuh tells us that we need to cross the river of blood, the river of pus to gain entrance. We need water, subterranean channels—and there aren't any at Choja Q'eq."

I furrowed my brow, studying the maps. Hun-Came remained mulishly silent as we worked, offering no help, essentially pouting.

"Not to state the obvious," Aedan said, "but why not this one?" He pointed to a spot labeled "Cueva del Xilbaba" in Petén, Guatemala. "Xilbaba Cave, right?"

"It's a possibility," Izzy said, eyebrows raised in approval. "That cave is part of the Chiquibul cave system that extends into Belize—about seven kilometers from the border. 150 hectares with chambers linked by an underground river. There hasn't been extensive research, but a survey in—" she shuffled some papers until she found what she wanted. "In the 1960's found artifacts, stone walls, and platforms built by the Maya, so we know it was used for rituals." She shifted in her seat, folding her hands before continuing. "On the Guatemala side, the cave system is officially closed. The entrance..." Her finger tapped the location on the map. "Is extremely remote, situated deep in the Petén jungle. Reaching it would require several days of hiking through dense, undeveloped rainforest. And since the site is closed, we would need permission."

"How hard would it be to get permission?" I asked.

Izzy shrugged. "It could be done—but it wouldn't be easy or cheap."

"The other option is we go to Belize." Her finger traced a straight line across the border. "The Chiquibul River flows through this area, creating a subterranean channel connecting Actun Tun Kul cave in Belize to Xilbaba Cave in Guatemala. If we choose this one, it would involve days of traveling underground and swimming—possibly requiring scuba gear."

Zen lifted his eyebrows. "Scuba gear?"

Izzy nodded.

I caught his eye. Actually, I wasn't sure I was up for traveling for days in a cave at all, not to mention swimming in one. My previous dream-scape experience of Xilbaba with Hun-Came had given me a healthy fear and respect for what we might find underground.

Hun-Came stirred within me, finally deigning to speak. *"As a mortal, the only way to avoid the journey to Xilbaba is to die a violent death."* His voice carried a hint of amusement.

Izzy continued. "Second option is here." She pointed to Chichen Itza on the Yucatan peninsula. "Site of human sacrifice—they've found a large cache of bones. Using electronic resistance surveys, archaeologists have identified a large cenote beneath El Castillo temple and a river under the Kukulkan temple." She glanced up at Aedan. "The feathered serpent of this temple is linked to visions connecting to supernatural realms." Gazing back at the map in front of her, she continued. "The channel below this temple was blocked by the ancient Maya—making it inaccessible but the river at the center could represent the center of the Maya's universe, which they thought of as a tree with roots reaching below ground." She traced the outline of the famous pyramid with her fingertip. "We wouldn't be able to access the archaeological site directly, but there might be another entrance."

"A back door?" Aedan suggested helpfully.

"Yes. Finding it would be challenging and time-consuming, but it could be done if we think that's where we should go."

Izzy's pencil tapped the third option. "Dzibanché in Quintana Roo, Mexico. Dzibanché was a major Maya city and the early capital and place of origin of the Kaan dynasty, a powerful Maya lineage. It has an Owl Temple associated with death. The nine doorway temples of the Plaza Xilbaba symbolize the gateway to the underworld's nine levels." Her voice took on a professorial tone. "There are a large number of cenotes in the area, which suggests some sort of underground river. There could be a subterranean channel linking it to..." Her finger traced a line from Dzibanché to Chichén Itzá to Actun Tun Kul in Belize to Xilbaba Cave in Guatemala.

The three of them looked at me expectantly.

"Any thoughts, love?" Aedan asked.

"I don't know which one it is," I said, feeling helpless. "Hun-Came's more or less giving me the silent treatment at the moment, at least when it comes to anything resembling helpful information."

"Guatemala," Zen said decisively. "Xilbaba Cave gives us the best chance. There are miles of unmapped caverns, it's remote, and it checks all the boxes. It hasn't been fully excavated and won't be overrun with tourists."

Aedan shook his head. "Scuba gear? It would take too long to explore, and frankly, you're not in any shape to be doing something like that."

Zen narrowed his eyes dangerously. "I will be."

"Look, I'm not saying it to insult you," Aedan replied, raising his hands placatingly. "But you're going to be dealing with... well, it takes more than a few days of sobriety. Withdrawal takes a physical toll."

"I'm fine," Zen growled.

Aedan shrugged, clearly unconvinced. "I vote for this one." He pointed to Dzibanché. "No need to spend days mucking about in the jungle searching for a back door, no need for scuba gear."

"If you're worried about getting your shoes muddy, you don't need to come," Zen snapped.

While they argued, I studied the three locations on the map. I knew Hun-Came. I had seen his sacred entrance in my dreams—a yawning maw carved into living stone. The air around it shimmered with unnatural heat. It wasn't just a cave; it was a throat waiting to swallow us whole.

I closed my eyes, trying to recall more details. In my dream, the entrance had been surrounded by towering ceiba trees, their massive trunks like pillars holding up the sky, obscuring the moon. The air had smelled of decay and jungle flowers. Inside a trickle of black water, the color of dried blood flowed from its depths to a large cavern with an underground lake.

"I've seen it," I said quietly.

The argument ceased immediately. All eyes turned to me.

"You've seen the entrance?" Izzy leaned forward, her voice tense with excitement. "Where?"

"In my dreams." I pointed to the map. "I think Zen's right. I think the entrance is in Guatemala." I looked at Izzy. "Are there any photos of the Xilbaba cave?"

She flipped through one of her books until she found what she was looking for—a black and white photograph of a cave entrance. "Here," she said, sliding the book toward me. "There are several more on the next page."

I studied the photographs. They looked familiar, but I wasn't one hundred percent certain. I looked at the map again.

"*Shall we make another bargain, my little vessel?*" Hun-Came's voice slithered inside my head, soft and seductive. "*I will give you the location. In exchange, you will hunt with me tonight. Willingly, without resistance.*" I could sense his eager anticipation. Frighteningly, it was matched by my own.

"Yes," I agreed, my whisper barely audible.

My hand, without any conscious effort on my part,

picked up a pen and moved toward the map, drawing a red circle on the paper.

Izzy pulled the map toward her, her brow furrowing as she read the small words. "There's nothing marked on the map at this location." She glanced up at me. "Are you sure?"

I nodded numbly.

"Most likely, it's part of the same cave system as the Xilbaba Cave. Like Zen said, the area is remote and most of the underground caves haven't been explored or mapped."

Zen nodded, a grim satisfaction in his eyes. "Then it's settled."

"I hate to be the one who tosses the spanner into the works," Aedan interjected. "But the lady did say the site was closed and inaccessible. Not to mention it involved us either growing gills or learning to scuba dive."

"There must be another way in," I said.

"There might be." Zen rifled through the papers on the table, pulling out a topographical map of the Petén region. "Li Xul runs his smuggling operations through this area. I could…"

"No!" The word exploded from my lips and Izzy's simultaneously. Surprised, I flicked a glance her way before turning back to face Zen. "No contact with Li Xul. It's too dangerous. We'll find another way in *without* Li Xul."

Zen held my gaze for a moment, then nodded.

Izzy's lips curved into a smile. "Actually, now that you mention it, there might be another option, but I need to check with my father."

I regarded her suspiciously. "Your father?"

She shrugged. "My family also conducts business operations in the Petén area."

"What does that mean?"

Izzy met my gaze evenly. "Some of my family's past businesses have been…extractive."

"Extractive?" I challenged.

"Yes," Izzy replied without a hint of shame. "The point is, I have access to maps and information that aren't in the public domain. There are old tunnels and caverns that intersect with the cave system which might help us avoid the underwater portion of the journey."

Aedan rubbed his chin thoughtfully. "In for a penny, in for a pound, I guess. How dangerous are these tunnels?"

"Less dangerous than drowning," Izzy pointed out. "Though there is the minor issue of structural integrity. Most of them haven't been maintained in decades."

"Wonderful," I muttered.

"And your father is going to be good with this?" Zen asked.

"Zen, you should know by now I always get what I want." The smile she gave Zen made me think of a wicked version of the Cheshire cat preparing to pounce on an unsuspecting songbird. Something twisted in my stomach—a feeling I refused to acknowledge as jealousy. There was an easy familiarity between them that needled me in places I didn't want to examine too closely.

Izzy picked up the map I'd marked with the red circle, her manicured fingers tracing the route we'd discussed. "I need to see my father. I'll let the staff know to serve dinner at the usual time and not to wait for me."

As she turned to leave, I couldn't help but notice how her hand lingered on Zen's shoulder just a second too long. My jaw clenched involuntarily.

"Charming," Aedan said dryly as we watched her sashay out of the room, the click of her heels on the tile floors echoing like tiny punctuation marks of privilege.

I waited until she was out of earshot before turning toward Zen. "Can we trust her?" My voice came out sharper than I intended, but I couldn't help it. Everything about this place—and her—felt dangerous in ways that had nothing to do with death gods and everything to do with the calculating look in her eyes whenever she glanced my way.

"Yes." Zen held my gaze. "I would trust Izzy with my life."

"Would you trust her with my life?"

"You don't have to worry about Izzy."

The loyalty in his voice sent another unexpected pang through me. *Defend her, why don't you*, I thought bitterly. I'd been possessed by a death god, nearly died, and somehow, I was the one feeling like I needed to justify my suspicions.

"She may not be directly involved with anything criminal," I commented tartly, letting my gaze travel around the large room with its expensive decorations and furnishings. "But she is certainly enjoying the benefits of her family's connection to the criminal elements."

I wondered how much of this luxury was built on suffering—addiction, violence, and blood. The jade jaguar at my throat suddenly felt heavy, as if it too recognized the weight of ill-gotten wealth when surrounded by it. Hun-Came stirred within me, amused by my moral indignation.

"Izzy has been nothing but helpful." Zen rose to her defense, his tone carrying a warning edge. "She's risking a lot by helping us, Niki."

Helping you while I'm risking everything, I wanted to scream. Instead, I bit the inside of my cheek, tasting blood as jealousy and self-pity warred inside me.

"Sorry to break up the fight between mother and father," Aedan interjected, his Irish lilt more pronounced as he attempted to diffuse the tension. "But do we have any idea what we'll face once we're inside this cave?"

Grateful for the interruption, I sank back in my chair, crossing my arms protectively over my chest. I knew I was being petty, but I couldn't shake the feeling that Izzy was playing us—playing Zen especially—for reasons of her own. No one with her connections and resources would risk everything just to help a former fling and his possessed tagalong.

Zen tapped the worn copy of the Popol Vuh beside him. "According to this, the Hero Twins faced several trials—the Houses of Darkness, Razors, Cold, Fire, Bats, and Jaguars. Each designed to kill those who sought entrance to Xibalba."

"And then there's the matter of the Lords of Xibalba themselves," he continued. "Hun-Came and Vucub-Came are just two of many. There are others—Scab Stripper, Blood Gatherer, Demon of Pus, Bone Scepter..."

"We get the picture," I interrupted, suppressing a shudder. Part of me wondered if even these horrors would be preferable to watching Zen and Izzy dance around whatever unresolved tension still existed between them. Then I immediately felt awful for the thought. My petty jealousy was nothing compared to what was at stake.

"So, our plan is to voluntarily enter the realm of death gods who enjoy torturing and killing intruders," Aedan summarized, his expression skeptical as he looked between Zen and me.

Not voluntarily, I thought. *Necessarily*. I touched the jade jaguar pendant at my throat, feeling the cold stone warm to my touch. Hun-Came's presence inside me seemed to pulse with anticipation, as if already savoring our next hunt. Whatever fears I had about Izzy's true motives or her history with Zen would have to take a backseat to the more immediate threat—the death god slowly consuming me from within.

But I made a silent promise to myself: I would watch her. I would be ready. Because while Hun-Came was a known danger, Izzy remained an unpredictable one. And in my experience, those were often the deadliest kind.

"Well then. I'd best make sure Sky-Splitter is ready," Aedan said, rising from his chair. "I suggest two of you get some rest while we wait for our lovely hostess to return."

Zen pushed back his chair and paused, his eyes lingering on me with a questioning look.

"I want to look at a few more of the photos," I told him. He nodded.

After Zen and Aedan left, I remained seated, staring at the photograph of the cave entrance. It pulsed with malevolence even in static black and white.

"*Are you afraid, little vessel?*" Hun-Came whispered inside my mind.

"*Yes*," I admitted silently.

His laughter echoed through my consciousness. "*Good. Fear keeps mortals' alert. You will need all your wits about you for what lies ahead. The journey to Xilbaba is an arduous path. You will need to prove yourself worthy.*"

I closed the book with a snap, trying to sever the connection, but his presence lingered.

CHAPTER SIXTEEN

"*It is time.*" Hun-Came's voice whispered seductively. "*As agreed, you must submit willingly and without barriers.*"

I sat on the edge of my bed in the darkened room, staring at the iron bracelet encircling my wrist. Every instinct screamed against what I was about to do, but I had made a promise.

I slipped the iron bracelet from my wrist, feeling it cool against my palm one last time before setting it on the nightstand. The protective barrier it provided—the thin line between his consciousness and mine—was now gone. My fingers brushed against the jade jaguar pendant resting against my sternum, and I settled back against the pillows, my heart racing with a mixture of fear and anticipation.

I closed my eyes and opened my mind to the death god, anticipation tingling under my skin. Hun-Came slid inside me, infiltrating my bloodstream like liquid fire. My entire body began to hum with energy, then convulse as bones began to shift beneath my skin in sharp bursts of pain that somehow felt ecstatic rather than agonizing. I could feel each vertebra in my spine pop and realign, muscle fibers tearing and rebuilding themselves stronger, denser, made for hunting.

He coursed through my veins, infusing me with demanding hunger, a burning need that eclipsed all rational thought. My vision sharpened until I could count dust motes in the darkness. Scents assaulted me—the lingering traces of perfume on my sheets, the distant aroma of dinner hours past, the tantalizing musk of living bodies throughout the compound. My arms and legs twitched and flexed, muscles and sinews growing stronger as he obliterated the last traces of my consciousness.

***

I want this. I need this. Death. Blood. Chaos.

Roaring like a wild beast, I am instantly transported outside. A cold moon rises behind the iron gates surrounding Izzy's family compound, silvering the manicured landscape. I raise my head, scenting prey, growling low in my throat. Every sound is amplified—insects chirping in the grass, small creatures scurrying in the underbrush, the distant murmur of the security staff patrolling the perimeter. The night is alive with heartbeats, each one a drumbeat calling to me.

And then I catch it—the scent of a larger animal. A Doberman patrolling the grounds. The smell of its sweat, its breath, the oils on its coat—all create a perfect olfactory image in my mind. I can almost taste its flesh already. I sink low into the shadows, tracking its movement, waiting for the perfect moment to strike. The dog pauses, sniffs the air, its ears perk up, sensing something amiss, but it is already too late.

I launch myself in a silent attack, raking its hind quarters with my claws, drawing blood and a yelp of pain. The scent of fresh blood hits me like a drug—metallic, warm, intoxicating. My pupils dilate with pleasure as the first drops splash against my muzzle. But the dog is trained for this—it recovers quickly, circling and snapping, saliva flying from its jaws. I snarl, muscles coiled, waiting for my opening. The anticipation of the kill sends electric pulses through my limbs, making my fur stand on end with exhilarating pleasure.

The dog darts in, teeth bared, and I pounce, landing on its back with crushing force. I hear the satisfying crack of ribs beneath my weight. It twists and turns beneath me, desperate to escape, whimpering sounds that only sharpen my hunger. My claws hold my writhing prey in place, sinking deeper with each struggling movement, tearing through muscle with wet, ripping sounds. I sink my canines into its neck, feeling the resistance of skin, then the yielding pop as I penetrate jugular and windpipe simultaneously. There is a satisfying crunch of bone, followed by a burst of hot blood in my mouth. I drink it greedily, the coppery taste igniting something primal within me. Each swallow feels like pure power flowing into my body, the dog's life force becoming my own. The animal's struggles weaken, its limbs twitching in death throes that only heighten my savage joy.

A sudden sharp pain in my flank causes me to roar in surprise—not just the pressure of teeth but the tearing of my own flesh, nerve endings screaming in white-hot protest. A second dog has its teeth in my hind quarters, ripping through skin and muscle, leaving me with a wound that throbs with each heartbeat. I spin, turning to attack the intruder, abandoning the lifeless body of the first dog. The corpse hits the ground with a meaty thud, blood pooling black in the moonlight.

The second dog backs away, growling low, its eyes wide with a fear I can smell—acrid and sweet simultaneously. I lunge, muscles bunching and releasing with explosive power, aiming for its throat. With one powerful snap of my jaws, I tear the soft flesh, feeling the warm spray of arterial blood against my face, the vibration of the dog's final yelp resonating through my teeth. Grasping the animal firmly in my jaw, I shake the limp carcass from side to side, hot blood spurting from the wound, spattering my chest and forelegs. The sensation of rending flesh is euphoric—each tear releasing more of the dog's essence for me to consume. I drop the body and throw my head back in a triumphant roar that rattles the night air.

I sense motion and whip around expecting to see another Doberman. Instead, a second jaguar leaps effortlessly over the wall surrounding the compound. A rival predator. Golden-eyed and powerful, it roars its challenge. The territorial rage that floods my system is instant and overwhelming—my kills, my hunting ground, my night to feast.

I growl at the interloper—these are my kills; I will not share. The bodies still radiate heat, the blood still flows, and the need to protect my prey burns hotter than hunger itself. I snarl a warning, fur bristling along my spine like needles, but the second jaguar does not back away. Instead, it holds its ground, meeting my threat with a low growl of its own that rumbles through the earth between us.

We circle each other, tension building with each step—the ripple of muscle beneath fur, the scent of raw power, the measured cadence of his breathing. Time slows and stretches between us until—Snap!

We launch simultaneously, colliding in midair in a fury of fur and bone, flashing dagger-like teeth. I attack with feral abandon, claws raking across sleek muscle, leaving hot furrows that release the copper scent of fresh blood. The impact of our bodies sends shock waves through my skeleton, but the pain only feeds my rage.

The other jaguar is bigger and stronger. In moments, he is on top of me, my throat in his mouth. I can feel teeth pressing against my neck, the pressure points exactly where a killing bite would sever arteries and crush my windpipe. I struggle, but each movement drives those teeth a millimeter closer to ending me. Hot breath steams against my throat, saliva mingling with the blood already matting my fur.

Zen.

The name rises unbidden in the back of my mind, a fragment of my human consciousness breaking through Hun-Came's control. I freeze in submission, waiting for him to kill me, surrendering to the inevitable. The world narrows to the pressure of teeth against my jugular, each hammering heartbeat pushing my flesh against those deadly points.

In that moment, Zen's image morphs before my eyes, transforming into Li Xul—the jaguar's eyes now ringed with red, hungry for my death, for Hun-Came's power. Fear jolts through me, a visceral terror that even Hun-Came cannot suppress.

The fierce cry of a quetzal bird pierces the night from above, and everything shatters.

***

I was outside on wet grass, Zen on top of me—both of us human again. Weakness swept through me, followed by waves of nausea that clenched my stomach and burned my throat. The world around the edges seemed blurred and indistinct, as if I was looking at everything from under water. I focused on the feeling of wet grass beneath my bare legs, blades pressing into my skin. The wound on my hip burned with painful clarity. The cold moon shone overhead as I drew strength from the natural world—moon, earth, the living things around me.

My mouth, neck, and hands were slick with blood. I could taste it on my tongue, the sharp metallic bite of it against my teeth, tacky as it dried between my fingers. Fragments of fur clung to my lips, a piece of something— muscle? tendon? —caught between my molars. The realization of what we had done—what Hun-Came and I had done—hit me with sickening clarity. Yet, beneath the horror was something worse—a lingering satisfaction, a fullness in my belly, a satiated hunger, and a memory of pleasure that made me hate myself more than the act itself.

Zen slowly rolled off of me. He was breathing hard from the exertion, his chest rising and falling rapidly. In the moonlight, I could see scratches across his torso, already beginning to heal—four parallel lines where my claws had opened his flesh to bone. Blood smeared his chin and throat, and his eyes still held a wildness that wasn't entirely human.

"Are you alright?" he asked, his voice hoarse.

I couldn't answer. The boundaries between Niki and Hun-Came, between human and predator, felt dangerously thin. I clutched the jaguar pendant around my neck and stared at the waxing moon, pulling its energy toward me as I recited the words my mother taught me like a mantra:

"Teorainn idir dá shaol, críoch idir dá fhód..."

"Boundary between two worlds, limit between two realms."

I was desperate to anchor myself to the here and now, to pull my consciousness back from the abyss of Hun-Came's hunger. I wasn't sure what had happened, unable to process anything but the need to tether my shadow soul to my mortal body. The echo of teeth tearing flesh still reverberated through my jaw. My fingers still twitched with the memory of claws extending, retracting.

"Niki," Zen said, his voice firmer now. "Focus on my voice. Focus on me."

I blinked, forcing my eyes to meet his. The gold of his irises caught the moonlight, glowing like embers in the darkness. For a terrifying moment, I thought I still saw Li Xul there, watching from behind Zen's eyes.

"I felt him," I whispered. "Li Xul. He was there." My voice sounded wrong—too rough, as if my vocal cords were not my own.

Zen's voice hardened. "I know. I felt him, too. He's watching us, through me." He reached out hesitantly, then drew back his hand before touching me, his hand leaving smears of blood on the grass between us.

I tried to sit up, my limbs leaden and uncooperative. The transformation—or whatever it had been—had drained me completely. Hun-Came had taken more than I'd been prepared to give. Every muscle ached as if I'd run for miles.

"Can you stand?" Zen asked, already on his feet.

I nodded, though I wasn't at all certain. He extended his hand, and after a moment's hesitation, I took it. The contact sent sparks shooting up my arm, a reminder of the connection between us—shifter and vessel, both bound to powers beyond our understanding.

He helped me to my feet, but my legs were shaky, barely able to support my weight. Zen slipped an arm around my waist, careful to minimize skin contact while still providing support.

"We need to talk about what happened," he said quietly as we made our way slowly back toward the house. "But not now."

I nodded again— all I could manage to do. It was taking every ounce of concentration just to put one foot in front of the other. The compound seemed miles away, though I knew it couldn't be far. With each step, flash images of the hunt bombarded me—teeth sinking into warm flesh, the struggle of prey, the hot rush of blood. Worse than the images, was the part of me that wanted to turn back to those cooling bodies and feast until dawn.

Aedan met us at the front door, his expression a mixture of concern and anger. Without a word, he lifted me into his arms, carrying me as easily as if I were a child. I didn't protest—couldn't protest. My head lolled against his shoulder as he carried me through the silent house to my room.

He set me gently on the bed, then reached for something on the nightstand.

"Put this back on," he said, holding out the iron bracelet. "Right now."

A stabbing pain erupted in my head as I reached for the iron bracelet. My fingers closed around it with desperate relief, and I slipped it back onto my wrist, feeling Hun-Came's presence recede slightly as the cold metal touched my skin. The weight of it was grounding, bringing me back to myself one heartbeat at a time.

"Better?" Aedan asked, studying my face with practiced intensity.

"A little," I managed.

He nodded, then pulled the blanket up over me. "Sleep if you can. I'll keep watch."

Like a stalled car, my physical body was on empty. I needed rest, but sleep felt dangerous—a surrender to darkness where Hun-Came waited, where the memory of blood and death lingered with seductive power. Unable to resist, my eyes closed of their own accord, the iron bracelet heavy on my wrist.

In the shadows of my mind, Hun-Came's satisfaction pulsed like a second heartbeat. *"You were magnificent. Soon, little vessel. Soon we will hunt in my kingdom."*

CHAPTER SEVENTEEN

When I woke, I had no idea what time it was. The heavy curtains blocked any hint of sunlight, leaving me disoriented in the half-darkness. My limbs felt leaden, my muscles sore in ways I'd never experienced before. I wobbled to the shower, vaguely worried what the household staff would make of the dried blood on the bed sheets. There was so much of it—rusty brown stains on the Egyptian cotton that no amount of bleach would likely remove.

Hun-Came had retreated to wherever he went when not actively possessing me...perhaps savoring his victory. I could still feel him, though—a satisfied purr at the edges of my consciousness, like a predator contentedly digesting after a successful hunt.

I turned the water as hot as I could stand it and scrubbed the blood from my body. Some had dried in the creases of my skin, under my fingernails, in my hair. As I watched crimson swirling down the drain, I couldn't help but think about what Izzy had said earlier—that I was risking physical corruption, spiritual consumption, and existential erasure. The words echoed in my head with each pass of the loofah over my skin.

"How many more nights can I survive this dance with

the death god before he consumes me completely?" I whispered to the steam.

I rinsed the soap and inspected my body for signs of putrefaction, half-expecting to find patches of decay, blackened veins, something to mark the corruption I felt inside. But there was nothing—my skin looked the same as always, unmarked except for old scars. Maybe Izzy was wrong. I desperately hoped she was wrong.

I dressed in jeans and a simple t-shirt, clothes that felt too normal for someone who had spent the night as a blood-thirsty jaguar and went in search of human company. My stomach growled, reminding me that whatever I'd consumed in jaguar form hadn't transferred to my human body.

The scent of breakfast hit me before I reached the dining room—eggs, chorizo, coffee, and something sweet. My heightened sense of smell hadn't completely faded, and the aromas were almost overwhelming in their intensity.

Zen and Aedan sat at the dining room table, tension crackling between them like static electricity. They weren't speaking, but their body language told a story of barely contained hostility. Aedan sat ramrod straight, his shoulders tense, while Zen lounged in his chair with deceptive casualness, his eyes never leaving Aedan.

"Morning," I said, my voice raspier than I'd expected.

They both looked up when I entered. Aedan's blue eyes narrowed, raking me up and down as if assessing me for damage. His healer's gaze cataloging symptoms and searching for wounds.

I dropped into an empty chair and a uniformed maid instantly appeared with a fresh pot of coffee. The aroma filled my nostrils—rich, dark, and bitter exactly what I needed to clean the taste of blood and death that still lingered in my mouth.

Zen's eyes met mine, sparking with amber fire. I could tell from the set of his jaw he was furious. "Please tell our Irish friend I was not responsible for last night," he said, the words clipped and precise.

I grabbed a mug and filled it with steaming brew, gulping it down, allowing the heat to scorch my tongue and throat before speaking. "Zen wasn't responsible for what happened last night," I said, meeting Aedan's skeptical gaze. "I was."

Aedan leaned back in his chair, arms crossed, an inquiring eyebrow lifted in my direction.

I took another swig of the hot coffee. "I made a deal with Hun-Came," I continued. "The location of the entrance to Xibalba in exchange for my hunting with him."

Both men erupted at once.

"What the hell were you thinking?" Aedan demanded, slamming his palm on the table hard enough to make the silverware jump. "Didn't you hear what Izzy said about the risks?"

"Are you trying to get yourself killed?" Zen's voice was quieter but no less intense. "Or worse than killed?"

I felt surprisingly calm in the face of their anger. "No." I looked at Zen. "I am not trying to get myself killed." I turned my gaze to Aedan. "Yes, I did hear what Izzy said. Which is why I struck a deal with Hun-Came. We don't have time to waste searching for the entrance on our own. I don't know how much time I have before..."

I let the sentence trail off before fixing my gaze on Zen. "What I don't understand is how you showed up. How did you know what was happening?"

Aedan leaned forward, arms folded once again across his chest, his hostile stare fixed on Zen. "Exactly my point."

Zen shrugged, shaking his head slowly. "I have no idea. I was asleep, and then suddenly I was—" He hesitated, perhaps remembering the transformation, the blood, the primal hunt. — "there."

"Roll up your sleeves," Aedan demanded abruptly.

"What?" Zen's expression hardened.

"You said you couldn't dream-walk unless you were in an altered state." Aedan's tone left no room for argument.

"Roll up your sleeves."

"Might not be a bad idea, Zen," I said softly. "I did see Li Xul last night and..." My words trailed off, the memory of those red-ringed eyes still chilling me to the bone.

Zen turned to me, furious. "Is this what you think of me? That I'd need to drug myself to find you?" He stood so abruptly his chair nearly toppled. His eyes gleamed dangerously.

I felt like a traitor for not trusting him, but I had to know. I refused to look away, uncomfortable under the intensity of his gaze. "I know what I saw."

With a muttered curse, Zen angrily shoved the sleeves of his shirt up to his elbows. His forearms were unmarked— no fresh puncture wounds, no track marks. Just smooth skin over lean muscle, and the faint remnants of old scars that had already healed.

"You want to know how I showed up?" he asked, voice razor-sharp. "The same way as before. You—" he pointed at me, — "pulled me into your dreamscape. Just like you have done since the beginning. Since before we ever met."

"But..." I protested. "I wasn't dreaming." I didn't tell him I'd been lost to Hun-Came, that last night I was no longer Niki but something else entirely. I didn't want to admit how far gone I'd been, how close I'd come to being consumed.

"We are linked," Zen said, his voice softening slightly as he sank back into his chair. "As much as you try to deny it, we are bound to one another."

He was right. He had shown up in my dreams long before I'd even met him in person. It was something I still didn't understand, wondering if our shared connection had something to do with Nayla. If my twin sister had somehow forged a link between the two of us.

Aedan watched, his eyes shifting between us like he was watching a tennis match, assessing, calculating.

I deflated like a balloon, the fight going out of me. "Sorry," I said. "I should have known better. I should have trusted you." I reached my hand toward Zen, but he pulled back his arm before I made contact, the rejection a stinging slap.

"How did you break the connection with Hun-Came?" Aedan asked, his curiosity apparently overriding his suspicion for the moment.

"I didn't. Zen did."

"She's right. I grabbed onto her when I transformed back into my human form," Zen explained. "I have more experience moving between supernatural and natural worlds." He glanced at me. "I wasn't sure it would work. I was hoping I wasn't going to find a jaguar beneath me when I changed into my human form."

I shuddered, remembering the taste of blood, the crunch of bone, the hot satisfaction of the kill. Something primal had been awakened in me, something that couldn't be contained by iron or ritual or will alone. I wasn't sure what would have happened if Zen hadn't appeared.

"Thanks," I said quietly. "For finding me. For bringing me back."

Zen's expression was worried, the anger fading into something more complex. "I brought you back," he acknowledged. "But our connection allowed Li Xul to connect with you again. I couldn't block him last night. He's tracking you through me, through our link."

Aedan leaned back in his chair, studying both of us. "Maybe it's time you two filled me in on Li Xul," he suggested.

Zen and I exchanged glances.

"Li Xul is a powerful shaman and narcotraficante," I explained. "He uses his ties to the supernatural world for evil—illegal mining, smuggling, drug trafficking, human trafficking. He uses migrants as mules to move contraband across borders."

"He's also completely without conscience," Zen added. "He'll sacrifice anyone, use everything within his means, to get what he wants."

"And what does he want?" Aedan pressed.

The answer came from the doorway, where Izzy stood watching us with cool, assessing eyes. "He wants what Niki has," she said, moving into the room with feline grace. "Power. He wants Hun-Came's power." Her gaze fixed on me, sharp and knowing. "I assume that's who we have to thank for the carnage the staff reported this morning? My father's guard dogs were eviscerated last night."

I couldn't meet her eyes, shame and guilt washing over me in equal measure.

"I spoke to my father," Izzy continued, taking a seat at the head of the table. "We can leave in two days." Her eyes fixed on me, unblinking. "Sooner would be better. Before she becomes something we don't want to let loose in this world."

The casual way she spoke of me—not to me—sent a chill down my spine.

"Niki's not a monster," Aedan said.

"Not yet," Izzy replied.

"Izzy," Zen's voice was tight. "That's enough."

"We'll see," Izzy replied, reaching for the coffee pot. "Won't we?"

The tension in the room was suffocating. I looked from Zen to Aedan to Izzy, each of them watching me with varying degrees of concern, suspicion, and calculation.

Hun-Came's voice whispered in the back of my mind, so faint I almost missed it: *"They fear what they cannot control, little vessel. But you and I... we will accomplish great things together."*

I tightened the iron bracelet on my wrist, turning it so the cold metal pressed against my pulse point. Two days until we leave for Xibalba. Two days to prove I could control the death god within me before we began our journey to find the entrance of hell.

CHAPTER EIGHTEEN

Sleep eluded me. I paced the perimeter of my bedroom like a caged animal, too restless to lie down, too exhausted to do anything productive. The events of the night before played on an endless loop in my mind—the hunt, the blood, the overwhelming sense of power and freedom. And beneath those memories lurked Hun-Came, watchful and patient.

The jade pendant around my neck felt heavier than usual, warm against my skin despite the cool night air drifting through the half-open window. I'd kept the iron bracelet firmly clasped on my wrist all day, pressing it into my skin whenever Hun-Came's whispers grew too seductive.

"*Little vessel,*" he murmured now, his voice a caress that made my skin prickle. "*You fear what lives inside you, but it has always been there. I merely awakened what was dormant.*"

"Shut up," I muttered, knowing it would do no good. The death god was persistent, if nothing else.

"*The druid warrior distrusts the wahy b'alam. The witch covets him. And you, little vessel—what do you covet?*"

I ignored him. Dawn was hours away, and the compound had settled into silence broken only by the occasional sound of the night patrol making their rounds.

After Izzy's thinly veiled threat at breakfast, the day had passed in tense preparation. Aedan and Zen had reached some sort of truce and spent hours making lists, gathering and sorting items for our upcoming jungle trek. Izzy had sequestered herself in her father's office making arrangements for our expedition, leaving me to my own devices.

I tried to distract myself with books from the extensive library, settling on an ancient text about Mayan death rituals that might provide clues about Hun-Came. But concentration was impossible with the death god's commentary and my own restless energy.

A soft knock at my door startled me from my thoughts. I hesitated, suddenly aware I wore only a thin tank top and sleep shorts.

"Who is it?" I called quietly.

"Zen," came the response, barely audible. "Can I come in?"

My heart rate kicked up a notch. "Just a second." I grabbed a robe from the back of a chair and belted it around my waist before opening the door.

Zen stood in the darkened hallway, shadows accentuating the sharp angles of his face. He looked as exhausted as I felt, with dark circles under his eyes and a tension in his shoulders that spoke of sleepless nights.

"Did I wake you?" he asked.

I shook my head. "I can't sleep."

"Neither can I." His amber eyes flicked past me to scan the room before returning to my face. "Can we talk?"

I stepped back to let him enter, acutely aware of Hun-Came's sudden attentiveness. The death god had gone silent, but I could feel him watching, waiting.

Zen moved into the room with the fluid grace that marked him as different—not quite human, not entirely other. He kept his distance, leaning against the wall near the window while I perched on the edge of the bed.

"I owe you an explanation," he said after a moment of silence.

"About what?"

"About Li Xul." Zen ran a hand through his disheveled hair. "About why he can find me... find us."

The temperature in the room seemed to drop several degrees. "I'm listening."

Zen's gaze shifted to the window, to the star-studded sky beyond. "When Li Xul killed Nayla, when he tried to kill you... after you destroyed the jade pectoral and escaped, he was desperate. He was using his contacts to search for you. I knew it was just a matter of time before he..." He paused, choosing his words carefully. "I took a leave of absence and went looking for him. He knew about my connection to you, about my abilities."

"Your abilities," I repeated flatly. "You mean shape-shifting."

Zen nodded. "Li Xul can't reach you directly. Hun-Came blocks him—territorial, I think. Death gods don't like to share." A humorless smile flickered across his face. "But I can reach you. I always have been able to."

"Because of Nayla?" I asked, thinking of my twin sister, whose death had set all this in motion.

"Maybe in part. But it's more than that." His eyes met mine, holding my gaze with an intensity that made my breath catch. "There's something between us, Niki. I don't know what it is, but I know you feel it, too."

I knew what he meant. The dreams I'd had of him long before we'd encountered each other in the flesh. The sense of recognition when we'd finally met. The undeniable pull that existed between us, despite all the reasons to resist it.

"So, Li Xul wanted to use that connection," I prompted, steering us back to the point.

Zen pushed away from the wall, moving restlessly to the other side of the room. "He offered me a deal. Information on rituals that might free you from Hun-Came, in exchange for my help."

"Your help doing what?"

"Dream-walk. Apparently, it's a latent skill for most shifters. He taught me how to dream-walk so I could help protect his shipments. Because of my work with the DEA, I knew the key players. He used me to plant suggestions, to locate rivals, to find people who had crossed him." Zen's voice was flat, devoid of emotion. "I said yes.

"I knew he was using his connection with me to try and find you, but I was also using him. I needed information." His eyes held mine, shining with a fierce light. "I knew you wouldn't approve, but I would do it again. If Li Xul is right and I can save you, then the sacrifice will have been worth it."

The confession hung in the air between us. Not just a confession, I realized, but also a declaration of love. "Zen," his name escaped my lips in a half-sob. I closed my eyes, ruthlessly rejecting the emotions threatening to overwhelm me in order to focus on the here and now.

"But your connection with Li Xul is still there," I said.

"It is. And he's using it." Zen turned to face me fully. "Last night, when you... when Hun-Came took over, when I found you, Li Xul followed. I've been blocking him. Aedan's protection spells help, but he's gotten stronger, Niki. The fact that he could manifest, even partially, in your dreamscape with Hun-Came—means he's found a way to get to you through me. But it goes both ways. I can enter his mind when he's linked through me."

A chill ran down my spine. "What does he want now?"

"Izzy was right. He wants the same thing he's always wanted. Hun-Came's power. But his approach has changed." Zen moved closer, lowering his voice though we were alone. "He doesn't need the jade pectoral anymore. He's found another way."

"What way?"

"You." Zen's eyes locked on mine. "If he can kill you while Hun-Came is active within you, he believes he can absorb the death god's essence directly."

The matter-of-fact way he delivered this news should have terrified me, but after everything that had happened, it felt almost inevitable. Of course, Li Xul would find another path to power. Of course, I would be at the center of it.

"And Izzy?" I asked, a new suspicion forming. "Where does she fit into all of this?"

Something closed off in Zen's expression. "Izzy is... complicated."

"She hates me."

"She doesn't know you." Zen sighed, dragging a hand across his face. "Izzy helped me contact Li Xul initially, through her family connections. She didn't know what I was planning, just that I needed to find him."

"And now?"

"Now she's helping us get to Xibalba." He frowned.

"She practically threatened to kill me," I reminded him.

"She was just making a point. It was just words, that's all." His certainty should have been reassuring, but it wasn't. "Sometimes, she can come across as cold or unfeeling, but Izzy is a good person."

"*The wahy b'alam is blind when it comes to the witch*," Hun-Came whispered in my mind. "*She has made bargains of her own.*"

I shivered, drawing my robe tighter around myself. "Hun-Came seems to think otherwise."

Zen's eyes narrowed. "What does he say?"

"That she's made bargains of her own." I hesitated. "He calls her a witch."

A flash of something—recognition? concern? —crossed Zen's face before he masked it. "Hun-Came is manipulative. He'll say anything to isolate you, to make you dependent upon him alone. You need to stop listening to him."

Zen had a point, but that didn't mean Hun-Came was wrong.

"You don't know what it's like," I said softly. "Having him in my head. Feeling what he feels. Wanting what he wants."

Zen moved closer, sitting beside me on the bed, careful to keep a sliver of space between us. "I can imagine."

"No." I shook my head. "You can't. Last night, when I was hunting... part of me loved it, Zen. The power, the freedom, the taste of blood..." My voice broke. "What does that make me?"

"Human," he said simply. "We all have darkness in us, Niki. The difference is in how we choose to face it."

I laughed bitterly. "Choice? Hun-Came doesn't leave much room for choice."

"You are stronger than you think." Zen's eyes locked onto me. "You embrace who you are and find a way to channel that darkness into light."

I thought of how Zen had learned to live with his shadow spirit. A spirit that compelled him to hunt if he was to survive. By joining the DEA, Zen had channeled the jaguar that lived within him into a force for fighting evil, pursuing bad guys instead of death.

"You learn to keep fighting the dark, one day at a time until it becomes second nature." Zen's hand found mine, warm and solid.

The contact sent a wave of heat through my body, awakening a different kind of hunger. I leaned toward him almost unconsciously, drawn by the promise of forgetting, of losing myself in something other than death and blood.

"Niki," Zen warned, his voice rough, but he didn't pull away.

"I need to feel something else," I whispered. "Something human. Something mine." I reached up to touch his face, tracing the line of his jaw with my fingertips. "Help me remember what that feels like." I pulled him toward my bed.

For a moment, I thought he would refuse. His eyes closed, his jaw clenched beneath my touch. But then he turned his face into my palm, lips grazing my wrist just above the iron bracelet.

"This is a bad idea," he murmured against my skin.

"Probably," I agreed, moving closer until our breath mingled. "I seem to be full of those lately."

His hand came up to cup the back of my neck, and I felt the tremor in his fingers—restraint, desire, fear, all tangled together. "If Li Xul follows the connection..."

"I don't care," I said, though part of me did. But that part was drowning in the need to chase away the darkness with something that felt like life instead of death. "Just for a little while. Make me forget."

Zen's eyes, when they opened, had darkened to molten gold. He leaned forward, his lips a breath away from mine— I surged up on my toes and kissed him. Our tongues twined and he groaned as his hands slid down my body waking every nerve ending. Each press of his mouth was a shot of electricity that surged through my bloodstream. Liquid heat pooled between my thighs.

In one fluid movement he released the belt of my robe, his hands slid under my tank top and found my breasts, kneading them, his fingers caressing my nipples, now rock-hard with desire. He buried his face in my neck breathing me in. "Niki," he groaned.

I leaned into him, tasting him, feeling his breath against my skin. His mouth whispered along my jaw line. Tilting my head back, I sucked his tongue into my mouth, devouring him. His teeth grazed my lower lip as his hands twined roughly through my hair.

His weight shifted, the hard planes of his body pressed against my belly, his thigh sliding between mine. Desire rushed at me like a Tsunami drowning every thought but one. Now! I wanted this man inside of me—now! A breathy cry escaped from the back of my throat as I pressed harder against him.

His hands slid down my back and cupped my hips. His fingers slipped under the elastic of my panties, exploring, delicate as butterfly wings. I closed my eyes enjoying the exquisite pleasure as he found my clitoris. Legs wobbling, I arched backward as the pleasure intensified, mewling with

143

need. "Zen, please."

Zen suddenly froze, his entire body going rigid.

"Zen?" I pulled back, alarmed by the sudden change.

When Zen spoke, the voice was his, but the cadence was all wrong. "You stole what was rightfully mine."

Ice flooded my veins. "Li Xul."

Zen's face contorted in a smile that didn't belong to him. "Nikita Balam, it's been too long."

I tried to pull away, but his grip was like iron. "Let him go."

"You and I have unfinished business, Nikita." Zen's hand—Li Xul's hand—moved to my throat, fingers pressing against my pulse point.

"Let. Him. Go." I grasped the jade pendant around my neck, focusing on its weight, its reality.

Li Xul laughed using Zen's mouth. "You destroyed my pectoral. Cost me years of work. Did you think I would simply give up?" The fingers around my throat tightened incrementally, his eye narrowed to slits as he studied me. "You've changed. I sense the darkness within you. You've acquired a taste for death. Intoxicating, isn't it? But, Hun-Came's power will be mine, one way or another."

"*He cannot touch me.*" Hun-Came's voice resonated with sudden urgency in my mind. "*But he can harm the shifter. The shifter can damage you. Let me help you, little vessel.*"

"No," I said aloud, uncertain if I was addressing Li Xul or Hun-Came. I wouldn't trade Zen's safety for submission to the death god. There had to be another way.

I focused on Zen's eyes, searching for any trace of him behind Li Xul's possession. "Zen, you need to block him from your mind."

Li Xul sneered. "The wahy b'alam is weak. Compromised by desire and need. So easy to—"

A spasm crossed Zen's face, cutting off Li Xul's words. His hand on my throat loosened fractionally. "Niki," Zen's voice broke through, strained and desperate.

His words choked off, face contorting in pain. Li Xul

was fighting to maintain control.

Zen couldn't block him alone. Without hesitating, I closed my eyes and dream-walked into his mind. The effect was immediate—Zen's body arched in pain, a cry tearing from his throat that might have been Li Xul's or his own. The fingers around my neck released completely as he fell back onto the bed, convulsing once, twice, before going still.

"Zen?" I leaned over him, checking for breath, for a pulse. Both were present, though rapid and irregular. "Zen, can you hear me?"

His eyes fluttered open, hazy with pain but his own again. "That was... unpleasant," he managed, voice rough.

Relief washed over me. "You're back."

"For now." He struggled to sit up, wincing. He pressed the heel of his hand to his forehead. "Having two of you in there at once, was a little rough."

I touched his shoulder gently. "I'm sorry."

"Don't be. It worked." Zen took a shaky breath. He exhaled slowly. "We can't risk this again. No physical contact until we reach Xibalba. It's too dangerous."

I knew he was right, but the thought of severing that connection, of facing what was to come without the comfort of touch, made the loneliness of Hun-Came's presence that much harder to bear.

"Li Xul said you were compromised," I told him. "By desire and need."

Zen's expression shuttered. "Li Xul exploits weakness. Any weakness." He closed his eyes as if he was in pain. "You are my weakness."

Zen stood, putting distance between us. "I need to talk to Aedan."

I walked him to the door, hyperaware of the careful space he maintained between us.

He paused at the threshold. "Niki." His voice was low, meant only for me. "What Li Xul said about you changing, acquiring a taste for death—don't believe him."

But part of me did believe him. Part of me recognized

the truth in Li Xul's words, in the hunger that had awakened during the hunt, in the way Hun-Came's whispers sometimes echoed my own thoughts.

"When we find the Boca de Xilbaba," I said instead of arguing. "We end this."

Zen nodded once, his eyes lingering on my face as if memorizing it, before he turned and walked away.

I closed the door, sliding the lock into place with trembling fingers.

"*The shaman Li Xul is not worthy,*" Hun-Came murmured. "*His motives are corrupt which is why I have chosen you. Once you submit, you will see that our coupling is not without its benefits*"

"Benefits?" My voice was filled with contemptuous disbelief.

"*Yes. I regain the freedom to travel in the physical realm. You gain the power of life and death. A power that only a god can bestow. Once you join me in my kingdom, neither the wahy b'alam nor the witch nor the shaman will matter.*"

I sank onto the bed, clutching the jade pendant like a lifeline. "What makes you think I'll survive Xibalba any better than your previous vessels? What if I refuse to become what you want? Will you kill me?"

"*I would never destroy something that was mine,*" he replied, a scornful note in his voice. "*You will prove yourself worthy. I have no doubt.*"

"I won't. I will fight you. I won't let you make me into your assassin. I become just another way for you to kill people."

"*Yes, you will.*" His laughter vibrated through my bones. "*Little vessel, you have already begun to change. The shaman is correct. You have tasted death and you have enjoyed it,*" Hun-Came whispered, his satisfaction curling through my veins like smoke.

I grasped the jade pendant around my neck, paralyzed by the most terrifying realization of all—that Hun-Came and Li Xul were right. I had tasted death and Hun-Came's power, something ancient and existential—a darkness that sought to consume both flesh and soul—that now resided inside of me.

I desperately needed to find a way to preserve my agency and humanity. Hun-Came whispered to me like a lover, his words vibrating under my skin. "*You have enjoyed it.*"

The death god's power was like a drug seeping into my bloodstream, infiltrating the very cells of my body, leaving me with an almost physical craving for more. I understood Li Xul more than I wanted to.

Hands trembling, I gazed out the window. The first faint light of dawn began to streak the eastern sky, but for me, the darkness had only just begun.

LISA DIETRICH

CHAPTER NINETEEN

After tossing and turning all night, I stared at the ceiling as dawn crept through the curtains. Every time I closed my eyes, I saw Zen's face contorting into Li Xul's cruel smile, felt those fingers tightening around my throat. But beneath the fear was something worse—the memory of how Hun-Came's power had surged through me when I'd dream-walked into Zen's mind, how intoxicating it had felt to wield that kind of strength.

I needed answers. Not just about what had happened last night, but about how to fight this darkness growing inside me, this almost physical craving that made me understand Li Xul's hunger for power more than I wanted to admit.

The rational part of me said to stay away from Zen, to give him space after what Li Xul had done to him. But Hun-Came was winning, pulling me deeper into the dark with each passing hour, and Zen was the only one who truly understood what I was facing. If I was going to find a way to fight this, I needed his help—even if being near him was dangerous for both of us.

I stood outside Zen's door for what felt like an eternity, my hand raised to knock, trembling slightly. What if Li Xul was still there, lurking beneath the surface? What if seeing me triggered another possession? But the alternative—facing this alone—was worse than the risk. I knocked softly, barely audible even to my own ears. A muffled sound came from within—maybe an acknowledgment, maybe just movement. Taking it as permission, I turned the handle and let myself in, my heart beating too fast from fear, adrenaline, and something else I didn't want to name.

I heard water running in the shower. The sound stopped, and moments later he emerged with a towel wrapped loosely around his hips, droplets of water still clinging to his shoulders.

He froze, one hand on his towel, his eyes lingering on me just a second too long. The muscles in his throat worked as he swallowed, his knuckles whitening where he gripped the fabric.

I couldn't help staring. His bare skin glistened, faint white scars across his shoulder accentuating his smooth hard muscles. My blood simmered at the sight of him, and with it came the faintest whisper of Hun-Came's pleasure at my desire. The two sensations twisted together until I couldn't tell where mine ended and the god's began.

"Niki, you should go."

I wanted nothing more than to lean into him, to have his arms wrap around me and let the warmth of him engulf me. To make me feel safe and whole and human. "Zen, don't shut me out. I need to talk to you."

His voice was tight, as if it took everything he had to keep it level and controlled. "Niki, please go."

A hot flush raced up my neck and face. Zen was rejecting me. But I was not too proud to beg. "Zen, please—" I reached out to him.

He stepped back so quickly he nearly stumbled, maintaining the distance between us with desperate precision. "Niki, please go."

Pulse galloping, I dropped my hand. "Please. I need you to help me. How do you fight it—the physical craving?" My gaze flicked to his forearms, searching for the old track marks I knew were there. "Do you still...?"

"No." His jaw locked, a muscle jumping in his cheek. "The drugs were a means to an end. The physical need is nothing but synapses firing in your brain. They can be controlled."

"But... the need to hunt? Do you crave that?" My voice shook. I could feel Hun-Came stirring within me at the mention of the hunt, his interest sharpening like a blade. "Because I do. I feel it crawling under my skin. The need to—" I couldn't finish the sentence.

"I'm a shapeshifter, so yes. I need to hunt." His eyes darkened, pupils dilating slightly. "It's what I am."

"But you don't kill indiscriminately." My eyes filled with tears. "Please, Zen. Tell me. How do I stop the wild thing inside of me? The thing that craves death. The thing that whispers how good it would feel to just... let go."

His expression softened for just a moment. "You learn control. You master those impulses and focus them elsewhere." His hands flexed at his sides—I recognized the movement, saw the way he counted his heartbeats to center himself. "You find an anchor to your humanity. Something stronger than the hunger."

"Teach me," I begged. "Please." I took a step toward him, and the air between us seemed to vibrate with tension.

He scowled, muscles coiling as if preparing to flee. "I can't. It's not safe. When I'm with you, I don't have control." He stilled, closing his eyes as if in pain. "Last night, I saw my hand on your throat. I could feel him—Li Xul. I know what he wanted. He wanted to kill you. To use me to kill you."

His breath hitched, and his face hardened into an expression like granite. The towel slipped slightly as his hands clenched into fists. "Not going to happen. Not going to let him use me like that."

"But you stopped him," I insisted, desperate. "You're stronger than he is. You fought him off."

"No. You stopped him. This time." The words hung heavy between us. His voice dropped to a whisper.

When Zen opened his eyes and looked at me, his expression distressed. "I couldn't live with myself if I hurt you, Niki. Please, go." The last words he whispered almost as if they were a prayer. Then he turned and walked back into the bathroom, shutting the door firmly behind him.

I stood there for a moment, hand outstretched toward the closed door, then let it fall to my side. The rejection stung, but beneath it was something worse—understanding. Because I knew exactly what he meant. The fear of what lived inside you. The terror of losing control for even a moment.

I slunk out of his room, a horrible ache ricocheting through me.

"*You do not need help from the shifter.*" Hun-Came's voice slithered into my thoughts. "*I am your destiny. Embrace the darkness.*"

"Leave me alone." I touched my jade pendant, focusing on Nayla, my parents. I resolutely shut my mind to him before returning to my room, hot tears pricking the back of my eyes.

***

We met in the dining room for breakfast.

The atmosphere was thick with unspoken tension. I picked at my food, appetite gone, while Zen sat rigid in his chair, his shoulders tense, jaw working as if perpetually biting back words. Every few seconds, I caught myself stealing glances at him, hungry for any acknowledgment. Each time our eyes nearly met, he'd shift his gaze just slightly, denying me even that small connection.

Aedan positioned himself strategically between us, his posture alert as though expecting Zen to lunge across the table at any moment. I wanted to scream at the absurdity of it all.

Izzy was the only one of us who was in good spirits. Her gaze whipsawed between the three of us with undisguised amusement at our discomfort. "We can leave tomorrow," she announced, breaking the suffocating silence. "My father's helicopter will take us to a landing area near the entrance of the tunnel shaft that should connect us to the cave system. It's all been arranged."

"Good," Zen said. He pushed his chair back from the table so forcefully it scraped against the floor, making me wince. "I'll finish putting together the packs."

Izzy perked up, practically glowing. "I'll help you. We can give my father a list of any other supplies we need."

"Fine." Zen shot a quick glance at me, his eyes unreadable, before leaving the table. Izzy followed happily behind him, throwing a triumphant look over her shoulder that made my stomach knot.

"Well, that was a trifle awkward," Aedan commented as he took a sip of his coffee. "I didn't think I'd be playing bodyguard for a shapeshifter."

"Is that what you're doing?" I asked, unable to keep the bitterness from my voice.

"That's what I've been asked to do," he replied carefully.

I stared at Aedan, my heart ripping in two. "What did Zen tell you?" My voice trembled despite my efforts to steady it.

"Enough."

"What?" I insisted, leaning forward. "What exactly did he say?"

Aedan sighed, setting his coffee down. "He said he lost control. Li Xul used him to get to you. He said he almost killed you."

"That's not true," I protested, heat rising to my face. "It wasn't like that. He just needed to shut Li Xul out. Which he did. It was Li Xul who tried to hurt me. Not Zen. Zen would never hurt me."

"That's not what he said." Aedan's gaze was cool, clinical. "He told me I'm to make sure he doesn't go near you again. It's too dangerous for you."

"Well, he's wrong!" I replied heatedly. "He just needs something like this." I held up my wrist with the iron bracelet, the metal catching the light. "Something to help him resist Li Xul." I laid a hand on Aedan's arm, squeezing desperately. "Can you make him something? An iron bracelet or anything?"

Aedan's blue eyes were full of compassion as he covered my hand with his. "I know you want to help him, but, Niki—he's a shapeshifter. I'm not sure anything I could make would be effective. Or that he'd accept something from me."

"*I can find you something to help him resist,*" Hun-Came's voice cooed in my ear, honey-sweet and tempting. "*But there will be a price to pay for the knowledge.*"

I touched my pendant and closed my eyes, focusing my thoughts on my family, muting his voice with effort. Every time Hun-Came spoke, it was getting harder to shut him out.

"What about something like this?" I asked, fingers trembling as I touched the jade pendant hanging around my neck. "What if I gave him this?"

Aedan studied me, his gaze lingering on my pendant. "I don't know. To be honest, your best bet would be to consult with our expert on the ancient Maya."

Dread filled me. I knew he was right, but every fiber of my being resisted asking Izzy for help. The thought of approaching her, with her smug smile and possessive stance toward Zen, made something dark and jealous twist inside me.

After a moment, I pushed my chair back from the table. "I'll talk to her later, but first I'm going to email my mom and see what she says."

Like Aedan, my mother's advice was limited. She also wasn't optimistic that anything she suggested would help Zen. Without any other options, I went in search of Izzy, my pride a bitter pill to swallow.

I found her in the library studying a map of the Chiquibul cave complex on her laptop. She looked up when I entered, her expression instantly closing, like shutters drawn against an unwelcome visitor.

"Hey, Izzy." I pasted a smile on my face that felt as brittle as glass. "I'm hoping you can help me with something."

"What?" she asked, arching one eyebrow in my direction. The single syllable dripped with reluctance.

I took a deep breath. "I'm—um—searching for something that can ward off dream-walkers. Specifically, Li Xul."

She flicked a glance at the iron bracelet encircling my wrist, her lips curling slightly. "Your druid charms aren't working?"

I bit back a sharp retort. "Please, if you know anything that might help, I'd appreciate it if you could tell me." The words cost me, each one like swallowing a thorn.

"Li Xul isn't just a dream-walker he's a dream-weaver. He can project his wahy at will into lightning, animals, people." Izzy leaned back in her chair, studying me. "There are things you can do to strengthen your tonal connection, to make it more difficult for him. Consuming cornmeal and amaranth for strength. Salt, rue, and obsidian mirrors to deflect evil spirits." She tapped her fingers on the table rhythmically. "I've also read that sleeping with an obsidian knife under your pillow can sever a dream-walker's connection, but I don't think most of these remedies will work against Li Xul." She shrugged, her indifference calculated. "Sorry."

"I'm not asking for me," I said quietly. "I'm asking for Zen."

Her expression sharpened instantly. "Zen?"

"I'm worried about what happens to him once we leave the compound and enter the jungle. He needs something to help him break Li Xul's connection to him."

Izzy shook her head, her dark hair catching the light.

"Anything Zen would use to keep Li Xul away weakens his own wahy. He is a wahy b'alam. These remedies are for protection of humans against beings like him." She leaned forward, her voice dropping to an intimate tone that made my skin crawl. "To protect himself, he needs to feed in order to strengthen his tonal and his shadow soul."

A chill ran down my spine. "By feeding…"

Dark eyes glittering like diamonds, Izzy nodded slowly, savoring my discomfort. "Exactly." Her voice hardened. "His strength comes from the same source as Li Xul. They are both shapeshifters."

"I know that," I spat out. "That doesn't mean there isn't some way for Zen to protect himself. Li Xul was able to subdue Zen's shadow soul. To make him do things. There has to be a way for him to fight back."

"You don't get it, do you? Zen is only a means to an end. Li Xul isn't interested in Zen. Li Xul wants you." Izzy's voice dripped with disdain. "The best thing Zen can do to protect himself is exactly what he is doing right now. Stay away from you."

Her words hung in the air between us like poison. The truth of it sank into me, a leaden weight in my chest. Zen was pulling away to protect me, yes—but also because getting close to me endangered his very soul.

"There has to be another way," I whispered, more to myself than to her.

Izzy's smile was cold, victorious. "There isn't. And the sooner you accept that, the better for everyone." She tilted her head, studying me with calculated cruelty. "Especially for Zen."

I stood there, hands clenched at my sides, wanting to scream at her, to deny everything she said. But I couldn't. Because deep down, I knew she was right.

And deep down, Hun-Came stirred, pleased at my despair.

"Don't worry. When the time comes, I'll help Zen," Izzy said after a moment. "Li Xul may be a powerful shaman, but he's not a god." Her eyes hardened. "Nothing will help you, though. If Zen's ritual doesn't work—and I won't let him sacrifice himself for you—then you will need to die. I will not allow you to unleash Hun-Came into this world."

She leaned closer, her voice dropping to a dangerous whisper. "Your exes don't want you to die—but I don't have that problem. If Zen's ritual fails and your ex-boyfriends won't kill you, I will."

CHAPTER TWENTY

I found myself hiking through the Guatemalan jungle—something I'd vowed never to do again. Yet here I was, the dense foliage closing around us as we moved away from the clearing where the helicopter had deposited us thirty minutes earlier.

The jungle hit all my senses at once, more intensely than I remembered. The air was thick with moisture, carrying the sweet-rot scent of decaying vegetation and the musty perfume of flowering plants. Every inhalation filled my lungs with life and death intermingled. Beneath my boots, the ground gave slightly, cushioned by layers of decomposing leaves. A symphony of insect calls filled the air—clicking, buzzing, chirping—punctuated by the occasional screech of a distant howler monkey that raised the hair on my arms.

Since Hun-Came had taken up residence within me, everything was different. Colors were more vibrant—the myriad shades of green so distinct I could almost taste them. Sounds separated themselves into individual threads that I could follow if I chose. And the scents... I caught whiffs of animals that had passed through hours earlier, the faint copper tang of blood from something recently killed, the mineral smell of an underground stream we hadn't yet reached.

"Do you sense it?" Hun-Came whispered inside me, his voice warm with pleasure. *"This is my domain. My power flows through every root and branch. Death, rebirth, death."*

I touched my jade pendant reflexively. Here in the jungle, Hun-Came's presence was stronger, more pervasive.

There were six of us in our expedition—seven if you included Hun-Came, which I was finding increasingly difficult not to do. Zen walked at the front with our guide, his movements fluid and predatory. Since our confrontation in his room, he'd barely spoken two words to me. Aedan stayed close to my side, ever the watchful guardian, while Izzy trailed a few steps behind, her dark eyes constantly tracking Zen's every move.

We'd also picked up Marco and Franco, two of Izzy's cousins. I thought of them as Tweedle Dee and Tweedle Dum—a pair of muscular, tight-lipped men who finished each other's sentences and carried themselves with an over-confident swagger. Neither seemed thrilled to be accompanying us. I got the feeling that Izzy's father had everything to do with their addition to our little group. They were our muscle. Tough guys with guns, protection from the human threats we might encounter in this remote region used by Li Xul and others for trafficking humans and contraband across the border to Mexico, then north to the US.

Leading our group was Ulices, a professional cave explorer hired by Izzy's father. He was a compact man in his forties with skin weathered like old leather and eyes that never stopped moving. A complex web of climbing rope was coiled around his torso, and a professional caving harness hung from his belt. Unlike the rest of us with our newly purchased hiking gear, his equipment showed the patina of extensive use. A battered and scratched hard hat was attached to his pack with a carabiner, bouncing lightly against his pack with each step.

The only one of us who seemed to be enjoying himself was Aedan. I shot a glance over my shoulder at him. He was in his element, druids loved spending time in nature. He grinned and whistled a little diddy that sounded suspiciously like the beginning notes of the Irish drinking song *Whiskey in the Jar*.

Just before we'd left the clearing, Izzy had reached into her pack and pulled out a small brown paper bag. "My father was able to find that item you requested," she'd said, handing it to Aedan with a knowing smile.

Aedan's face had lit up. "Bless you, darling," he'd said, quickly stuffing it into his pack.

"What's in the package?" I'd asked, curious.

"Ah, just a wee drop of the creature," he'd replied with a wink in my direction, patting his pack affectionately. "For medicinal purposes only, of course."

"He means whiskey," Izzy had explained, rolling her eyes. "Irish whiskey."

"A proper bottle of Redbreast 15-year," Aedan had corrected. "Hard to come by in these parts. And essential for any proper expedition into the unknown."

I rolled my eyes, though I have to admit I did find it comforting that Aedan believed we'd have an opportunity to enjoy a wee dram or two at some point during our journey to the Mayan underworld. Maybe the monsters, demons, and other-worldly beings waiting for us weren't going to be as bad as I feared.

We walked in single file along a narrow trail that seemed to appear and disappear at random. Each of us carried machetes except for Aedan, who had Sky-Splitter strapped across his back. Our packs were laden with supplies—water, purification tablets, freeze-dried food, insect repellent, helmets and headlamps, first aid kits, sleeping bags, and waterproof matches. Everything we might need for several days in the jungle and caves.

I glanced at Zen, wondering if he felt the same heightened awareness of our surroundings. As if sensing my thoughts, he turned slightly, his eyes meeting mine for just a moment before turning away. But in that brief connection, I saw it—the wildness that lurked just beneath his careful control. The same wildness that was growing in me.

"I could use a wee breeze about now." Aedan commented, wiping sweat from his brow, his happy whistle wilting as the humidity intensified. His Irish skin was flushed from the heat.

"Actually, it's quite pleasant today," Zen replied without turning around. "Wait until we get deeper in. There, the air will be so thick you will feel like you are swimming."

"Fantastic," Aedan muttered, his good humor quickly dissipating.

"It's the mosquitoes and bugs, I don't like," Izzy said, waving a hand at the insects buzzing around her wide-brimmed hat.

"They don't bite me much," I said, then realized with a start that it was true. Since entering the jungle, I hadn't felt a single insect landing on my exposed skin. I looked down at my arms, expecting to see the familiar angry red welts forming, but my skin was unmarked.

"*Another gift from me,*" Hun-Came whispered. "*No creature of this forest would dare feast on the vessel that carries a god.*"

I shuddered, and Aedan shot me a concerned look.

"You, okay?" he asked quietly.

"Just... taking it all in," I replied. I felt a strange stirring in my chest, like something unfurling. The longer we walked, the more at home I felt in this dangerous place. The jungle seemed to whisper secrets I could almost understand. The terrain that had initially appeared chaotic now revealed patterns—game trails, water sources, places where predators might lie in wait.

"*You begin to understand, my little vessel. This is power,*" Hun-Came murmured. "*True power. Not the weak magic of iron bracelets and jade pendants. Feel how the jungle recognizes us, welcomes us.*"

I wanted to deny it, but I couldn't. Something

fundamental was changing within me, resonating with this wild place. It terrified me, yet I couldn't help but wonder what other senses might awaken if I stopped fighting so hard against Hun-Came's influence.

We hiked in silence for another hour before Ulices paused, crouching down to examine something on the ground. We gathered around Ulices, peering at what had caught his attention—a clear footprint in the mud, much larger than any of ours.

"Jaguar," he said, his voice tinged with respect. "A big one. Fresh, maybe an hour old."

Zen knelt beside him, his fingers hovering just above the print without touching it. His nostrils flared slightly, and for a moment, something flickered across his features—recognition, perhaps. Or kinship.

"Will it be a problem?" Izzy asked, her hand moving almost imperceptibly toward the small of her back where I knew she kept a small pistol concealed.

Ulices shook his head. "Not likely. They avoid humans. Unless..." His eyes flickered to Zen, then to me, a puzzled expression crossing his face. "Unless something draws them to us."

"We should keep moving," Zen said abruptly, standing.

I looked over at Zen, one eyebrow raised inquiringly. "*Li Xul?*"

He gave his head an almost imperceptible nod.

"I agree with Zen. We shouldn't dally, lads and lassies. Law of the jungle—survival of the fittest and all that," Aedan commented adjusting the straps of his pack.

I rolled my eyes.

"That is not the law of the jungle. That's a misinterpretation of Darwin's Theory of Evolution," Izzy lectured from behind me.

Aedan raised an eyebrow. "My mistake, Professor. What is the law of the jungle then, if you're such an expert?"

"We are the law in the jungle," Franco interrupted, puffing out his chest and patting the semi-automatic rifle slung over his shoulder.

A derisive laugh escaped Aedan. "Ah yes, the gentlemen with the guns will protect us from the wild beasties of the jungle."

Franco and Marco exchanged glances. "This is not a laughing matter," Franco said, his hand resting on the rifle slung over his shoulder.

"It is not jaguars that you need to fear. The men who travel here are dangerous men," Marco chimed in from the rear.

"In the jungle, they take what they want. Anything soft and weak are fair game," Franco added with a coarse laugh, his eyes shifting between Izzy and myself, making it obvious who he thought was soft and weak. "That is why we are here."

"Charming," Izzy muttered, but I caught the subtle shift in her stance—weight forward, ready to move.

We resumed our trek in silence. I should have felt a fission of fear at Franco's words, but I didn't. I glanced over at Zen, who walked slightly apart from the group, his expression distant. Was the forest whispering to him as Hun-Came was to me? Was the jaguar spirit inside him also feeling the pull of something ancient and primal awakening in his blood?

"You're quiet," Aedan observed as we navigated around a fallen tree covered in luminous orange-colored fungi. He kept his voice low, meant for my ears alone.

"Just listening," I said. It wasn't entirely a lie. I was listening—to the jungle, to Hun-Came, to my own transforming body. I felt the weight of his concerned gaze boring between my shoulder blades.

"Niki, I can help, but only if you're honest with me. And yourself," he added gently.

Before I could respond, he switched to his normal volume. "Well, I for one would kill for a cold beer right about now. Or a shower. Preferably both."

No one responded to his comment, but I felt his hand

brush against mine—a small gesture of solidarity that made my throat tighten unexpectedly.

We took turns slashing our way through the never-ending sea of vines and plants in the stifling heat. Hot and moist, the dense air clung to me. Sweat dripped down my forehead and nose, stinging my eyes.

"How about a water break?" Aedan asked.

Ulices looked over his shoulder, then stopped without saying a word, waiting patiently while the rest of us shed our packs.

I drank my tepid water greedily, wiping my mouth with the back of my hand. Something was different. I could hear a strange shushing, rustling sound beneath the normal chirring of insects and trilling of birds.

"Do you hear that?" I asked, my voice barely above a whisper.

Ulices cocked his head to one side and listened carefully, his weathered face creasing with concern as the usual sounds of the jungle—the constant background hum of insects, the occasional bird call—became eerily quiet.

Zen stiffened, his head snapping up. His nostrils flared as he scanned the surrounding vegetation, every muscle in his body suddenly taut. "Something's wrong," he said, his voice low and urgent. "The animals—they're running."

"Running from what?" Marco asked, his hand moving to his rifle.

Before Zen could answer, the jungle erupted into chaos. As if the front gates of a zoo had burst open, thousands of crawling, hopping, and slithering creatures rushed out of the underbrush in a mad exodus. We found ourselves in the middle of a living highway—spiders, roaches, beetles, lizards, and small rodents all frantically scrambling to escape some unseen terror.

"Jesus, Mary, and Joseph," Aedan breathed, taking a step back as a tarantula the size of his hand scuttled over his boot.

Above us, a flock of birds appeared, swooping down like

dive bombers, picking off the parade of insects and reptiles scurrying over the leaf litter. The air filled with the sound of wings and desperate squeals.

Ulices' eyes widened with recognition and fear. "We must hurry," he said, his calm demeanor cracking. "We need to get to the river. Now! Follow me!"

"What the hell is going on?" Marco demanded, his weapon raised as if he could shoot whatever was coming.

"Army ants," Ulices explained, already moving. "Millions of them. They are marching."

"Ants?" Franco scoffed, though I noticed he'd gone pale. "We're running from ants?"

"Trust me," Zen said, his voice carrying an edge I'd never heard before. He grabbed Izzy's arm, pulling her forward. "Move. This isn't natural—a swarm this size, this coordinated. The jungle is... aware of us."

Inside me, Hun-Came's presence swelled with what could only be described as delight. *"Ah, my little vessel. Do you see? I have prepared a welcome for us. A demonstration of power. Watch how death moves through the living world like water through stone."*

"You did this?" I whispered, stumbling as Aedan pulled me forward.

"I merely... suggested. The jungle remembers me. These creatures serve the old gods, as all things must eventually serve death."

Ulices quickened his pace to almost a run. When we finally reached the river, he didn't hesitate, wading directly into the murky brown water until it reached his waist.

Franco folded his arms across his chest, watching as the rest of our group dutifully followed Ulices into the river. "I'm not getting in that water. There could be anything in there—caimans, leeches, parasites—"

"Franco, come on!" Izzy called, already knee-deep, her earlier bravado replaced by genuine fear.

Marco hesitated at the bank, glancing between his brother and the rest of us as the strange shushing noise grew increasingly louder, closer. It sounded like rain on leaves, but wrong somehow—purposeful, hungry.

Ulices stood calmly in the river, his eyes focused laser-like on the surrounding trees. "You do not want to be on land when they arrive."

The green wall of leaves and vines bordering the riverbank trembled and vibrated, as if something massive was pushing through from behind. A frightened squalling sound came from somewhere in the bushes—high-pitched, desperate.

A young coatimundi dragged itself out from the underbrush, its ringed tail matted with blood. The little animal yowled plaintively, pushing itself forward with its front paws while dragging an injured hind leg behind it. Its dark eyes were wide with terror.

"Oh, no," I breathed, my hand moving instinctively toward the bank. "We have to help it—"

Aedan's hand closed around my wrist, holding me back. "Niki, no. There's no time."

The shushing noise hit its crescendo quickly transforming into a roar. Then, like a volcanic explosion, millions of ants erupted from the jungle, pouring over everything in their path. They crawled up tree trunks in writhing columns, swarming over vines and branches until the very trees seemed to come alive, writhing like tormented giants.

Franco and Marco finally broke, splashing into the river with shouts of alarm.

The little coatimundi squealed in terror, trying desperately to pull itself forward, but its injured leg made escape impossible. The leading edge of the swarm reached it, and within seconds, the animal disappeared beneath a boiling, bubbling mass of insects.

"Don't look," Zen said quietly, but I couldn't tear my eyes away.

The coatimundi's squeals rose to an unbearable pitch as the tiny predators swarmed over it, their pincer-like jaws stripping flesh from bone with terrifying efficiency. Steam rose from the writhing mass as the ants digestive enzymes went to work. Within minutes, only bones remained, picked clean and gleaming white.

"This is wrong," Zen muttered, his face ashen. "A swarm this size—I've never heard of anything like this. It's as if something is driving them, directing them."

"Oh, God," Izzy gasped, her face pale. She looked at me, and I saw the realization dawning in her eyes. "This is because of us. Because of what we're doing."

Inside me, Hun-Came laughed, the sound reverberating through my bones. "*Beautiful, is it not? The dance of death and consumption. This is but a taste of what awaits in Xibalba. Life feeding on life, death giving birth to new life. The eternal cycle that mortals fear but cannot escape.*"

I wanted to feel horror, disgust, anything normal. But part of me—a growing, terrifying part—felt exhilarated. The raw power of it, the savage beauty of nature's most efficient killers working in perfect harmony. I pressed my jade pendant so hard against my chest that it would leave a mark.

"Niki?" Aedan's voice was sharp with concern. "What's happening? Your eyes—"

The swarm continued its march to the river's edge. They didn't stop or turn away at the water as I expected. Instead, they marched directly into the river without pausing, even as the first ranks drowned and floated to the surface.

"They're coming into the river!" Izzy shouted, panic cracking her voice.

"Stay calm," Ulices commanded, though his own voice was strained. "We can move out of their way. Watch—they will build a bridge."

And they did. The ants kept pouring into the water, drowning by the thousands. But the ants behind them climbed over their dead comrades, forming a bridge of floating carcasses that allowed the rest of the swarm to cross. It was simultaneously horrifying and mesmerizing— the perfect sacrifice of individuals for the survival of the collective.

We shifted out of their path, the water lapping at our chests as we gave the living bridge a wide berth. The column was at least six feet wide, millions upon millions of bodies creating a highway across the water.

"I've never seen anything like this," Ulices whispered, his professional composure finally cracking. "Not in thirty years of exploring these jungles."

When the ants reached the opposite bank, they spread out once again in a wide column, their shushing sound gradually fading as they moved deeper into the forest.

We stood in the water for close to an hour, watching as the miniature army marched past in an endless stream. The sound was maddening—like rain on leaves, but underneath it, I could hear something else. The clicking of millions of miniature jaws munching, devouring everything in their path.

"How much longer?" Marco asked, his voice tight.

"Until the colony moves on," Ulices replied. "We wait."

As suddenly as the ants had appeared, they were gone, leaving the jungle completely silent. No birds sang. No insects chirped. Even the ever-present hum of the rainforest had ceased, as if the jungle itself was holding its breath.

"Can we get out now?" Izzy asked, her teeth chattering despite the warm water.

Ulices nodded slowly, wading toward the bank. We followed, our movements slow and cautious, as if afraid any noise might summon the swarm back.

On the riverbank, where the coatimundi had fallen, only scattered bones remained. The surrounding vegetation had been stripped clean—leaves, bark, even the softer wood had been consumed. The ground itself looked scoured.

"Oh my, God. There's nothing left," Izzy breathed. I heard the tremor in her voice.

Zen crouched beside the bones, not touching them. When he looked up at me, his expression was grave. "This was a message. A warning," he said quietly, his eyes meeting mine.

I felt Hun-Came's presence surge with satisfaction.

"Fucking ants," Marco said, his earlier bravado completely gone.

"What do we do now? Go back or keep following the fucking ants?" Franco demanded, though he kept his distance from the cleaned bones.

"Turning back won't make us safer," I said quietly.

They all turned to look at me.

Ulices checked his watch, then the sky visible through the canopy. "She's right. We should keep moving. We've lost time, and there's weather coming."

As if to punctuate his words, distant thunder rumbled across the sky. The sound seemed to echo the memory of millions of tiny jaws clicking in unison.

We began following our guide in silence, each of us processing what we'd witnessed. Franco and Marco stayed close together, their earlier swagger replaced by watchful tension. Izzy couldn't seem to stop glancing over her shoulder. Even Aedan had lost his good humor, his hand never straying far from Sky-Splitter's hilt.

Only Zen seemed unsurprised, moving with the same fluid grace as before, though I caught him studying me when he thought I wasn't looking.

"Well," Aedan finally said as we resumed our march, his attempt at levity falling flat. "I'm thinking that bottle of whiskey might not last as long as I'd hoped."

No one laughed.

As we walked, Hun-Came's voice whispered in my mind, intimate and terrible. *"You felt it, didn't you? The beauty of it. The rightness. This is what you are becoming, my vessel. Not weak and afraid, but powerful. A force of nature, like the swarm. Accept it, and so much more awaits you."*

I touched my jade pendant, but it felt warm against my skin, its protection wearing thin. With each step deeper into the jungle, toward the entrance to Xibalba. I could feel the boundaries between myself and the death god blurring.

And the most terrifying part? I was no longer sure I wanted to stop it.

CHAPTER TWENTY-ONE

The jungle slowly returned to normal, though the memory of witnessing nature's violent hunger did not leave us. The trail began to descend, and the character of the jungle changed subtly. The trees grew taller, their canopies knitting together to block out much of the sunlight. The undergrowth thinned, replaced by massive buttress roots that twisted across our path like petrified serpents. The air grew cooler and damper, carrying the unmistakable mineral scent of underground water.

"We're getting close," Ulices announced. "The tunnel entrance is just beyond that ridge."

As if on cue, a distant rumble of thunder rolled across the sky. I looked up, but the dense canopy revealed only occasional patches of darkening sky.

"Storm coming," Ulices said, quickening his pace. "We should hurry."

The first fat raindrop hit my face like a cold finger tap. Within seconds, the sky opened up, unleashing a deluge that turned the forest canopy into a sieve. Water cascaded through the leaves in sheets, drenching us instantly.

"Bloody hell!" Aedan shouted over the roar of the downpour, fumbling with his pack.

Ulices was already pulling his waterproof poncho from his bag, with practiced efficiency.

I struggled into mine, the plastic material clinging to my wet skin. The rain drummed against the hood pulled tight around my face, creating a hollow echo chamber where Hun-Came's whispers seemed to amplify.

"The storm heralds your approach to Xibalba," he murmured, his voice almost gleeful. *"The Lords of Death await your arrival with eager anticipation."*

We pressed forward, slipping on the sudden mud, the trail transforming into a shallow creek bed before our eyes. Lightning split the sky, illuminating Zen's face ahead of me—his features sharp and intent, seemingly unbothered by the downpour.

Another crack of thunder, this one so close it vibrated in my chest. I startled, my foot sliding on a slick root. Before I could fall, Aedan's hand shot out, steadying me with a firm grip on my elbow.

"I've got you," he said, his Irish lilt more pronounced in his concern.

"Thanks," I managed, acutely aware of Zen glancing back at us, his eyes narrowing slightly at Aedan's hand still on my arm.

After what felt like hours but was likely only forty minutes of grueling progress, we arrived at the tunnel entrance—or what was supposed to be the entrance. Instead of an opening into the earth, we found a pile of rubble and limestone. The entire face of the small cliff had collapsed, massive boulders blocking what once had been a passage.

"Jesus, Mary, and Joseph," Aedan breathed, wiping rain from his eyes. "That's not exactly welcoming, is it?"

Ulices approached the rockfall, examining it. "This is recent," he said, his voice tight. "Very recent."

"How recent?" Izzy demanded, pushing her way forward.

He ran his hand over a jagged edge of stone. "Days.

Perhaps less." He looked back at us, his expression grim. "This was not natural. See these marks?" He pointed to several indentations in the rock face. "Explosives."

Franco spat on the ground. "One of the narcos, sealing access to a rival's mine shaft."

"Or the military," Marco added. "They sometimes seal old mines if they find traffickers using them."

"Either way," Zen said, "this entrance is useless to us now."

We huddled beneath the scant shelter of a limestone overhang, the rain still pouring around us. Izzy looked furious, her dark eyes flashing as she paced the small dry space.

"All this way for nothing," she snapped.

"Not necessarily," Ulices said slowly. He pulled out a worn topographical map protected in plastic, spreading it against the rock wall. "There is another way. A smaller cave entrance, about a day's hike from here." He traced a path with his finger.

I read the name on the map, Cueva de Navajas. "The Cave of Razors," I translated out loud.

"It's more difficult terrain, but the cave connects to the larger system," Ulices continued.

Izzy's expression turned thoughtful. "Cave of Razors." Her eyes swept over us. "It's from the Popol Vuh. One of the challenges the hero twins had to face before entering Xilbaba."

Zen's eyes found mine. "Damn."

I gritted my teeth as Hun-Came's laughter reverberated inside my head. *The bruja is not wrong. The Lords of Xilbaba prepare to welcome you.*

"A day's hike? To someplace called the Cave of Razors. In this?" Aedan caught my eye, gesturing at the torrential rain. "What a perfect holiday. You certainly know how to show a lad a good time."

"Feel free to leave anytime," I said tartly. "It's not as if I actually asked you to come with me to Guatemala."

"I wouldn't have missed this for the world, love," Aedan remarked with a grin. "Besides, as you know, I'm very good with sharp objects."

Ulices ignored our bickering. "If you wish to continue to the cave, we should make camp here for the night. Start fresh in the morning."

Izzy looked like she wanted to argue but then nodded sharply. "Fine. Let's get the tents up."

As we began unpacking our gear, I noticed Zen standing apart, staring at the collapsed entrance with an unsettling intensity. I moved to his side, keeping my voice low.

"What is it?"

"Li Xul," he said simply. "I can feel him. He was here."

A chill that had nothing to do with my wet clothes slid down my spine. "Recently?"

"Yes." His dark eyes met mine, and for a brief moment, I saw a flash of the wildness within him—the jaguar spirit that made him a shapeshifter. "He's hunting us, Niki."

A sound between a sob and laugh escaped from my throat. "Well, I guess he'll just have to get in line behind the Mayan god of death."

Aedan called out, "Niki! Give us a hand with these tents, would you, love?"

I hesitated, not wanting to break the fragile connection with Zen, but he had already turned away, moving to help Marco with one of the tarps.

Setting up camp in the rain was miserable work. By the time we had the tents secured on the least muddy ground we could find, the downpour had slackened to a steady drizzle, but we were all soaked to the bone.

"Right," Aedan said, clapping his hands together. "Sleeping arrangements. We've got three two-person tents."

"I prefer to sleep outside," Ulices interjected, already using his machete to construct a simple shelter from palm fronds. "I sleep better beneath the sky."

Marco nodded. "The women should not sleep in the same tent. We need a man with a weapon in each tent for protection."

Izzy held up the dainty pistol she carried. "I have a weapon."

Franco and Marco exchanged looks, before guffawing derisively. "That is not a weapon." Franco raised the submachine gun he carried. "This is a weapon."

"No offense, love," Aedan added with a grin. "But that does look more like a fashion accessory than a weapon."

Izzy's eyes narrowed to slits.

"I'll bunk with Niki," Zen said quickly.

Aedan's head swiveled toward Zen, his eyes hardened. "I don't think so, mate. My job is to keep her safe."

"And you think I can't?" Zen challenged, stepping closer.

"I know you can't," Aedan replied, his voice dangerously soft. "Not from yourself." The tension between them crackled like the lightning that had just torn through the sky. I opened my mouth to intervene, but Izzy beat me to it.

"Oh, for God's sake," she said, rolling her eyes. "Zen will share with me. Aedan can share with Niki. Marco and Franco will protect each other. Problem solved."

The flash of jealousy that shot through me was so sudden and intense it momentarily took my breath away. Izzy must have seen it on my face because her lips curved into a knowing smile.

"Unless there's some reason that any of you think that wouldn't work?" she purred, her eyes flicking between Zen and me.

"It's fine," I said, my voice tight. "That makes sense."

Aedan looked smug, hooking an arm around my shoulders. "That's settled then. Niki's with me, Zen's with Izzy, and the cousins share the third tent."

Franco stepped forward, water still dripping from his poncho. "We need to establish a watch for tonight."

"Not even those ants we met earlier would be willing to march in this weather," Aedan scoffed. "It's raining cats and dogs. Any predator with sense is tucked away somewhere dry."

"Those aren't the predators we're worried about," Marco said grimly. "You heard Ulices. Someone blew that entrance. They could still be nearby."

Aedan and Zen exchanged a glance that contained an entire conversation. I knew what they were thinking—Their guns would be no protection against the supernatural forces hunting us. Between Aedan's druid abilities and Zen's jaguar senses, we had protection beyond what Franco and Marco could understand.

"Fine," Aedan conceded. "You want a watch; we'll have a watch."

"I'll take the first shift," I volunteered.

Marco shook his head. "You don't have a weapon."

I bristled at his dismissal. "I can still watch and shout if I see anything."

"I'll take first watch," Zen said, his tone brooking no argument. "Then Aedan, then Franco. Then Marco. Izzy and Niki can take the last shift."

I glared at him.

"What are we going to do about food?" Izzy asked, hugging herself against the chill. "We can't light a fire in this."

"Cold soak your rations tonight," Zen replied, pulling out a dehydrated meal from his pack. "Save the cooking for morning."

We huddled under the partial shelter of the limestone overhang, glumly eating our partially rehydrated food. The silence was broken only by the patter of rain and occasional distant thunder. As darkness fell, the jungle transformed around us, the shadows deepening, strange calls echoing through the trees.

I felt Hun-Came stir within me, more restless than before. "*So close,*" he whispered. "*Can you feel the strength and power in this place? The thin veil between worlds?*"

When it was time to sleep, I crawled into the tent I'd be sharing with Aedan. The small space felt intimate in a way that stirred memories I'd rather keep buried. He entered a few minutes later, carefully removing his wet outer layers before slipping into his sleeping bag.

"I'm happy to offer my services as a sleeping bag warmer, should you be interested," he said, his face illuminated by the small lantern between us.

"No thanks," I replied, turning onto my side to face him. "There are already two of us in here and I don't think there's room for three."

He chuckled, the sound warm and familiar. "Fair point." He reached out, his fingertips hovering near my face before dropping back to his sleeping bag. "I'm worried about you, Niki."

"I know."

"Do you?" His eyes searched mine. "Whatever's happening to you—this Hun-Came business—I can see it changing you."

I swallowed hard. "I'm still me."

"Are you?" he asked gently. "Because sometimes when I look at you, I see something else looking back." He shifted closer. "Just... don't forget who you are, love. Promise me that."

The genuine concern in his voice made my chest ache. "I promise I'm trying."

He stretched his arm toward the lantern. "Good. Because I've promised your mother I will bring you back to her. I wouldn't want you to make a liar out of me."

"I won't," I whispered.

He nodded, seeming satisfied with that answer before extinguishing the lantern. "Well, then we'd best get some sleep while we can."

I closed my eyes, lulled by the rhythmic sound of rain on the tent. Sleep came quickly, dragging me down into darkness that soon transformed into a vivid dream.

***

Wet fur clung to my powerful body as I moved silently through the underbrush. The rain had softened the earth beneath my paws, making each step soundless. My whiskers twitched, capturing the faintest vibrations in the air. Every sense was heightened—the scent of rich soil, the gentle tap of water droplets on leaves, the distant heartbeat of my prey.

I could taste it on the air—the warm musk of deer, its body heat creating a ghost of steam in the cool night. I stalked closer, my muscles rippling beneath sleek fur. My body moved with liquid grace, hardly disturbing a leaf as I crept forward.

The young white-tailed doe stood in a small clearing, head raised, nostrils flaring. It sensed danger but couldn't place it. Its heartbeat quickened—a sound so delicious it made my mouth flood with saliva. I sank lower, my belly nearly touching the ground, feeling the coiled power in my haunches.

The rain masked my scent, the thunder covered any sound I might make. Perfect hunting conditions. I gathered myself; every fiber of my being focused on the moment of release to come.

The doe took one step, then another, its hooves sinking into the mud. So vulnerable. So beautiful.

I launched forward; a shadow made of flesh. Time slowed as I sailed through the air, my claws extending, my jaws opening wide. The doe tried to leap away, but too late—I landed on her back, my weight driving it down. My teeth found the tender flesh of its throat, clamping down with exquisite precision.

The doe's struggle was brief, its life pulsing hot and copper-sweet against my tongue. Power flooded through me—not just from the kill, but from being exactly what nature intended. Predator. Hunter. Death embodied. Every nerve ending in my body sang with the rightness of it all.

As the doe's final breath rattled out, pleasure coursed through me—primal, raw, and perfect. I ripped in the soft underbelly, savaging her still warm flesh with ravenous fervor.

***

I jolted awake, gasping. The tent was empty—Aedan

must have left for his watch. My heart hammered against my ribs, and I could still feel the phantom sensation of powerful muscles beneath my skin. My body hummed with a lingering, uncomfortable pleasure that made me feel both ashamed and vibrantly alive.

"Beautiful, isn't it?" Hun-Came's voice slid through my mind. *"The hunt. The power. You feel it through your bond with the wahy b'alam."*

"What?" I whispered into the darkness.

"He hunts tonight. The wahy b'alam prowls while the man keeps watch. And you, little shadow-soul, you feel it because you are connected. This is why you are my chosen vessel—you walk in both worlds, just as he does."

I sat up, pushing my hair back from my sweaty forehead. The rain had stopped, I realized. The constant patter on the tent had ceased, replaced by the drip of water from leaves and the chorus of night insects.

Driven by some instinct I couldn't name, I slipped from my sleeping bag and out of the tent. The night air was cool against my skin, heavy with moisture. The clouds had parted, revealing a waxing moon and patches of star-strewn sky between the canopy.

I stood still, letting my eyes adjust to the darkness. Aedan sat watch under the overhang. His silhouette blending into the shadows. Something moved at the edge of our camp— a shadow detached itself from the deep night of the surrounding jungle.

Gleaming eyes reflecting the moonlight, Zen emerged from the undergrowth, his clothes clinging to his body, his hair wild. He raised a hand to Aedan, who returned the gesture.

When he caught sight of me, he froze for a moment, then approached with that fluid grace that seemed more pronounced now, more inhuman.

"You should be asleep," he said, his voice a low rumble.

"I felt you," I replied simply. "Hunting."

He went very still. "What did you feel?"

"Everything. The rain on fur. The scent of prey. The power in... in your body." I swallowed. "Hun-Came says we're connected. I can feel it when you shift. I think I've been able to do that for a while. I just didn't realize it. Not when you were away. I couldn't then when I was in California, but before and now..." I trailed off at the look on his face.

Zen's eyes narrowed slightly. "You felt the hunt? Through me?" He ran a hand through his damp hair, agitation evident in the gesture. "This is not good, Niki."

"Why were you hunting?" I asked, trying to ignore the lingering thrill in my blood, the echo of that primal power.

"I need to," he said, voice dropping lower. "Here, in the jungle... my control isn't what it should be." He looked away, into the darkness. "Your father and Rosa taught me to maintain balance with my wahy, to keep the jaguar spirit in check. But here—" He gestured at the surrounding jungle. "The jaguar spirit inside me is stronger here. Hungrier."

"And you need to feed it," I finished for him. "So that you can protect yourself from Li Xul."

"Yes." His eyes locked with mine again. "I need my wahy at full strength. Controlling this part of me takes a toll, physically and spiritually. Li Xul is a powerful shapeshifter, Niki. More experienced than I am." He moved closer, stopping just inches away. I could feel the heat radiating from him despite his wet clothes, smell the wild scent of him—earth and musk and something distinctly feline.

"But this connection between us... it's dangerous," he murmured. "Especially for you."

"Because of Hun-Came?"

"Yes." His voice hardened. "He wants this. Wants you to feel the power, the freedom of the hunt. It's another way to seduce you into surrendering."

I swallowed hard, unable to deny the truth in his words. The hunt had felt... exhilarating. Natural. Right. "I liked it," I admitted in a whisper.

"I know," he said softly. His hand rose to my face, fingers tracing my jawline with excruciating gentleness. "And that's what scares me. Hun-Came is using what we have—this connection—against you." He gave his head a shake. "We need to find a way to block the connection between us."

I leaned into his touch before I could stop myself. Blocking the connection between us was the last thing I wanted to do. "Zen, I—"

"You should go back to your tent," he interrupted, dropping his hand.

I stepped back, wrapping my arms around myself. "Did you find anything out there? Any sign of Li Xul?"

Zen's expression shuttered. "No. But he's close. I can feel him. Another predator in the same territory." He glanced toward the tent. "You should try to get more rest."

I nodded, turning back toward my tent. I paused, looking over my shoulder at him. "Be careful, Zen. Please."

Something flickered in his eyes. "Always, Niki."

I slipped back into the tent, my skin still tingling where he'd touched me. As I settled into my sleeping bag, I heard Hun-Came's amused whisper.

"Such an interesting combination. So fraught with possibilities. The wahy b'alam and my little vessel."

"I know what you're trying to do, and it won't work," I hissed.

His laughter sounded like the rattling of dry leaves and brittle tree limbs. *"You enjoy it—the power to command life and death,"* he continued, his voice caressing my mind. *"This is what I offer you, little vessel. Not just survival, but dominance. The forest bows to us."*

I closed my eyes, trying to ignore him, but I couldn't deny the truth—part of me had reveled in the raw power of the hunt. That was what made Hun-Came's influence so insidious. He wasn't forcing me to become something I wasn't; he was awakening something that already existed within me.

LISA DIETRICH

CHAPTER TWENTY-TWO

Rain poured relentlessly from above, at times in violent sheets that stung like needles, other times softening to mere showers, but it did not stop—would never stop, it seemed. We slogged our way through thick mud that sucked at our boots with each step, threatening to claim them as trophies. We scrambled over rocks made treacherously slippery by rivulets of water cascading down them and fought our way through an almost impregnable thicket of thorns.

These weren't gentle brambles but vicious, hooked daggers that seemed to reach for us with malevolent intent. The barbs caught and tore at our flesh, drawing beads of blood that mixed with rainwater and sweat, leaving trails of pink down our arms and legs. We had to remove our ponchos to preserve them from being shredded, but this left our exposed skin to bear the brunt of the jungle's hostility—each branch we pushed aside exacting its payment in scratches and gashes.

The metallic scent of blood hung heavy in the humid air, and I had to clench my fists to keep from breathing it in too deeply. Hun-Came stirred within me, pleased by the offering, and I felt an unwanted hunger unfurl in my chest—not for food, but for more of that copper-sweet perfume that made my pulse quicken with dark anticipation.

"We should be calling this the Trail of Razors," Aedan complained, wincing as he pulled a two-inch thorn from his forearm, a fresh crimson stream marking its exit.

I caught myself licking my lips as I stared at the bright ribbon of blood trailing down his skin and jerked my gaze away, disgusted by my own fascination and desire. Through the rain, I glimpsed Zen ahead of us, his jaw rigid with tension, nostrils flared slightly as if he too was fighting some primal response to the scent saturating the air. The jaguar in him recognized what Hun-Came craved, and for a moment our eyes met—predator acknowledging predator—before he looked away.

We tried to hack our way around the worst of the thicket, machetes ringing against the woody stems, but the thorns seemed to mock our efforts. Where we cut one branch, two more twisted into existence, fresh and green and hungry. The very path we had just cleared would be choked with new growth when we glanced back, as if the jungle was healing itself behind us, sealing off any hope of retreat.

"This is impossible," Marco panted, his blade dulled and nicked from the futile battle.

The brambles writhed with an almost serpentine intelligence, curling around our ankles and wrists when we paused too long, drawing us deeper into their thorny embrace. Blood seemed to make them stronger—each drop we shed appeared to nourish the soil beneath our feet, sending up fresh shoots that sprouted thorns like teeth. Hun-Came's satisfaction pulsed through me at the sight, and I had to bite down hard on my tongue to keep from smiling.

It was Aedan who finally drew Sky-Splitter, the ancient blade singing as it left its sheath. The sword's edge gleamed with an inner light that made the raindrops dance like scattered diamonds along its length. Where the enchanted steel touched the brambles, they didn't just part—they recoiled, shrinking back with an almost audible hiss. The thorns that had seemed so eager to taste our blood now cowered away from the blade's radiance, creating a corridor of safety that remained open in our wake.

"Stay close," Aedan called over the drumming rain, holding Sky-Splitter before him like a torch against the darkness. The sword carved through the supernatural thicket as if it were mere shadow, leaving behind a path that the jungle, for once, did not dare to reclaim.

My thoughts darkened with each step. The connection I'd felt with Zen during his hunt pulsed inside me like something alive, something growing. The smell of everyone's blood perfuming the air made it difficult to concentrate. Hun-Came's presence within me seemed to expand with every mile, filling the spaces where my own identity had once been secure. The constant threat of Li Xul lurking somewhere in this merciless jungle—it all swirled in my mind like the muddy water rushing past our boots, threatening to drown my sense of self.

But mostly, I feared what I was becoming. The power that flowed through me when Hun-Came's presence was strongest felt intoxicating—addictive even. I was terrified that when the time came, I might not want to let go of who—or what—I was becoming. Would I even recognize myself by journey's end? Or would Niki be washed away in this deluge, replaced by something ancient and terrible?

Our forward progress came to an abrupt halt when we reached a rushing torrent of foaming, muddied water. What had once been a moderate river was now a churning, seething freshwater sea. Brown frothy spray shot into the air as water crashed into boulders and downed tree trunks. The roaring sound of the river drowned out any ability to communicate, a deafening wall of noise that isolated each of us in our own private hell.

We resorted to shouting and frantic hand signals, our words torn away by the thundering water almost before they left our mouths. Zen, Aedan, and Ulices scouted along the bank, eventually managing to hack limbs from a fallen log.

We worked to wrestle it across the narrowest section—a makeshift bridge over the raging current—while Marco and Franco stood silent on the bank, rifles slung over their shoulders, their expressions increasingly resentful and dour, eyes darting nervously to the surrounding jungle as if expecting death to emerge at any moment.

"Unfasten the waist belt of your packs before crossing," Ulices instructed, raising his voice over the roar of the water. "If you fall in, the pack will drown you. Ditch it and keep your head above water, swim at an angle toward the shore." His words chilled me to the bone as I imagined myself being dragged under, lungs filling with the same mud-choked water that raged before us.

Ulices tested our log bridge, slowly and carefully inching his way over the turbulent water. Zen followed, nimbly crossing the log with a sure-footed feline grace. Then it was my turn.

The crossing was slippery and treacherous. I inched my way across the log, acutely aware of the raging current below that could sweep me away in seconds. Halfway across, my foot slipped on a patch of slick moss. The weight of my pack threw me off balance, and I lurched sideways, my stomach dropping as gravity began to claim me. Terror seized my chest, constricting my breathing as the hungry waters reached up for me.

In a panic, I threw my weight forward, diving for the safety of the log bridge. The force of the impact knocked the air from my lungs, and I scrabbled desperately for purchase, wrapping my arms around the slippery wood, my fingernails digging desperately into the soggy bark. I lay with half my torso on the tree trunk, my legs frantically scissoring in the air as I tried to haul myself back to safety. The roar of the water filled my ears, but beneath it, I could hear my own frantic heartbeat, a drumming countdown to disaster.

"Hold on!" Zen shouted from the far bank. He was already moving back onto the log, his movements sure despite the danger.

Before he could reach me, Hun-Came's voice slithered through my mind, cold and amused. *"Remember the river of blood from the Popol Vuh?"* The voice paused, letting the implications sink in. *"This river hungers for sacrifice, just as the blood river did. It wants to carry you down to the underworld, to me..."*

As I dangled there, Hun-Came's words merged with the river's roar. Was this my test? Was I meant to fall? The water below seemed to darken before my eyes, transforming from muddy brown to a thick, arterial red—a vision of the mythic river of blood that had swallowed so many before me.

Zen's strong hand gripped my wrist, pulling me back to reality as he hauled me onto the log. "I've got you," he said, his eyes meeting mine with an intensity that momentarily drove Hun-Came's whispers from my mind. "One step at a time." His touch anchored me to the present, yet I couldn't shake the feeling I'd glimpsed something in those waters—something waiting for me.

With his help, I made it to the far bank, legs trembling so badly I could barely stand. The others followed, each crossing with varying degrees of difficulty. Franco nearly fell in, saved only by Marco's quick reflexes. By the time we were all safely across, the rain had intensified again, beating down on us in heavy sheets. I stared back at the raging water, unable to shake Hun-Came's words from my mind.

After another hour of slogging through mud and jungle, each step a battle against exhaustion and nature's hostility, we finally reached the cave a tall, narrow fissure in a limestone cliff face. The dark slash of the cave's entrance against solid rock appeared before us like an ancient wound in the earth. A small thatch hut stood near the opening, weathered and sagging under the relentless rain. As we approached, a local man emerged from the hut, a semi-automatic rifle cradled in his arms with the casual familiarity of someone who had used it before and wouldn't hesitate to do so again.

His eyes were hard and watchful, scanning our bedraggled group with calculated assessment. He seemed to know Ulices, who offered a traditional greeting in Q'eqchi': "Ma sa laa ch'ool." Meaning, "How is your heart?"—a question that seemed eerily profound given our circumstances.

Ulices signaled to Marco and Franco to stay back. They glowered, fingering their weapons and shooting menacing looks at both Ulices and the armed guard as the two men began conversing in rapid Q'eqchi'.

"What's going on?" Aedan asked, shifting his weight impatiently, his hand instinctively moving to rest on Sky-Splitter.

Zen listened for a moment, his face impassive but alert, then translated for us. "He's a local campesino," he explained. "He's being paid to protect the entrance. Ulices is negotiating for our passage."

"We work for Don Ricardo. We don't negotiate." Franco's voice was a low growl, his knuckles white around his weapon.

Zen's expression turned glacial when he turned toward Franco. "Izzy's father is not the only player out here. Illegal loggers and gold miners, smugglers, traffickers, palm plantations, campesinos, they are all in Petén. Each one of them circling the others, waiting for a chance to stake their claim." He jerked a thumb in the direction of Ulices and the guard. "All this guy knows is that he is being paid to keep the wrong people out of the cave. Ulices is trying to convince him that we aren't the wrong people."

"Do you think he's working for Li Xul?" I asked, eyeing the guard's weapon, my mouth dry with fear at the mention of that name. The very air seemed to darken around us at the utterance.

Zen shrugged, but the tension in his shoulders betrayed his concern. "It's a definite possibility, though there are other groups operating here. They're less visible, but they're just as vigilant. Like I said, everyone has a stake and they jealously guard and protect control over their trafficking routes."

After fifteen minutes of intense discussion, Ulices returned to our group, his expression grim. "We can pass into the cave," he said. "But we have to pay a piso—a tax to enter. It goes to the local traficante."

"How much?" Marco growled menacingly, his hand tightening on his weapon.

"We don't pay," Franco said, slipping the rifle from his shoulder and lifting the muzzle, pointing it threateningly at the guard. "There are seven of us and only one of him."

Zen quickly pushed the muzzle down toward the ground, his movements controlled but urgent. "Don't be stupid," he hissed, his voice low and dangerous. "If Li Xul controls the trafficking routes in this area, he will kill to protect his interests. I've seen what he does—he doesn't just kill people—he mutilates and dismembers them before putting them on public display."

Franco exchanged glances with Marco, their expressions mulish, a volatile mix of pride and anger battling across their faces. "We are not afraid."

"You're here to protect us, not get us killed," Izzy snapped, stepping forward, her patience clearly frayed. "My father has a large number of business interests in this area. If you do something stupid, it could cause problems for him as well as us."

The cousins wavered, looking at each other, then at Izzy, reluctance etched in every line of their bodies.

"Tomorrow," Ulices said abruptly. "We do not enter tonight. We will enter in the morning. We must be well rested. Tonight, we will prepare."

As if the gods themselves heard him, the rain suddenly stopped.

Aedan squinted up at the sky. "I'm thinking this might be a good time to set up the tents."

Zen nodded. "Agreed."

I felt a wave of relief at the prospect of doing so without the relentless rain. I hadn't realized how tired and hungry I was until I slipped off my pack, my shoulders immediately lightening as the weight fell away.

Under the watchful eye of the man in the guard shack, we set up our camp. The ground squelched beneath our feet, and the humid air clung to our skin like a second layer. Despite the rain having stopped, the jungle around us continued to drip rhythmically, as if the trees themselves were weeping.

Ulices managed to get a sputtering fire started, somehow finding semi-dry wood in the surrounding sodden landscape. We formed a circle around the fire, sitting directly on the ground. Already wet with our clothes caked with mud, it didn't seem worth the effort to find logs. I deliberately chose to sit next to Zen, my thigh almost brushing his. Aedan caught my eye with a lifted eyebrow and took a seat on the other side of me.

Gathered around our little fire, we silently heated up water and poured it into our dehydrated food. The tension was palpable, hanging in the air like the lingering moisture. Occasional conversation sputtered and died as quickly as the flames threatened to. Izzy was in a foul mood, her jaw clenched tight as she viciously stabbed at her rehydrated meal. Her eyes narrowed as her gaze shifted between Zen, Aedan, and me, tracking our interactions with the calculation of a predator.

"I can't help but wonder what it's like?" She paused, her eyes glittering with malice as they rested on me. "I've never experienced a ménage à trois. Maybe you can tell me. What was the sex like?" Her eyes flicked to Zen with a familiarity that made my stomach clench. "Do things get confusing with the three of you?"

Marco and Franco snickered, looking at Aedan, Zen, and me with lewd interest.

I shot a look at the cousins, unsure how much they had been told about my—situation. Ulices remained stoic, his weathered face unreadable in the flickering firelight, but his attention was fixed on the exchange with unmistakable interest.

My pulse pounded in my ears, and I could feel Hun-Came's anger mingling with my own, a dangerous alchemy. The death god's presence expanded inside me like ice crystals forming in water, sharp-edged and spreading.

"Izzy," Zen said, voice dangerously soft. "Don't."

Her eyes widened innocently, long lashes fluttering. "What? Am I wrong?" she asked. "How does the sex work when there are three of you in bed together?"

"Izzy, stop." Zen's expression was cool, but his eyes flashed a warning.

"It makes sense that you'd be willing to walk on the wild side," she said, holding Zen's gaze for a moment before continuing, her voice a silken purr. "Though I have to admit I am surprised you're willing to share even with Niki's special guest." She paused, her eyes flicking toward me with an appraising sweep that made me feel stripped bare.

Marco and Franco's eyes gleefully darted between Izzy and me, as if they were watching a tennis match.

Heat flashed through my body, a mixture of embarrassment and rage. I felt Hun-Came's presence swell within me, feeding on my emotions, amplifying them. The bracelet at my wrist felt suddenly cold, the iron's protective influence weakening under the surge of power.

The darkening sky seemed to flicker, though I couldn't be sure if it was my imagination.

"That's enough," Zen growled, the sound rumbling from deep in his chest.

The corners of Izzy's mouth lifted into a lazy smile, triumphant at having provoked a reaction. "Sorry. I suppose it's just my professional curiosity getting the better of me." She turned toward me, her eyes glittering with cruel interest. "I'm not asking for every detail, just a basic overview of the physical practicalities of the situation. Is it good for your—special guest? Or does he get off on watching?"

Furious, I felt something snap inside me. The carefully maintained barrier between Hun-Came and myself thinned to transparency. Power surged through my veins, cold and ancient. My vision sharpened until I could see the slight quiver of her pulse at her throat. I could smell her perfume, her sweat, the acrid scent of her jealousy. And beneath it all, the tantalizing scent of her fear, which she was trying desperately to mask with bravado.

"*Let me show her what real fear tastes like,*" Hun-Came whispered in my mind, his voice silky with anticipation.

Shadows seemed to deepen around us, pooling under dripping vegetation and stretching toward us like living things. The sky suddenly darkened as a loud crash of thunder exploded, causing everyone to gasp. Marco dropped his food container, cursing in Spanish as it splattered across his boots.

Startled by the sudden noise, Aedan and Zen both jumped to their feet. I remained seated, staring at Izzy. My hands were flat on my thighs, fingers splayed. I could feel energy radiating from my palms, spreading through me, heating my blood like molten lava. The jade jaguar pendant against my chest grew warm, pulsing with each beat of my heart.

The sky flickered again, heat lightning, longer this time.

"Too bad for you, that I'm not. Willing to share that is," I said, baring my teeth in her direction, more warning than smile. My voice sounded strange to my own ears, deeper, with an echo that wasn't quite my own. The sky grew darker still, and I could see Izzy's breath misting slightly in the air between us as the temperature around our fire plummeted.

There was a sudden crack of thunder, and a bolt of lightning streaked across the sky, illuminating everything around us in stark, blue-white relief. For a moment, I saw actual fear flash across Izzy's face—genuine, unfiltered terror that cracked her perfect composure. She masked it quickly, but not before I'd witnessed it, not before Hun-Came and I had tasted it together in a moment of perfect, terrible union.

"Localized storm. Directly over us," Aedan explained, his voice strained as he looked between me and the rapidly darkening sky. "Thunder without rain. Lightning striking the same spot repeatedly. Not exactly subtle, is it?" His eyes were fixed on me, concern warring with apprehension. "I'd say our uninvited guest is not happy with us at the moment. I'm hoping you can do something about that, love."

I felt Zen's hand on my shoulder, warm and grounding. "Niki," he said softly, just my name, but I understood the message. I took a deep breath, forcing the cold rage back down, feeling Hun-Came's presence reluctantly recede like a tide pulling back from shore.

"It's been a long day. I am going to bed," Izzy said matter-of-factly, but I could hear the slightest tremor in her voice. She set down her spoon and folded her hands as she worked to regain her composure. I met Izzy's eyes across the firepit, a silent understanding passing between us. She may have had wealth, education, and a history with Zen, but I had something far more dangerous—and we both knew it now.

Raising her gaze to where Zen stood behind me, hands still resting on my shoulders, she cleared her throat. Her voice was brittle as thin ice. "Will you be joining me?" she asked, her eyes locked onto Zen.

"I'll take first watch," Zen announced, his thumb absently stroking the nape of my neck in a gesture that did not go unnoticed.

"Good idea, mate," Aedan murmured.

Izzy's face contorted. A muscle twitched violently along her jawline, and her nostrils flared with each sharp intake of breath. She snatched up her water bottle, knuckles white around its neck as if she were strangling it. For a moment, I thought she might hurl it into the fire.

"How considerate of you," she hissed, each word dripping with venom. She rose to her feet in one fluid motion, her movements tight and controlled like a wound spring. "Always so noble, aren't you, Zen?" She swept her gaze over our small group, her eyes lingering on me with undisguised loathing before returning to Zen. "Just remember who organized this expedition. Who has the maps. Who knows the way forward."

Without waiting for a response, she turned on her heel and stalked toward her tent. The zipper hissed loudly as she yanked it open with unnecessary force, the sound echoing through the sudden silence around the campfire. She disappeared inside with a final glare in our direction, the tent fabric shuddering as she violently zipped it closed behind her.

Marco and Franco watched silently, twin expressions of confusion and wary fascination on their faces as if they'd just witnessed an exotic animal attack. They quickly finished eating their meals and retired to their own tent, murmuring to each other in low voices.

Aedan rummaged in his pack and pulled out the bottle of whisky Izzy had procured for him. "I'm thinking this might be a good time for a wee dram," he said, uncorking the bottle and offering it to me first.

I took it gratefully, the smooth burn of alcohol a welcome distraction from the lingering taste of Izzy's fear and Hun-Came's satisfaction.

CHAPTER TWENTY-THREE

I wasn't sure if it was the whisky, the lingering memory of Zen's thumb caressing my neck, or the exhilarating sensation of power I'd shared with Hun-Came, but something fundamental had shifted within me. Fear of Li Xul no longer paralyzed me. I was done letting him dictate what—or who—I could have. And what I wanted, with every fiber of my being, was Zen. Right here. Right now.

It might have been nothing more than a primal instinct to mark what I considered mine, but in that moment, I was going to do whatever it took to claim him. I jabbed our meager fire with a stick, sending a constellation of orange sparks dancing toward the night sky.

Aedan passed the whisky bottle to Zen, who took a long, deliberate pull before returning it. Their fingers brushed during the exchange, a subtle tension passing between them.

"Well then," Aedan said, replacing the cap with exaggerated care. "I best turn in now, get some sleep before my watch." His eyes found mine, searching. "Will you be joining me?"

I shook my head, holding his gaze.

"I thought as much." He stood, touching my shoulder with surprising gentleness. "Be careful," he murmured, the warning clear in his voice. He tucked his whisky bottle into his pack before slipping off his boots and disappearing inside our tent.

The crackling fire filled the silence between us until Zen spoke.

"Sorry about that," he said, his voice low. "Izzy isn't happy with me at the moment. She's taking it out on you."

I found his hand in the darkness and laced our fingers together, savoring the feel of his skin. "Izzy wants you."

"You don't have to worry." He sighed heavily, his eyes fixed on the flames. "I've made it quite clear to Izzy I'm not interested in rekindling our past relationship." He turned toward me then, his amber eyes blazing with such raw desire that my breath caught. "You are the only one I want."

I leaned against him, relishing the warmth of his breath whispering down my neck. I lifted his hand to my lips, pressing a kiss against his palm before gently but insistently pulling him closer. I nuzzled the sensitive hollow of his neck, breathing in his scent.

He groaned; a sound caught between pleasure and pain. "Niki, don't."

I traced his jawline with my lips and tongue, feeling his pulse quicken beneath my touch. When I reached his ear, I nipped at the lobe, drawing another shudder from him. "I want you inside me," I breathed, my words barely audible.

His entire body tensed, muscles coiling like he was fighting for control. "Please," he whispered hoarsely. "Don't make this harder than it already is. It's not safe for you."

In one fluid movement, I shifted, straddling him, my thighs gripping his hips as I ground against his abundantly apparent desire. The friction sent delicious shocks of electricity shooting through my entire body, igniting me from within. I captured his gaze, refusing to look away from those blazing eyes.

"I'm not afraid."

His hands slid along my back as I rocked against him.

He groaned, then with one powerful thrust of his hips he flipped me on my back, pinning me in place with the weight of his body.

Oblivious to everything but my raging desire, my only thought was I wanted more. More of this. More of him.

He captured my arms trapping them above my head as I writhed beneath him, every nerve-ending firing with anticipation and need.

"Is this what you want?" he growled, his voice rough with barely restrained hunger.

"Yes," I breathed, arching against him.

Hun-Came's silky and sensuous voice slipped into my mind. "*You begin to understand the ecstasy of submission, little vessel. Something to remember when it is our time.*"

Zen suddenly stiffened and rolled off of me. We lay on the wet ground panting, the chill night air rushing between us like an unwelcome intruder.

"Li Xul?" I asked, the name tasting like poison on my tongue.

Zen nodded grimly. "He's watching. Always watching." He sat up, running his hands through his disheveled hair. "You may not be afraid, but I am."

I pushed myself up onto my elbows, my body still humming with unfulfilled desire. "I don't care if he sees."

"You should." Zen's eyes had lost their amber glow, replaced by something darker, more guarded. "What we just did—what we almost did—it creates a connection. And he can use that connection to hurt you."

"He can't hurt me," I replied with more confidence than I felt. "Hun-Came won't let him."

"Hun-Came is not the answer!"

I startled at the harsh tone of his voice.

Zen inhaled deeply as if working to center himself. When he spoke again, his voice was once again steady, his words measured. "Hun-Came wants you to become dependent upon him. Every time you defer to him, his connection to you becomes stronger." His eyes locked onto me, pleading with me to understand. "Don't let him in. You need to resist him."

"So, you're just going to push me away?" I couldn't keep the hurt from my voice.

He reached out, his fingertips brushing my cheek so lightly I might have imagined it. "I'm trying to keep you alive, Niki."

The tenderness in his voice nearly undid me. I wanted to argue, to tell him we could face Li Xul together, but the resolute set of his jaw told me it would be futile.

"Get some rest," he said softly.

Pride made me stand without his help, though my legs trembled beneath me. I brushed the mud from my clothes, trying to recover some dignity. "Goodnight, then," I managed, my voice steadier than I felt.

"Goodnight, Niki." His eyes followed me as I walked away.

The few steps to the tent felt like miles. Inside, Aedan's steady breathing told me he was either asleep or pretending to be—a kindness I appreciated. I slipped out of my damp clothes, my body still aflame with need, my mind churning with frustration.

Outside, I could see Zen's silhouette against the dying fire. He sat motionless, his back rigid as he stared into the flames. The loneliness of his vigil made my chest ache.

I slid into my sleeping bag and closed my eyes. As I drifted toward sleep, Hun-Came's voice whispered at the edges of my consciousness, promising pleasures that Zen denied me and power that would make Li Xul insignificant. All I had to do was surrender.

CHAPTER TWENTY-FOUR

I woke to the sound of rustling fabric as Aedan slipped from the tent. The whispered exchange between him and Zen barely registered—my senses were already focused beyond their conversation, tuned to a different frequency. I lay perfectly still, my body motionless while my mind hummed with anticipation.

Maybe it was our physical proximity, or his distraction of having to block Li Xul, or Hun-Came's increasing potency, but whatever Zen had been doing to block me was no longer able to keep me out. Now that I knew I could reach into his mind, I was going to find my way to Zen.

Jaguars, I remembered from some half-forgotten nature documentary, were patient ambush hunters. Tonight, that's exactly what I would be.

I counted minutes by my heartbeats, allowing thirty to pass before I closed my eyes and began constructing my dreamscape. The dense jungle materialized first—massive ceiba trees stretching skyward, their buttressed roots creating secret hollows. Vines draped like living curtains between branches festooned with orchids, silvered with moonlight. The air hung thick with moisture, each breath drawing in the heady perfume of night-blooming flowers and fertile earth.

I felt Hun-Came's presence, his satisfaction vibrating through me as I surrendered to sleep. Not a surrender of weakness, but of power—knowing exactly what I was unleashing.

"This is exquisite, little vessel." His voice purred through my consciousness. *"You begin to understand what we can be together."*

***

My shadow soul begins its transformation—a strange tightening of my skin, then a delicious stretch as my body reconfigures itself. Black rosettes erupt across my pale golden fur, each one a perfect dark halo. My bones shift, muscle coiling with new density around them. The world sharpens, the darkness of the jungle revealing its secrets to me— speaking to me through scent.

Every creature, every plant, every drop of water carries its own signature. And cutting through them all, the unmistakable musk of another jaguar. Zen.

I inhale deeply, drawing his scent over the sensitive organ in the roof of my mouth. He had passed this way recently. Hungry. Restless.

I pad forward on silent paws, my body moving with liquid grace. The boundary between spiritual and physical realms blurred—this is neither fully a dream nor fully reality, but something more powerful than either.

I can sense Zen's hunger now, not just for food but for connection. For release. For me.

A twig snaps somewhere ahead. Not carelessness—a signal. He knows I am here. He is leading me deeper.

I catch a flicker of movement—dark fur illuminated briefly by shafts of moonlight penetrating the canopy. He is magnificent, larger than my form, muscles rippling beneath his spotted coat. He pauses, turning his massive head toward me, amber eyes gleaming with challenge and desire.

Then suddenly, I feel them—Li Xul and Hun-Came, voyeurs at the edge of my consciousness. Their presence should have angered me, but instead I feel a perverse thrill. Let them watch. Let them see.

Li Xul's frustration radiates like heat waves, I rebuff his attempts to intrude with surprising ease. This is my dreamscape, shaped by my will, strengthened by Hun-Came's ancient power flowing through me. I block Li Xul as effortlessly as swatting away an insect, feeling Hun-Came's dark amusement at my pleasure of his rival's impotence.

"You are stronger than he is now in this realm," Hun-Came whispered through our connection. "Through me, you have become something he cannot touch."

Zen growls, drawing my attention back to the hunt. He disappears into the underbrush, and I follow, my heart pounding with excitement. The chase has begun.

I track him through the jungle, across a shallow stream where the water cooled my paws, around massive tree trunks whose bark held the scratched signatures of generations of jaguars. Always he remains just ahead, leading me ever deeper into the wilds of my own creation.

Then suddenly, the trees open into a small clearing, moonlight streaming down to illuminate a flat stone outcropping. He stands at its center, waiting, his body tense with anticipation.

I emerge from the shadows, and our eyes lock. No more running. No more chase. He is my willing prey.

I approach slowly, muscles rippling beneath my spotted coat. A warning rumble builds in his chest—not rejection but ancient ritual. I answer with a sound halfway between purr and growl.

We circle each other, these powerful bodies moving with primal grace. When we meet, it is a collision of muscle and fur, rolling across the moonlit stone. His scent envelopes me—musky, wild, intoxicating. His teeth find the scruff of my neck, holding me with gentle dominance that sends shudders of pleasure down my spine.

Our jaguar forms move together with none of the hesitation of our human selves. There is only instinct here, only need. His weight presses me into the cool stone as he mounts me, our bodies joining in a union that transcends the merely physical.

The sensation is overwhelming—raw pleasure mixes with something more profound, a connection that vibrates through every cell. My consciousness expands outward, touching the edges of something vast and ancient with each powerful thrust. Through our joined bodies, I can feel the pulse of the jungle itself, the heartbeat of earth and sky.

I surrender to it completely, to the rhythmic joining of our bodies, to the primal force that tears through me like wildfire. My jaguar form arches and writhes beneath him, accepting him fully while claiming something of him in return.

When release comes, it consumes me utterly—stars bursting behind my eyes, my body convulsing with wave after wave of pleasure so intense it borders on pain. Together we roar our completion to the night sky, the sound echoing through the dreamscape jungle.

I watch the moon track across the starlit sky, aware of Hun-Came's satisfaction and Li Xul's impotent rage at the periphery of my consciousness.

The dream begins dissolving around the edges, the jungle fading like mist in morning sun. I fight to hold onto it, but reality is already reclaiming me.

***

"Niki?" Aedan's concerned voice penetrated my consciousness. "You cried out in your sleep. Are you alright, love?"

I opened my eyes to the dark interior of the tent, my body still throbbing with the echoes of pleasure. I smiled. "Yes. I'm good."

CHAPTER TWENTY-FIVE

"Pay the man," Izzy said firmly. "And let's enter the cave." Her words sent a shiver down my spine, as if the cave itself was listening, waiting to claim us.

Franco's jaw worked as he wrestled with his pride, but eventually he reached into his pocket and pulled out a wad of bills. He counted out a stack and thrust them at the guard, who accepted them with a slight nod that conveyed neither gratitude nor respect—merely a business transaction completed.

As the guard stepped aside, Zen moved ahead of me, his shoulder brushing mine as he passed. The brief contact sent a jolt of electricity through my body. His fingers briefly touched the small of my back, hidden from the others' view. "When you dream-walk, you are able to block Li Xul?" he murmured, his voice so low only I could hear it, amber eyes holding mine with an intensity that made my breath catch.

I nodded. It wasn't exactly a lie. I had blocked him, with Hun-Came's help.

A ghost of a smile touched his lips. His gaze dropped briefly to the jaguar-shaped pendant at my throat. "That was amazing last night."

"Zen, you need to help Ulices with the packs." Izzy

stared at the two of us stone-faced.

"Remove your packs. I will enter first," Ulices announced. "You will hand them to me, then follow one at a time."

We fell into a line behind Ulices as he led the way to the narrow opening in the limestone cliff.

When I passed the guard, his eyes met mine, and I felt a chill that pierced to my marrow, having nothing to do with my damp clothes or the lingering sensations from Zen's touch. There was recognition there—not of me personally, but of something within me. Hun-Came stirred, pressing against the boundaries of my consciousness with newfound vigor, as if the proximity to the cave had awakened him fully.

"He knows what you carry," Hun-Came whispered, his voice like dry leaves scraping against stone. *"They all sense it, even if they cannot name it. The closer we get to Xibalba, the more they will feel my presence."*

"Shut up," I muttered under my breath, earning a curious look from Aedan, who was right behind me.

"Are you having a private conversation?" he asked, his voice light despite the tension in his shoulders. "Anything you care to share with the rest of us?"

"Just thinking out loud," I lied, forcing a smile I didn't feel, my heart hammering against my ribs like a trapped animal sensing danger.

Aedan didn't look convinced, but he let it drop as we dutifully passed our packs into the darkness of the cave before squeezing through the narrow fissure. The air inside was cool and damp, smelling of wet stone and something else—sour and dank.

The entrance quickly opened into a larger cavern, the ceiling soaring above us, lost in shadow. Ulices flicked on his headlamp.

We stood in silent awe. Embedded in the limestone along one of the walls, catching and reflecting the light from Ulices's helmet were hundreds—perhaps thousands—of obsidian blades. They jutted from the wall at every angle, their edges still razor-sharp despite the centuries.

For a brief moment, I thought I saw blood dripping from the glittering black stones. I gasped, blinking in shocked surprise. When Ulice's light passed over them a second time, the blood was gone.

"Cave of Razors?" Aedan asked, running his fingers over a nearby limestone formation hanging over his head, his voice hushed as if afraid to disturb whatever might be listening in the darkness.

"Natural obsidian formations," Ulices explained, though his tone suggested he wasn't entirely convinced of his own explanation. "The Maya believed they were placed here by the gods."

"Or one god in particular," Zen said quietly, his eyes meeting mine over Ulices's shoulder.

Aedan walked over to inspect the wall. "As of right now, no flying blades threatening to chop off our heads—feeling good about this one," he said with forced levity, though his eyes darted around the chamber, assessing it for potential threats.

We all pulled out headlamps from our packs, illuminating the cave in overlapping cones of light. In the eerie red glow of our headlights, we could see cracked ceramics lying on the cave's damp, clay floor. Ulices swept his light across the formations, and his beam caught something else—the unmistakable gleam of a human skull half-buried in the clay, its front teeth cracked, and the bone long-ago crystallized into calcite.

I gasped, my hand flying to my mouth as I stared at the grim discovery. Its empty eye sockets seemed to watch us, judging our intrusion, a silent sentinel from an age long past. It wasn't alone—as our lights swept the chamber, more bones became visible, scattered throughout the clay like grim seeds planted by death itself.

My stomach clenched at the sight, and Hun-Came's presence swelled within me, feeding on my distress.

207

"Holy offerings from those willing to place their children's lives into the hands of the gods," Hun-Came whispered.

A sudden wave of images flooded my mind—small figures bound with rope, their eyes wide with terror, swaying unsteadily on their feet as priests in elaborate headdresses led them into this very chamber. I could almost hear their cries echoing across time.

Hun-Came's voice was now a grotesque mixture of reverence and hunger. *"Death is always sweeter when it comes for the young and pure."*

"Stop it," I hissed under my breath, my hands trembling as I tried to block out the visions. I stumbled backward, nearly colliding with Aedan, who steadied me, sending a concerned look my way.

"This is amazing." Izzy's voice echoed eerily inside the chamber, directing her light toward some glyphs that had been carved into one of the caverns walls. Her fingers traced the rough stone with reverence.

"These tell of a journey to the underworld," she murmured, her voice barely above a whisper. "A warning to those who would enter unprepared... and a promise of what awaits those who are worthy."

Kneeling by one of the skeletal remains, her fingers hovered just above the tiny bones, not touching but tracing their outline in the air.

"These are children," she said softly, her voice a mixture of academic fascination and genuine sorrow. She looked up, the beam from her headlamp flickering across the cavern walls and coming to rest on me. Something in my expression made her pause briefly before continuing.

"Possibly offerings to Hun-Came," she added, her eyes searching mine. I felt exposed, as if she could somehow see the death god lurking behind my eyes. "Though they may have been offerings to Chaac, the rain god or even the Maize god."

She looked down again, her light illuminating the calcified small skull in front of her. I could see her shifting fully into her role as an archaeologist. "We hardly see human sacrifice, certainly nothing on the scale of what is in this cave, until the period right before the Maya collapse."

I stared at the bones, sparkling like macabre jewels in the light of my headlamp. They were so small. A child who had been led into this dark place, never to see daylight again. My vision blurred with unexpected tears.

"Their souls strengthened me," Hun-Came whispered. *"Death is nourishment. Without death there is no life."*

I felt bile rising in my throat. The cave suddenly seemed too small, the air too thick. These children had died here, terrified and alone, all to appease the very entity that now resided within me. Was I walking the same path to the same fate? Would I end up another sacrifice to Hun-Came's insatiable hunger?

Ulices must have sensed the growing unease in our group. He adjusted his headlamp, directing our attention away from the grim remains and toward a narrow passage ahead.

"This way," he said, his voice tight with tension. "Watch your step and stay close. This cave has many passages, and it would be easy to become lost."

I hesitated, looking back at the children's remains one last time. "'I'm sorry," I whispered, though I wasn't sure if I was apologizing to the ancient victims or to my companions for what I was bringing into their midst. With each step deeper into the cave, I could feel Hun-Came's presence growing stronger, feeding off the ancient power of this sacred, terrible place.

"How far does it go?" Izzy asked, her scientific curiosity battling with growing apprehension.

"No one knows. This cave has not been fully explored," Ulices replied, his voice echoing ominously in the chamber. A brief survey was completed a decade ago for possible excavation, but the authorities determined to leave everything as they found it."

"Why?" Aedan asked.

Ulices shrugged. "Lack of accessibility. Dangerous location. Lack of funds. And superstition. Several of the members of the exploration team died."

"And we're following in their footsteps," I said quietly, fighting the urge to turn back, to flee toward the daylight we had left behind.

Hun-Came's laughter echoed in my mind, a sound like dry corn husks rustling in the wind, like bones rattling together in ancient tombs, followed by the gleeful jingling of bells. The sound seemed to reverberate through the very stone around us, though I knew I was the only one who could hear it.

As we moved deeper into the cave, the passage narrowed until we had to walk single file, the walls closing in on either side like the slowly tightening grip of a stone fist. Water trickled down the walls in silvery rivulets, catching the light of our headlamps and creating an illusion of movement in the surrounding stone. The sound of our breathing and footsteps was amplified in the confined space, punctuated by the occasional drip of water from overhead stalactites— a liquid metronome counting down our journey into darkness.

I tried to focus on the physical reality around me—the cool stone against my fingertips, smooth in some places, jagged in others; the sound of our footsteps echoing off the walls; the occasional brush of a low-hanging formation against my hair. Anything to ground myself against Hun-Came's growing presence.

But with each step we took into the darkness, I could feel him becoming stronger, more distinct within me. His consciousness seemed to expand, fed by the ancient power of this place, by the proximity to what must be one of the entrances to Xibalba itself. The boundary between us was thinning, becoming permeable, and I found myself experiencing flashes of memory that weren't mine—rituals performed in this very cave centuries ago, blood offerings made to appease the Lords of Death, the screams of sacrifices echoing through these same passages.

I wondered if, by the time we reached the heart of Xibalba, there would be enough of me left to resist him, or if Niki would be swallowed completely by the ancient death god.

"The Lords of Death await us," Hun-Came whispered, his voice now clearer than it had ever been, as if the cave itself amplified his words within my mind. *"Can you feel them, little vessel? They sense our coming."*

And the terrible thing was, I could. As we descended deeper into the earth, following Ulices, I felt a weight settling over me—the awareness of ancient, hungry eyes watching our approach with anticipation. The air grew heavier, harder to breathe, thick with the dust of centuries and something else—a palpable malevolence that seemed to press against my skin.

We were entering their domain now, and they were waiting. The Lords of Xibalba, the rulers of the Maya underworld, were preparing to receive us—or perhaps to judge us. And as the passage continued its relentless descent into the earth, I couldn't shake the terrible certainty that not all of us would be returning to the world above.

CHAPTER TWENTY-SIX

We shed our packs eyeing the small opening before us with trepidation. Ulices alone had come prepared with knee and elbow pads.

The entrance—no more than a three-foot wide hole carved into the wall of the cavern.

Aedan eyed the opening dubiously. "You expect us to go in there? I haven't been that size since I was six years old."

Ulices measured Aedan with a calibrated eye, before turning and doing the same for the other men. "You will fit, but it will not be comfortable."

"I hope you're right, mate. Wouldn't want to get stuck in there."

Ulices shed his pack. "If you go slowly and carefully, you will not." He climbed up to the tunnel, stuffing his pack into the opening before lying down on his stomach. He shoved his pack in front of him and began using his elbows to propel himself into the tunnel.

I waited until Zen's feet had disappeared into the hole, before levering myself into the opening and dropping to my stomach. Prostrate on the ground, I stared into the small black void. Breath hitching, I fought to control my rising panic. *Breathe,* I commanded myself, anxiety clawing at my throat. *Slowly. Deeply. Breathe.*

With one last inhale, I crawled into the narrow opening, pushing my pack in front of me as I slithered forward.

"Jesus, Mary, and Joseph." Aedan's muttered curses echoed eerily from somewhere behind me. "How the hell am I supposed to fit through this?"

As I inched forward, my breath came in shallow, ragged gasps that echoed in the cramped tunnel, the sound of prey in a trap. My mind reeled with calculations—how many minutes of oxygen remained in this stone coffin? How many tons of ancient rock hovered mere inches above, waiting for the slightest geological hiccup to pulverize bone and flesh into red paste?

The stone chute wasn't merely tight; it was predatory—a constricting serpent of limestone with a hide of jagged protrusions that threatened to flay the skin from my back with each movement. A sharp obsidian fragment embedded in the floor sliced into one of my palms. I felt the heat of blood as it welled from the wound, the sharp biting smell filling my nostrils as I added my slippery handprints to the macabre trail of bloody handprints marking this passage.

Every forward drag of my body was warfare against the screaming instinct to thrash and claw my way backward toward light and air. The cave itself seemed to inhale as I exhaled, the walls contracting infinitesimally with malicious intent, threatening to suffocate me. Fifteen excruciating yards of belly-crawling through stone-scraped agony.

"I see your light, Niki. You're almost through." Zen called encouragement from the other side.

The air hung heavy and stagnant in my lungs, a potent mixture tasting of minerals, decay and fresh blood. I focused my attention on his voice and the light dancing at the end of the chute. The passage gripped me like a birth canal—squeezing, constricting, wringing me through its geological sphincter until, with a final push, I shoved my pack through the opening. I followed quickly, pulling myself forward with bleeding fingers.

Zen offered me his hand, pulling me to my feet. "Well done."

"Thanks." I dropped from the opening scrambling aside on trembling limbs to clear the way for Aedan's emergence. My heart thundering against my ribs like a frantic animal seeking escape as I stared at the cavern in front of me.

Colossal stalactites descended from the shadowed ceiling like the petrified fangs of some primordial deity— some needle-thin and translucent, others thick and ridged with millennia of mineral accretion. From below, stalagmites thrust upward to meet them, creating columns where they joined. A small shallow pool of water filled the very center of the chamber reflecting the anemic lights of our headlamps, transforming the formations into the dental architecture of a large animal that had swallowed us whole, its calcified digestive tract surrounding us in grotesque splendor.

A shallow creek bisected the chamber floor, its current vanishing into another yawning chute at the far end of the cavern. I was relieved to note that the passage appeared wide enough for upright passage, despite the water coursing through its channel.

Cautiously, I climbed down from the ledge to the cavern floor. Flipping over my hands, I examined the bloody scrapes and scratches on my palms with a clinical eye.

Then I heard them.

The Lords of Death.

Their voices permeated the chamber—not mere echoes but invasions of consciousness, a cacophony both ancient and immediate. They bartered and bargained over us like vultures squabbling over carrion, dividing living souls with the casual cruelty of children sorting candies.

A voice sharp as a serrated blade sawed through my thoughts: "*I am the lord of sharp pains and sudden death. I will take my due from their blood and sinew.*"

A second voice growled hungrily. "*They journey through my*

domain—their breath and bone should all be mine."

"There are many, choose one. Leave the others for us." A third voice whose utterance was nothing more than a raspy whisper as cold as frost.

"Yes," hissed the unctuous voice of yet another Lord, intoned. *"Their bodies will bloom with my touch, flowering with pustules and weeping wounds."*

Several of the Lords laughed, a wet, gurgling laugh like the sound of infected lungs drowning in their own fluids reverberated in the empty space of the chamber.

I gasped, frantically scanning the faces of my companions. Ulices—checking equipment with methodical precision. Aedan—massaging life back into cramped muscles. Zen—crouching in front of the opening, calling encouragement to Marco and Franco. Izzy—brushing dust from her clothing with disgusted flicks. Not one of them reacted to the chorus of voices reverberating through the cavern.

"The others cannot hear them, but do not worry, my little vessel. You are under my protection," Hun-Came whispered comfortingly to me.

Ulices shattered the moment, his voice painfully ordinary after the unearthly chorus. "This river joins with the one that flows from the Cave of Xilbaba."

I looked at the river and now saw the truth of what it was, wishing desperately for blindness.

I beheld a river of viscous horror—not water tinged with minerals or clay, but actual blood and pus, thick as warm honey and reeking of iron and rot. Corpses bobbed and rolled in the sluggish current, their flesh swollen and mottled with decomposition, organs protruding from ruptured abdomens, eye sockets crawling with pale, segmented things. The stench assaulted me in physical waves—the sweet-putrid miasma of decay so potent I could taste it coating my tongue and throat, forcing me to swallow convulsively against rising bile.

No one else flinched at the abomination before us.

River of blood. River of pus. River of souls.

The Popol Vuh's warning incarnate before my eyes.

Aedan picked up on my distress. "You alright, love?"

Mutely, I shook my head. "I am seeing things and hearing voices," I whispered.

He reached for my arm, his fingers clasping the iron bracelet around my wrist. "Bind yourself to the earth." He pulled me over to one of the limestone columns and placed my hand on it.

The rock felt cool and healing, a counterpoint to the burning wounds on my palm.

"Focus on channeling the earth's energy." He turned his head and called over his shoulder. "Izzy, love. Have you got a moment? I think Niki could use a bit of help."

Izzy's eyes flashed with annoyance. Zen looked up from where he was shouting helpful suggestions to Franco and Marco who were apparently stuck in the chute, but Aedan waved him off. "We've got this. You focus on getting the lads out of the tunnel."

"Teorainn idir dá shaol, críoch idir dá fhód—Boundary between two worlds, limit between two realms." I closed my eyes, chanting my mother's words and the earth's healing energy flowed through me.

Marco's and Franco's angry profanity punctured the supernatural conversation echoing inside my head as the voices of the Lords of Death slowly began to fade.

Izzy approached us. "Have you got a little something to help quiet some troublesome supernatural entities?" Aedan asked quietly.

I opened my eyes to find Izzy studying me, her expression guarded. She nodded brusquely and walked over to her pack, returning with a small obsidian mirror. "Put this in your pocket, it will help deflect the spirits."

With my free hand I slipped the polished black stone into my front pocket. "Thank you."

Her eyes narrowed dangerously. "Don't thank me. I'm not doing this for you. I'm doing this for Zen." She turned abruptly.

"Hell hath no fury like a woman scorned," Aedan commented, his eyes following the angry set of her shoulders as she marched back to where Zen and Ulices were still trying to coax Marco and Franco through the chute. "You and your shapeshifter might want to be a bit more subtle about your night-time activities in the future."

My gaze drifted to the flowing water—once again returned to its natural state. The Lords of Death's voices had completely faded, though I could still sense an ominous current of malice flowing through the cavern much like the river at our feet.

Aedan's fingers rested atop my iron bangle lending his healing power to my mother's runes. "Better?" he asked.

I nodded and slowly removed my hand from the limestone column.

After much sweating, grunting, and profanity, Marco and Franco finally made it through the narrow fissure.

"We're all here," Ulices announced, unslinging his pack. "We'll rest, eat lunch, hydrate before continuing."

I sank down against a relatively smooth section of wall, my limbs leaden with exhaustion. From my pack, I extracted a meal of couscous, dumped some water into the package and waited, eating an energy bar while my lunch rehydrated itself.

I barely tasted the food, forcing myself to chew and swallow as I battled a mixture of anxiety and claustrophobia. With the six of us crowded into the small chamber, it felt incredibly small. My chest felt tight, each breath requiring conscious effort. The air hung stagnant and heavy in my lungs, carrying the metallic tang of limestone and something else—something darker. I studied the faces of my companions, counting their breathing patterns, trying to calculate if there was enough oxygen for all of us in this subterranean prison. The math refused to cooperate with my rattled mind.

Ulices paused mid-bite, head cocked as if listening. A

distant rumble permeated the stone around us, so subtle it might have been imagination.

"The weather is becoming unsafe," he said, abandoning his meal and moving toward the river channel. "There is too much water here already. The rain is feeding this river." His voice carried the weight of professional concern. "It would be best to return to the entrance and continue our journey another day."

Franco's face contorted with indignation. "Return? I am not going back into that fucking rathole. He gestured angrily at the small opening we'd just finished crawling through.

"There is plenty of room. The river is not deep," Marco added, pointing at the water flowing through the center of the cavern. "We should continue."

Izzy stood, brushing stone dust from her pants. "We're paying you good money to get us to Cueva de Xibalba, Ulices. That was the agreement."

Ulices looked to Zen, perhaps hoping for an ally in reason.

"How long is the tunnel?" Zen asked instead, studying the channel where the creek disappeared into darkness.

"Twenty-five meters, maybe less," Ulices replied, resignation coloring his voice.

Aedan and Zen exchanged glances. "What's on the other side?" Zen asked.

"A cavern. Two more tunnels. The one on the left connects with the cave you are seeking. But the channel isn't safe when it rains."

"The thing of it is," Aedan's eyes flicked to me before returning to rest on Ulices. "We're a bit pressed for time. We need to reach that cave as quickly as possible."

"If we leave now, would it be safe?" Zen asked.

"Better to go now than to wait for the rain." Ulices stood, stuffing the remnants of his lunch into his pack. "With rain, the channel becomes extremely dangerous," Ulices continued, his eyes darting toward the ceiling. "A downpour above will cause the river to rise and turn this chamber into a death trap."

"Then we should go now," Zen confirmed.

"Yes. Without delay." Ulice's expression was grim.

Zen nodded then turned to look at the rest of us. "Is everyone in agreement? We continue forward?"

We all nodded.

Hun-Came's laughter rippled through my consciousness. *They walk willingly into the mouth of death. Such delicious irony.*

Ulices approached the channel where the river entered the next passage. He unwound the rope he'd worn strapped across his body, attaching it with a carabiner to a piton that had been pounded into the rock wall beside the entrance. I took comfort in the thought that we weren't the first to make this journey.

"I will go first and secure the rope at the other end," he said, his movements precise despite his obvious reluctance. "You will wait until I return for my pack. We'll use the rope as a hand-hold to make our way through. The water has eroded the cave floor, so keep to the edges where it isn't deep. The rocks are slippery. You will need to go slowly and watch your step."

As if punctuating his warning, a deep, resonant boom echoed through the cavern—the sound of thunder transmitted through miles of limestone.

I shivered, not entirely from the cold that radiated from the water. Something in Ulices's words had triggered a response from the Lords of Death—their voices rising in gleeful anticipation, like predators scenting blood on the wind.

I watched Ulices work his way into the tunnel, stepping carefully to avoid the water at the center, one hand braced against the wall, the other feeding out the rope behind him. His headlamp created a bobbing orb of light that grew smaller and dimmer until it vanished around a bend.

The minutes stretched like hours as we waited. The air grew heavier, charged with a static tension that had nothing to do with atmospheric pressure. A steady dripping sound from somewhere deep in the cavern marked time with maddening irregularity.

Then I felt it—vibration through the stone beneath my feet, a rhythmic trembling that intensified with each pulse.

"Do you feel that?" I asked, glancing at the others.

Before anyone could answer, a sound like the cave itself drawing breath filled the chamber. We turned as one toward the passage through which we'd entered. Water surged into the cavern—not a gentle flow but a violent, frothing deluge that submerged the lower opening within seconds, turning the floor beneath our feet into a churning turbulent lake.

"Damn it all to hell," Franco cursed, scrambling backward.

We clambered higher, seeking refuge on the elevated edges of the cavern as the water level rose with terrifying speed.

As the lake level rose, the creek of water flowing through the tunnel had now become a frothing river.

"One for me," whispered one of the Lords of Death, his voice serpentine with pleasure. *"Soon."*

Ulices reappeared at the river channel, soaked and breathing hard. His eyes widened at the transformed cavern.

"The water's rising. We best get a move on," Aedan called to him.

Ulices nodded grimly. He retrieved his pack and returned to the channel entrance. "The rope is secured. We must move quickly now."

We shouldered our packs and prepared to follow him through the tunnel.

"Hold onto the rope. Follow me. Walk quickly. Take care with your footing. Once you are in the tunnel, do not stop for any reason. You must be careful exiting the tunnel. There is a long drop at the exit." He grabbed the rope and disappeared.

Izzy followed behind him, grimacing as she stepped into the river.

Aedan swore audibly as he entered the water. He turned and caught my eye and grinned. "In for a penny, in for a pound." He turned and disappeared into the tunnel.

I stared at the rising water, unable to banish the image of the river of blood from my mind. Zen held my gaze for a moment, noting the fear behind my eyes. "I'm right behind you, Niki. I won't let anything happen to you."

Taking a deep breath, I grabbed hold of the rope and stepped into the water.

The shock of the cold water rocketed up my spine, causing me to gasp. The once shallow creek had risen to mid-thigh as the rain from above continued to funnel into the chamber. I gripped the rope with white knuckled determination, as the water continued to rise. "Twenty-five meters. Twenty-five meters," I chanted to myself. I could do this. All I needed to do was walk the length of a swimming pool. I focused my light on the rocks and water in front of me, moving as quickly as possible.

It couldn't have taken more than a few minutes, but by the time I exited the tunnel the water had reached my waist. I grabbed onto Aedan's hand, scrambling and slipping on wet rocks, my entire lower body numb from the cold.

"That's three down. Three more to go," he said, cheerfully. "You'll want to head for high ground. Take care to stay away from the drain." He tilted his head illuminating a hole in the floor of the cavern that seemed to swallow the frothing water surging from the mouth of the tunnel.

I nodded and climbed upward, careful to secure good handholds as water crashed and cascaded beneath me.

I had just clambered up to the dry ledge below the twin tunnels when it happened.

The thunder that had been distant now crashed directly overhead, the sound reverberating through the cave system like the voice of an angry god. The water in the channel surged violently, rising several inches in an instant.

Marco, the last one of us to exit the tunnel, lost his footing on the slick stone. For one suspended moment, he maintained his grip on the rope, his face a mask of pure terror illuminated in the beam of his headlamp.

"Hold on!" Zen and Aedan shouted, both reaching toward him.

But the current strengthened, wrapping around Marco's legs with liquid hands. He tried to brace himself against the force of the water pushing him forward, but the weight of his rifle and his pack worked against him. His feet went out from underneath him and he fell backward, desperately clinging to the rope with one arm.

I watched in silent horror as his fingers, numbed by the frigid water, slipped from the rope.

Unable to stop his forward momentum, the surge of water carried him from the exit. His head cracked on a rock, staining the water red as the river dropped him into the gaping maw in the floor with the swift efficiency of a predator, dragging him under and away from us in a heartbeat.

Franco lunged forward, but Zen held him back with an iron grip. "'You'll both be lost!"

Marco's headlamp created an eerie underwater light show as the current pulled him deeper into the channel. It flickered once, twice, then winked out completely.

"Mine." A voice echoed inside my head with satisfied finality.

The Lords of Death fell silent, their bargain fulfilled. For now.

CHAPTER TWENTY-SEVEN

Silent, each one of us battling our own demons—grief, guilt, anger. Ulices, Zen, and Aedan all wore expressions of grim determination, focused solely on getting the rest of us out of this cave alive. Franco's face was a wooden mask. He'd seen death before, but that didn't mean the loss of his brother didn't cut deep.

And then there was Izzy. Her silent, accusing rage directed at me with laser precision. Eyes like obsidian knives slicing me open, flaying me to the bone. I couldn't help but think she was right. My fault. This was all my fault. How much more damage would I cause before this was over?

I'd left four dead bodies in California. I'd turned Zen into an addict who'd betrayed everything he believed in to form a pact with Li Xul. Only Aedan remained unscathed... but for how much longer? Everyone I touched seemed doomed to suffer.

In the cave there was no night or day, just an eerie semi-darkness. The glow of our headlamps generated strange shadows that seemed to stretch and grow like living things as we made our way past the rock walls that entombed us.

I had no way of telling what time it was, but when Ulices told us it was time to stop, I was more than ready. I slumped tiredly on the ground and opened another package of dehydrated food. I had no idea what it was, didn't even bother to look at the label on the package. Food and drink had become nothing more than a means to fuel my body.

The dense silence of our camp site was broken only by our exhausted chewing.

"Do you even care that Marco died!" Izzy's voice suddenly lashed out at me, her words sharper than any machete. The light from her headlamp pinned me in place like an animal caught in the headlights of an oncoming vehicle.

"I care," I whispered miserably.

"Do you?" she asked, her voice full of cold fury. "You can't deny that part of you craves death. What I want to know is how much? How much of you is celebrating the death of my cousin?"

"Izzy, that's enough." Zen's tone was gentle but firm.

She whipped her head round, turning her grief and fury on him. "Don't you dare defend her! You know what she is! Even if you won't admit it!"

"We all chose to be here." Zen glanced at me, his eyes softened by understanding. "'It's not your fault, Niki. None of us could have predicted this."

But his kindness only made me more miserable, consumed by the guilt that had become my constant companion.

Izzy stood and walked away from our small group. Zen stood as if to follow her, but Franco blocked his path with an outstretched arm. "Not you," he said gruffly.

Aedan, Zen, Ulices and I sat in awkward silence listening to Izzy's quiet weeping as Franco murmured to her.

I felt sick with the knowledge that Izzy was right. I felt sad and guilty about Marco's death, but I couldn't deny that another part of me accepted his death as if it were my due.

"Death is necessary for life," Hun-Came whispered irritably. *"Why is it that mortals fail to understand and accept this?"*

I touched the jade jaguar at the base of my neck and

recited my mother's words, quieting Hun-Came's voice.

"It would be best to conserve our lights. We will need them tomorrow," Ulices announced. He unrolled his sleeping bag, slid inside, and promptly turned off his headlamp.

The rest of us followed suit, spreading our tarps on the hard rock floor and laying sleeping bags on top of them. Our headlamps clicked off one by one leaving us in Stygian darkness. I held my hand up in front of my face unable to see even the faintest outline of my fingers.

The silence was oppressive after days in the jungle—accompanied by the constant chirring and buzzing, trilling and hooting, now there was nothing more than the occasional drip of water from stalactites and our own breathing.

In the darkness, I felt Zen reach over, his fingers brushing mine. Despite everything, I took comfort in that small connection, that reminder that I wasn't completely alone in this hell we'd descended into.

Exhausted—physically and emotionally drained of all energy—I didn't fall asleep so much as collapsed into unconsciousness.

At first, I thought I was dreaming. I opened my eyes, unable to see anything in the pitch blackness. Then I heard it again—a high-pitched squeaky noise, like rusty wheels being dragged over metal tracks, accompanied by the whirring, fluttering sound of thousands of wings in motion.

Izzy screamed from somewhere nearby, and suddenly we were enveloped in a swarm of wings as hundreds of small furry bodies launched themselves at us. I was pummeled from all sides, small projectiles thudded against my sleeping bag. I frantically waved my arms above my head to ward off the unseen attackers.

"Bats!" Ulices shouted. "Cover your faces!"

But as my eyes adjusted to the darkness, aided by the frantic beams of headlamps being switched on, I saw something impossible. The bats were... changing. Their bodies elongating, wings growing fingers, faces contorting into something ancient and malevolent.

Unlike the others who saw only a terrifying swarm of bats, I could see them as they truly were—messengers from the Popol Vuh. Supernatural guardians transforming into death incarnate, their eyes glowing with netherworld fire, their mouths open in silent screams that somehow echoed louder than any sound.

And they were coming for us all.

I buried myself inside my sleeping bag, squeezing my eyes closed and whimpering like a child as the winged assault continued.

Then I heard it. The call of a quetzal echoing against the rock walls of the cavern. Impossible, but there was no mistaking it.

Nayla!

The quetzal called again and again as she attacked the Death Lords' bat-spirits. I clasped the jade pendant around my neck listening until the whir and flutter of their wings slowly fell silent.

I cautiously stuck my head out from my down-filled cocoon. My sister's wahy, her wings tinted with sunlight, spiraled upward through the darkened cavern, trailing light like stardust, leaving the cave suffused with a soft golden light.

"What the hell was that?" Aedan stood next to me, still grasping Sky-Splitter in his hands.

"Bats," Ulices answered, his voice unsteady.

"Those weren't bats, mate," Aedan said firmly. "I've seen bats, and those things weren't bats."

I glanced over at Aedan, surprised. "You saw them?"

He nodded grimly.

"They weren't bats," Izzy agreed, her eyes finding mine across the dim space. "They were Camazotz—bat spirits."

I turned to her, shocked. "You saw them, too?"

Franco slammed his palm against the cave wall. "What the hell is going on here?" he demanded, his gaze shifting between each of us, fury etched into every line of his face.

For a moment no one spoke. Aedan lowered his sword, exchanging a meaningful look with Zen. "You got it in one go, mate. Hell."

Zen remained uncharacteristically quiet. After a long pause, he looked at Izzy. "You might as well tell him everything."

Franco's eyes darted between them. "What do you mean 'tell him everything?'"

LISA DIETRICH

CHAPTER TWENTY-EIGHT

Franco's rifle was pointed directly at my chest, his finger hovering dangerously close to the trigger. The hatred in his eyes was unmistakable—cold, calculated, and utterly certain.

"You brought death to us," he said, his voice steady despite the rage that twisted his features. "My brother is dead because of you."

Zen stepped between us, his movements fluid and unhurried. To the casual observer, he might have appeared relaxed, even nonchalant, but I could see the predator lurking beneath that calm exterior—muscles coiled and ready, eyes gleaming with dangerous intent.

"Lower the gun, Franco," Zen said, his voice slipping into a deceptive calm that made everyone shift uncomfortably. "Niki is not a threat."

Franco's laugh was bitter. "Maybe she isn't, but the thing inside her is. We need to kill it."

I felt a chill sweep through me at his words. Not because of the threat, but because of the truth they contained. I was dangerous.

Behind Franco, I caught a glimpse of movement. Aedan had somehow circled around, silent as a ghost. The tip of Sky-Splitter now pressed against Franco's back, its ancient metal gleaming faintly in the dim light of our headlamps.

"I wouldn't if I were you, mate," Aedan's voice was conversational, almost friendly. "You'd be dead before she hit the ground."

Franco didn't flinch. "I will take that chance."

"It's not Aedan you have to worry about," Zen interjected, his voice still unnervingly calm. "It's Hun-Came. He's a death god. If you kill his chosen vessel, he won't just come for you. He'll kill everyone in your family."

I saw a flicker of doubt cross Franco's face, quickly masked by defiance. "They're protected. No one can touch them."

"Are you sure?" Zen asked, stepping closer to Franco. "Are they protected from the wrath of a god? You saw the bats. We're not dealing with normal, everyday threats."

The rifle wavered slightly in Franco's grip.

"He's right, Franco," Izzy said, her voice subdued. "Listen to him. If you kill her, we'll all die."

Franco's gaze shifted to Izzy, then back to me. The gun lowered a fraction of an inch. "That gold thing—the thing that went after the bats. What was it? Another god?"

I met his eyes steadily. "That was my sister. My dead sister." I paused, letting my words sink in. "You're not the only one who's lost a sibling."

Something in Franco's expression shifted. Recognition, perhaps.

Ulices, who had remained silent throughout the confrontation, finally spoke. "We cannot stay here. The bats may return."

"As soon as Franco puts down his gun, we can break camp," Zen added, his eyes tracking Franco's movements with a feral intensity.

Franco stood motionless for several long seconds, his internal struggle playing across his face. Then, with a muttered curse, he lowered the gun.

"If any more of us die," he said, his eyes boring into mine. "I will not hesitate."

"Understood," I replied.

Aedan withdrew Sky-Splitter but remained close, his eyes never straying too far from Franco.

We packed up our camp in tense silence, the memory of Marco's death and the bat attack hanging heavy in the air. As I rolled my sleeping bag and prepared my pack, I felt the weight of Franco's accusation and my guilt pressing down on me like the tons of rock above our heads.

"*Such hubris. The dead are not marked for death by you, little vessel,*" Hun-Came whispered in my mind, his voice carrying a note of amusement. "*Death is not a gift you bestow. It is my gift to the world. The natural conclusion of all things.*"

I ignored him, focusing instead on rolling up my sleeping bag with trembling hands.

As we resumed our trek, Ulices assumed his usual position at the head of our procession. Zen positioned himself directly behind Ulices, with me following. Aedan stayed close behind me—a protective shadow. Izzy and Franco brought up the rear. Franco's one hand fingering the Virgen of Guatemala medal around his neck, the other never straying far from the safety on his rifle.

We moved single file through narrow passages where the walls pressed in on either side.

After what felt like hours of walking, Ulices called for a brief rest. We huddled in a small chamber, drinking water and chewing energy bars in silence.

Zen touched my arm. "Walk with me," he murmured, nodding toward a small alcove at the edge of the chamber.

I followed him, aware of Franco's watchful gaze tracking our movement.

Once we were partially concealed by a limestone column, Zen turned to me, his expression serious. He reached out, his fingers brushing a strand of hair away from my face with a gentleness that made my heart ache. "You don't need to worry about Franco."

"His brother is dead. And he blames me."

"That wasn't your fault."

"Wasn't it?" I whispered, voicing the doubt that had been gnawing at me. "Everyone around me seems to end up dead or corrupted. Four bodies in California. Marco. You—" I stopped abruptly.

His brow furrowed. "Me?"

I couldn't meet his eyes. "The pact you made with Li Xul. That's on me, too."

Zen's fingers caught my chin, tilting my face up to meet his gaze. "Listen to me, Niki. I made my choices. Not you. Not Hun-Came. Me." His eyes, amber in the dim light, held mine with fierce intensity. "And I would make them again."

"Why?" The question escaped before I could stop it.

For a moment, he said nothing, his thumb tracing the line of my jaw. Then, "Because some things are worth the sacrifice."

The simplicity of his answer stole my breath. Before I could respond, he leaned in, his lips brushing against mine—not a passionate kiss, but something deeper. A promise. A declaration.

When he pulled back, I saw something in his eyes I hadn't noticed before—a vulnerability beneath the strength, a fear beneath the courage.

"I can't lose you," he said quietly. "Not to Franco. Not to Hun-Came. Not to whatever waits for us in Xibalba."

I reached up, my fingers tracing the contours of his face, committing them to memory.

He leaned forward, his forehead touching mine, breathing me in as if I were oxygen. "You are my soulmate, Niki. Nothing will change that. We are bound together."

"For how long?" The question hung between us, unanswered.

Hun-Came's voice slithered through my consciousness. *"Forever, if you choose it. Tell the wahy b'alam that death is eternal. It is life that is fleeting."*

I shivered at the intrusion, and Zen's arms tightened around me, mistaking my reaction for being cold.

"We should get back," I said, reluctantly pulling away.

Zen caught my hand as I turned to leave. "We'll find a way through this. All of it."

I wanted to believe him. God, how I wanted to believe him. But as we rejoined the others, Franco's hostile glare and Izzy's wounded silence were stark reminders of the cost my presence had already exacted.

Ulices stood, adjusting his pack. "We must continue. The Cave of Xibalba is not far now."

As we prepared to resume our journey, I felt Hun-Came stirring within me, his anticipation growing with every step that brought us closer to his domain.

"The Lords of Death await," he whispered, his voice like dry bones rattling. *"Soon, little vessel. Soon."*

I touched the jade jaguar at my throat and thought of Nayla, of the golden light she had brought to the darkness. If death had a presence in this underworld, perhaps life did, too.

With that fragile hope, we followed Ulices toward whatever fate awaited us in the heart of Xibalba.

CHAPTER TWENTY-NINE

Time and direction had lost all meaning. Without the sun or stars to guide us, we wandered through stone arteries like blood cells pushed along by some primal current. West, east, north—these words had become hollow sounds, devoid of significance in the womb of the earth.

I had no idea how long we'd been walking, minutes and hours blurring together in the steady rhythm of footsteps and labored breathing. The only change I noticed was the gradual incline of the passage. We were moving upward.

And there was something else—a sound that had been growing steadily louder over the past hour. A distant rushing, like wind through trees, but deeper, more primal.

"Water," Ulices confirmed when I mentioned it. "We are approaching the river."

My stomach clenched at the memory of Marco's death, of that surging current dragging him into darkness. I glanced over my shoulder at Franco. He must have been thinking the same thing; his face had hardened into stone.

The passage widened abruptly, opening into a vast cavern that took my breath away. Our headlamps barely penetrated the darkness, but the sound was unmistakable now—a thundering roar that vibrated in my chest.

"The Garganta de Xibalba," Ulices said, his voice filled with a mixture of awe and fear. "The Throat of Xibalba."

As we moved deeper into the chamber, the beams of our headlamps revealed a massive waterfall cascading from high above us, plummeting down into a churning pool at least twenty feet below where we stood. Mist filled the air, catching the light in ghostly swirls, creating a halo effect around our lamps.

"How do we get across?" I asked, raising my voice to be heard over the thundering water.

Ulices pointed upward. "We climb."

Following his gesture, I saw a narrow ledge running alongside the waterfall, ascending toward a faint glow far above us.

"That's our only option?" Aedan's skepticism was evident.

"Unless you wish to turn back," Ulices replied.

Franco snorted. "That's not an option."

"We'll need to leave our packs," Ulices said, already slipping out of his harness. "Too bulky for the climb. Without a rope it would be dangerous."

"I'm not leaving Sky-Splitter," Aedan stated flatly, patting the ancient blade strapped to his back.

Franco's hand tightened on his gun. "The rifle stays with me."

No one argued. After the attack of the bats, we all felt the vulnerability of being unarmed, though against what, I wasn't entirely sure.

We stashed our packs in a dry alcove. The rope that might have made our climb safer had been lost with Marco, a fact no one mentioned but we all felt keenly as we approached the base of the climb.

"Stay close to the wall," Ulices instructed. "The mist makes the rocks slippery. Go slowly."

One by one, we began the ascent. Ulices led the way, his experienced hands finding holds invisible to the rest of us. Izzy followed, then Zen, with Aedan and me close behind.

Franco brought up the rear, his rifle slung across his back, his eyes constantly scanning for threats.

The climb was treacherous. Water sprayed across the ledge, turning the stone slick as ice. Each handhold required careful testing with cold cramped fingers before trusting it with my full weight. My palms, still raw from the earlier scrapes, protested with every grip. Several times, I felt my foot slip, my heart leaping into my throat before I caught myself.

I fought the urge to look down, blocking the image of Marco's fall and death from my mind and focused on climbing upward, my arm's shaking from cold and fatigue.

"You're doing great," Zen called down to me over the roar of the waterfall. "Just a little further."

I tilted my head back to see him extending his hand toward me from a wider section of ledge. Gratefully, I reached for him, allowing him to pull me up to relative safety.

I rolled awkwardly into a seated position and scooted away from the edge, pressing my back against the solid rock surface with a sigh of relief, as I waited for Aedan and Franco to join us.

From my new vantage point, I gazed at the water splashing down the rocks to the cavern below. An eerie blue-green light seemed to infuse the misty spray with a glow that pulsed with a life of its own.

Hun-Came stirred within me, his presence expanding like a shadow stretching at sunset. "*Home*," he whispered, the word carrying a weight of longing that momentarily overwhelmed my own consciousness.

After everyone had a moment to catch their breath, we continued upward. The ledge widened as we climbed higher, making the going easier, but the mist grew thicker, obscuring our vision. I focused on the sound of Zen's footsteps ahead of me, using it to anchor myself in the swirling vapor.

The roar of the waterfall began to diminish, though the

mist remained thick around us. The ledge leveled out, becoming a proper path that curved away from the falls.

"We're nearly there," Ulices said, his voice tight with anticipation or fear—I couldn't tell which.

The path led us through a narrow fissure in the rock wall, barely wide enough for us to squeeze through single file. And then, abruptly, we emerged into a space so vast our headlamps couldn't reach the ceiling or the far walls.

But we didn't need our lights. The entire cavern was illuminated by that same blue-green glow we'd seen from below, emanating from what appeared to be a perfectly circular pool of water at the center of the chamber—a cenote. The black water of the sacred pool seemed to glow with an otherworldly light.

The sickly-sweet smell of putrefaction filled my nostrils as I stared wide-eyed at the ancient stone altar with its piles of disarticulated bones. I thought I heard the faint echo of lost souls reverberating like a thousand plucked guitar strings against the cavern's stone walls.

I knew this cave. Recognition surged through me, visceral and absolute. I had once stood at this very cenote and faced One-Death in a vision.

As if in response to my thoughts, Hun-Came's presence swelled within me, his consciousness pressing against the boundaries of my own. I clutched the jade jaguar at my throat, fighting to maintain control.

"Well, well," a voice echoed from the shadows beyond the cenote. "You've arrived at last."

I froze, my attention snapping toward the sound.

From the darkness emerged a figure that made my blood run cold—a familiar figure wearing a jaguar pelt over his shoulders instead of the priest's collar he'd worn when I first met him.

His face was painted with intricate designs in black and red, and around his neck hung dozens of small amulets made from bone, feathers, and what looked horribly like human teeth. His eyes, when they met mine, were rimmed with red.

Li Xul.

Behind him emerged half a dozen men, armed with modern weapons.

"Zen," Li Xul said, his smile cold. "Did you really think I would let you perform the K'ex ritual? That I would allow you to take back what is rightfully mine?"

Zen stepped forward, placing himself between me and Li Xul. "It was never yours to begin with."

Li Xul's laughter was like rocks grinding together. "I've sacrificed to Hun-Came for decades. I earned One-Death's esteem with the gift of blood." His black eyes shifted to me. "This girl and her sister interfered with what is rightfully mine." His gaze returned to Zen. "And now you want to perform the soul transfer ritual and take his power. This time, I will not be denied."

I looked at Zen, shock rippling through me. Was that truly his plan? To take Hun-Came's power for himself?

Zen's face remained impassive, revealing nothing.

"No one is performing a ritual," Franco growled, moving forward with his rifle raised. "No more death. No more gods. This ends now."

Several of Li Xul's men raised their weapons in response.

"Franco, don't," Izzy warned, but he ignored her.

"You killed my brother," Franco continued, his rifle aimed squarely at me now. "You and whatever demon lives inside you."

"How amusing," Li Xul said. "Do you think you can fight gods with bullets?"

"*Enough!*"

The voice that thundered through the cavern wasn't mine, though it came from my lips. It resonated with power ancient as the stones around us, deep as the earth itself. Hun-Came had taken control.

Everyone—Li Xul included—took an involuntary step backward.

"*You, Li Xul, have defiled my sacred pool,*" Hun-Came

continued, using my voice but transforming it into something otherworldly. *"You must pay for your insolence and your disrespect."*

I felt my body straighten, my arms spreading wide as Hun-Came channeled his power through me. The blue-green light from the cenote intensified, casting grotesque shadows across the ancient altar.

Aedan's face had drained of color. "Niki?"

"She can hear you," Hun-Came replied. *"But I speak now."*

Franco's rifle wavered, his eyes wide with shock. Izzy made a small, frightened sound. Even Ulices, who had maintained his stoic façade throughout our journey, looked shaken.

"One-Death," Li Xul whispered reverentially as he dropped to his knees.

"Yes," Hun-Came replied. *"And you have entered my domain uninvited."*

From the shadows around the cavern came an echoing chorus of unearthly voices—the other Lords of Death, their presence palpable though their forms remained hidden. *"Death to those who desecrate the sacred portal. Death. Death. Death,"* they chanted.

My arm raised of its own accord slashed through the air in a wide arc. I watched in shocked horror as Hun-Came sliced through Li Xul's men as if he were cutting stalks of corn with a scythe. They fell to the ground without a sound. Their blood disappearing into the dry dust as if the earth itself were swallowing it.

Li Xul's eyes never flickered toward his fallen men, not even a glance at their crumpled bodies. Instead, he straightened his spine and stepped over the corpse of his closest guard. An obsequious smile spread across his face as he dropped to one knee before me.

"Hun-Came, most exalted Lord of Death," he said, voice dripping with reverence. "I thank you for cleansing my expedition of these... inadequate servants. I humbly offer myself as your vessel. The girl is nothing—unrefined, untrained. My body and mind have been preparing for this sacred honor since before her birth."

"*He must prove himself worthy*," a raspy guttural voice insisted.

"*A game*," one croaked. "*They must play the game.*"

"*Yes, a competition*," another agreed, the words dripping with malicious glee. "*As it was in the   beginning.*"

"*A game to the death*," a different voice hissed eagerly. "*As it was in the beginning.*"

"*A game*," Hun-Came agreed. "*Choose your champion*," Hun-Came commanded me, his gaze—my gaze—sweeping across the gathered humans. "*Who will face the trials of Xilbaba on your behalf?*"

Inside my own mind, I fought to regain control. *No,* I thought desperately. *I won't let anyone else die for me.*

With an effort that felt like I was tearing myself in half, I pushed Hun-Came back, reclaiming my voice. "I will face him," I declared, pointing at Li Xul. "This is between us."

Hun-Came's presence surged forward again, wrestling control from me. "*No!*" he thundered, my voice transforming into something ancient and terrible that echoed off the cavern walls. "*You are the prize. You must choose your champion.*"

Again, I fought back, the struggle visible to everyone as my body trembled with the effort. Blue-green light from the cenote pulsed in time with my heartbeat, casting writhing shadows across the faces of those watching. "I will not risk anyone else's life but my own," I insisted, my voice my own again, though strained. "No more death. No more sacrifices."

"*Gods do not bargain with mortals.*" Hun-Came's voice dropped to a dangerous whisper that somehow filled the entire chamber. The stone beneath our feet began to tremble. "*I make the rules in Xilbaba, and I will not ask again.*" His rage built with each word, causing stalactites to shudder overhead. "*Choose your champion. Or I will choose for you.*"

Li Xul watched with greedy fascination, his black eyes

gleaming in the supernatural light. Franco tightened his grip on his weapon, shifting nervously as the very air grew heavy with ancient power.

Aedan unsheathed Sky-Splitter, the ancient blade catching the eerie light as he stepped forward. Zen placed a hand on his shoulder, stopping him. For a moment, everything went still—even the shadows seemed to hold their breath.

Then, Zen stood in front of me, facing Hun-Came. His body transformed subtly, taking on the fluid grace of the jaguar spirit within him. "I will fight for Niki," he declared, the words echoing.

The Death Lords' excited laughter erupted from the shadows, a cacophony of inhuman sounds that scraped against the mind like obsidian knives. *"Pitz! Pitz! Pitz!"* they chanted in unison, their voices building to a frenzy that made the water in the cenote ripple and dance.

Franco and Izzy backed away, terror plain on their faces. Ulices dropped to his knees, crossing himself frantically as he whispered prayers in rapid Spanish.

Aedan stepped forward, undaunted by the supernatural display, positioning himself shoulder to shoulder with Zen. Sky-Splitter glowed with an inner light, as if the ancient weapon recognized the presence of the death gods. "I will also fight for Niki," he echoed, his Irish accent thickened by emotion.

Li Xul's lips curled into a smile that revealed his teeth. "And I," he said, stepping forward. "Will fight for myself. For what is rightfully mine."

For a moment, Hun-Came was silent, his consciousness coiled like a serpent within me. Then I felt him smile— a terrible, ancient expression that had nothing to do with joy.

"Pitz," Hun-Came thundered, his voice causing dust and small stones to rain down from above. The cenote's waters began to swirl, forming a vortex that revealed glimpses of another world beneath—a world of shadow and bone. *"We shall play the ball game to determine who is worthy. As it was in the*

beginning," Hun-Came intoned, his voice now filled with dark anticipation. "*So it shall be again.*"

.

CHAPTER THIRTY

The sound of bones clacking filled the darkness, a macabre percussion that seemed to come from everywhere and nowhere. I felt it in my chest before I heard it with my ears—hollow, ancient, and hungry. The eerie blue-green glow of the cenote brightened around us, water rippling though no wind disturbed its surface. Somewhere in the darkness, hands began to clap, feet stomped in rhythm, the tempo increasing with each beat until the very ground beneath us vibrated.

"What's happening?" Izzy whispered, her eyes searching mine, her fingers digging into Franco's arm.

I couldn't answer. The walls of the cavern trembled, dust and small stones raining down. The edges of my vision blurred, the ground beneath us no longer solid but shifting, dissolving.

And then we were falling.

Plummeting through absolute darkness, spinning, my stomach lurching into my throat. I wanted to scream but I couldn't draw a breath, couldn't think, couldn't do anything but fall through the endless void.

Until suddenly, we weren't.

We emerged from darkness onto solid ground, the

transition so abrupt that my knees buckled. I blinked rapidly, my eyes adjusting to the sudden brightness. We stood on the edge of a massive stone structure—a ball court like those that had once dominated the plazas of great Maya cities, only impossibly pristine, as if freshly constructed. A long, narrow playing field stretched before us, bordered on each side by sloping limestone walls. Two stone hoops, one on each side of the court, six feet off the ground, marked the center of the field.

My breath caught in my throat. I knew this place from the codices, from the ancient stories.

"Pitz. The game that decided the fate of the Hero Twins," I whispered.

"What did you say?" Ulices asked, his voice tight with fear.

"The sacred ball game," I said. "We're in Xibalba's ball court."

From my position at the side of the field, I stared around me, my body feeling as though a million insects were crawling beneath my skin. Izzy and Ulices stood on either side of me, all of us perched on what appeared to be a flat stone bench—or perhaps a sacrificial altar—along the edge of the ball court.

Above us, at the top of the stone walls, a crowd had gathered—not people, not exactly. Shapes both human and not, some translucent, others solid as stone. Among them, I recognized the Lords of Death: One Death with his bone scepter and obsidian crown; Seven Death with his necklace of eyeballs; Flying Scab, his skin peeling away in layers; Bone Scepter with his staff of femurs; Blood Gatherer with his bowl of still-warm hearts; and all the others—eleven in total, watching with hungry, expectant eyes.

Beside me, Izzy gasped. I followed her gaze to the middle of the ball court where four figures had appeared as if from nowhere.

Zen and Aedan stood on one side of the court. Li Xul and Franco on the other. Their heads swiveled in shocked surprise as they took in their surroundings. Their bodies had been painted—Zen and Aedan in deep black with red stripes across their chests and faces; Li Xul and Franco in red with black markings that looked like claw marks. All four wore thick leather guards strapped to their hips and forearms.

A tall figure strode onto the field from the far end—Hun-Came, no longer inhabiting my body but present in his full glory. He wore a headdress of quetzal feathers that cascaded down his back, a jade pectoral over his bare chest, and a skirt of jaguar skin. His face was painted half-white, half-black, and his eyes glowed with unearthly fire.

I reached into my mind, searching for him, realizing with a start that he was no longer there. The heaviness that had pressed against my thoughts was gone, the hunger that had simmered beneath my consciousness vanished. My body felt lighter, my thoughts clearer—like emerging from murky water into fresh air.

Hun-Came carried a large, perfectly round ball that seemed to absorb rather than reflect light. He stopped at the center of the court.

Zen strode forward to meet him. Li Xul followed suit, his movements predatory. Because of the court's acoustics—sounds bounced off the stone walls—I could hear every word they spoke.

"What is this?" Zen demanded, his voice echoing.

Hun-Came held up the ball. "The sacred game will decide the fate of your souls." His voice reverberated across the court.

Li Xul's lips curled into a smile.

"My team-mate is not familiar with this game. He will not know how to play," Zen said, casting a concerned glance at Aedan.

Hun-Came raised a skeletal finger at Zen. "You may explain."

Zen nodded. He turned to face Aedan. "This is a ball court for the ancient Mayan game called Pitz. I'm a little vague on the rules but I do know the game is a lot like soccer. What you call football. Except you can't use your feet or hands."

"No feet. No hands," Aedan replied, eyeing the ball. "Going to be a bit of a challenge."

Zen pointed to the ball in Hun-Came's hand. "Right. You move the ball using your hips, forearms, and knees. The ball is solid rubber and very heavy. Whatever you do, do *not* head the ball."

"Hips, knees, forearms... a bit different, but I'm game," Aedan said, gesturing to the stone rings. "Our job is to get it through one of those, right?"

"Yes," Zen said. "If we get it through the hoop, we win. Only I think there might be a penalty if you miss." He glanced at Hun-Came for confirmation, but the god only watched with amused detachment, remaining stubbornly silent.

Zen's brow furrowed. "Probably best to only shoot for it if you have a good shot. We'll have to figure out the rules and scoring as we play."

Hun-Came raised his hand for silence. "Enough. The game begins."

He threw the ball high into the air.

On the sidelines, Izzy, Ulices, and I tensed. I gripped the edge of the stone bench so hard my knuckles turned white.

The ball reached its apex and began to fall. Aedan positioned himself beneath it, ready to bounce it off his protected hip. When the ball connected, he let out a shocked grunt, nearly buckling under its weight. The ball fell to the ground with a dull thud on their side of the court.

"Point to the challengers," Hun-Came declared, gesturing to Li Xul and Franco.

Li Xul smiled, a cold, predatory expression. He picked up the ball and served, bouncing it off the sloping wall. It ricocheted with surprising speed toward Zen, who barely managed to deflect it with his forearm guard.

"Gods, that stings," he hissed.

The game was brutal. The ball moved with unnatural speed and weight, leaving bruises even through the thick padding. Franco and Li Xul, lacking Zen and Aedan's athleticism, played with vicious precision, aiming for vulnerable spots—throats, ribs, groins. With each impact, the stone walls seemed to pulse, as if the ancient court itself hungered for their pain.

Aedan and Zen quickly found a rhythm. They moved in tandem, anticipating each other's positions, their eyes laser-focused on the ball as they leaped and twisted their bodies seeking to stop its forward progress. I could hear and see everything—the dull sound of a heavy object striking muscle and flesh, the grimace of pain, the sweat coating their bodies like sacrificial oil—and at the center stood Hun-Came, awarding seemingly random points to each side. Try as I might, I could not fathom the scoring of this game. I had no idea who was winning or losing.

From the shadows above, the Lords of Death watched with gleaming obsidian eyes. Their bone-white fingers tapped in unison against the stone, creating a rhythm like a heartbeat—a counterpoint to the thud of the ball and the labored breathing of the players below.

When Li Xul sent a particularly vicious serve directly at Aedan's face, Zen dove in front, deflecting it with his hip. The ball ricocheted off the wall at a perfect angle.

"There!" Izzy grabbed my arm, her fingers digging into my flesh. "It's going for the hoop!"

The ball arced through the air, heading straight for the stone ring. Li Xul's face contorted with rage, his eyes flashing, glowing an inhuman red.

"No!" he snarled, the word transforming into a growl midway through.

Li Xul's body bent forward, his spine elongating with audible cracks, his face stretching into a muzzle. Fur erupted from his skin, obliterating the red paint. His hands became massive paws tipped with curved claws that scraped against the stone floor, sending up sparks. Where Li Xul had stood, a massive jaguar now crouched, muscles bunching beneath its spotted coat. The air around him shimmered with heat, the scent of jungle and blood suddenly thick in the air.

The jaguar—Li Xul—leapt, crossing the court in a single bound, jaws open to reveal teeth, each one shining like polished ivory.

Time seemed to slow.

I felt something deep inside me shift, ancient power flowing through my blood, my bones. The world around me took on a reddish hue, as if I were seeing through a veil of blood. Without thinking, I reached out with my mind, searching for Zen across the distance. I could feel him—not just see him, but *feel* him—his heartbeat, his fear, his determination.

Change! I commanded, a word that wasn't a word but pure intention, written in the language of the universe. My voice echoed not in the air but in the spaces between worlds, and the glyph for transformation burned bright in my mind's eye.

Zen turned, his eyes widening at the sight of the beast flying toward him. The ball passed through the stone hoop with a hollow sound that echoed across the court like the toll of a death bell.

Zen's body blurred, his form shifting, shrinking, then expanding into that of a sleek black jaguar, its amber eyes blazing with Zen's intelligence. His transformation was more fluid than Li Xul's—as if this form were a natural extension of his being.

The two great cats collided in midair, a tangle of fur and fury, claws raking, teeth snapping. They crashed to the stone floor, rolling, snarling, a tornado of violence.

Izzy screamed beside me, her hands covering her mouth. A roar of approval arose from the ghoulish spectators lining the top of the walls as the two cats tore into each other. The Lords of Death leaned forward in unison, their skeletal fingers gripping the stone ledge, their hollow eyes devouring the scene below them.

My eyes were fixed on the battle, my heart hammering against my ribs. Blood spattered the stone court, black in the eerie light, impossible to tell whose it was. Each drop that hit the ground sizzled like water on hot stone, the court drinking it in.

With a sudden shout that was more war cry than human sound, Franco charged forward. He heaved the ball with all his might, smashing it into Zen's side and knocking him to the ground. The impact echoed across the court like thunder, and I felt it in my own ribs as if I'd been struck myself.

Li Xul pounced on the stunned Zen; his massive jaws snapping closed on the soft flesh of his throat and ripped it open. The sound—wet, tearing—cut through me like a blade.

"No!" The scream tore from me as Zen's blood spilled from the gaping wound, steam rising from it in the cool air of the underworld. The world around me pulsed red, my vision tunneling to focus only on Zen's fallen form. In that moment, I felt our connection pull taut and begin to fray.

Hun-Came raised his hand, bone-white against the darkness. "The game is decided."

Li Xul threw back his head and roared, the sound echoing off the stone walls and through my bones. The spectral audience responded with a hollow cheer that sounded like wind through dry bones.

My feet carried me to Zen before I made the conscious decision to move. I fell to my knees beside him, tears cascading down my face, my fingers trying in vain to staunch the blood matting his dark fur and staining the court red. The blood warm, so warm, against my cold fingers.

His eyes found mine, amber now clouding with pain but still unmistakably Zen's.

"Don't leave me," I begged, my voice breaking. I pressed harder against the wound, as if I could hold his life inside through sheer force of will.

"Soulmates." I heard his voice as clearly as if he had spoken it aloud. I stared into his eyes, one hand clutched to his bleeding throat, his blood bubbling between my fingers, and watched as the light in those beautiful amber eyes slowly dimmed.

I felt it when he left—a snap, like a thread breaking, somewhere deep inside me. A part of me went with him, disappearing into the darkness.

I crumpled to the ground weeping; my forehead pressed against his cooling fur. Above us, the Lords of Death began to chant, a low, rhythmic sound that seemed to pull at Zen's essence. I could almost see it—a pale mist rising from his body, being drawn upward toward them.

Aedan approached and laid a consoling hand on my shoulder. At his touch, my grief blazed into a white-hot rage and a need for death that wasn't mine but somehow was. It consumed me, filled me, until there was nothing left of Niki Balam but a vessel for vengeful fury.

I leaped to my feet, spun around to point a trembling finger at Li Xul. My hand glowed with an inner light, casting stark shadows across the court. "Kill him!" I commanded Hun-Came, my voice resonating with power that made the stone walls vibrate. I turned and pointed at Franco, who cowered back from me. "Kill them both!"

"You begin to understand, little vessel." Hun-Came's skull split into a grotesque smile, his teeth too numerous, too sharp. "Strike down your enemies and join with me." He extended his hand toward me, offering power, offering vengeance.

"Niki, love, don't do this." Aedan's voice was urgent, pleading, breaking through the red haze of my rage. "Zen would not want this."

I heard his words, but was deaf to their meaning. I had moved to a space beyond reason, beyond humanity. I felt Hun-Came's presence expanding inside me, filling the hollow space left by Zen's departure. I turned to face Li Xul, my entire body shaking as Hun-Came's power swelled inside of me. The air around me grew cold, so cold Aedan's breath fogged before him.

"Change!" I ordered the shaman, the word carrying the weight of divine command. "I want to see your face when I kill you."

The shaman shifted back to his human form and stood in front of me, chin raised, defiant. Strange symbols glowed beneath his skin, protection spells and wards that would be useless against what I had become. Franco, beside him, fell to his knees, shaking and whimpering.

"You will die today," I intoned, raising my hand. I could feel the power gathering in my palm. The Lords of Death leaned forward as one, eager for the spectacle of more death.

"*Soulmates.*" The word, no more than a faint whisper, pierced the haze of rage and grief clouding my mind. It came from beyond, carried on a breath of wind that shouldn't exist in this stagnant underworld.

I glanced to where Zen lay, and my heart stopped. His jaguar form shimmered, returning to human shape, a pale light surrounded him, pulsing with each beat of his heart.

"*Soulmates.*" The word echoed again, this time in my bones, in my blood.

LISA DIETRICH

CHAPTER THIRTY-ONE

I closed my eyes and reached for Zen with my mind but found only emptiness where he should have been. The connection that had always hummed between us—faint but constant—was severed, leaving a hollow ache in my chest.

"What's happening?" I heard Izzy's voice, distant and faint.

I couldn't answer. My consciousness felt untethered, floating somewhere between the world of the living and the realm of the dead. The ballcourt began to fade around us, its ancient stones dissolving like mist. The Lords of Death raised their skeletal hands in unison, their hollow laughter echoing as they began to retreat into shadow. Hun-Came's eyes met mine across the fading distance—satisfied, victorious.

Then everything went black.

When awareness returned, I found myself back in the cenote cavern, the blue-green glow of the water casting ghostly patterns across the stone walls. But something fundamental had changed—I could feel the boundary between worlds had grown thin here, gossamer-fine and permeable.

Zen lay motionless beside me, his human form pale and

still. The wound at his throat had stopped bleeding, but his chest didn't rise and fall with breath. His skin was growing cold under my trembling fingers.

"He's gone," Aedan said quietly, his hand gentle on my shoulder. "I'm sorry, love."

"No." The word emerged as barely a whisper. I pressed my palm against Zen's chest, feeling for any flutter of life. Nothing. "His life-force—it's still connected to this world. Hun-Came took his jaguar spirit, but not all of him."

I remembered the stories my father had told me, the old ways that predated the Spanish conquest. The Maya understood that each person carried multiple souls—the soul that resided in the blood and gave life to the body, the soul that could travel in dreams and visions, and the wahy the animal spirit companion that could be shared or stolen.

"What are you saying?" Ulices asked, crossing himself nervously.

"I'm saying Hun-Came made a mistake." I pulled the obsidian blade from my belt, the one I'd carried since our journey began. Its edge gleamed wickedly in the cenote's ethereal light. "He took Zen's jaguar spirit, but his other soul... is still tethered to this world. To me."

Without hesitation, I drew the blade across my left palm. The cut was deep, deliberate—pain sharp as lightning followed by the warm flow of blood. Dark red drops fell onto Zen's still chest, spreading across his skin like ink in water.

"Blood calls to blood," I murmured, pressing my bleeding palm directly over Zen's heart. "Life calls to life." I closed my eyes, and placed my other palm on the ground, drawing on the life nourishing power of the earth and sky, merging my druid inheritance with my Mayan bloodline.

The cavern around us stilled. Even the constant sound of dripping water fell silent. I could feel something stirring in the space between worlds—not Hun-Came's cold presence, but something warmer, more familiar.

"Alejandro Lorenzo Rafael Ignacio Cazares y

Mendoza." I spoke his true name aloud, the syllables carrying power in the sacred space. "By blood we are bound. By breath we share life. I call your soul back from the threshold of death."

My blood began to glow where it touched his skin, not with the harsh light of divine power, but with a softer radiance like candleflame. The glow spread outward from the point of contact, tracing the pathways of his circulatory system in faint golden lines beneath his skin.

"Come back to me," I whispered. "Your animal spirit may belong to Xibalba now, but your human soul is mine to call home."

The air shimmered above his body like heat waves rising from sunbaked stone. I felt rather than saw his wahy—his free soul—hovering nearby, caught between worlds, unsure which way to go.

I leaned down and breathed across his lips, a soft exhalation that carried all my will, all my love, all my desperate need for him to return. "Follow my breath back to your body. Follow my blood back to life."

For a long moment, nothing happened. Then Zen's body gave the slightest shudder. His chest rose fractionally, fell, rose again. The cut at his throat began to close, the edges of the wound pulling together as if drawn by invisible thread.

"Impossible," Ulices breathed.

Zen's eyes fluttered open, unfocused at first, then finding mine with laser precision. When our gazes met, I felt it—not the complete soul-deep connection we'd shared before, but something quieter, more fragile. Like a conversation conducted in whispers.

"Niki," he said, his voice hoarse. He lifted a trembling hand to touch my face. "I can feel... something's missing."

I helped him sit up, supporting his weight against me. "Hun-Came claimed your shadow soul."

Zen nodded slowly, understanding. He touched his chest, right over his heart. "But you brought the rest of me back."

"Yes," I said. "The soul that makes you human. It is still yours."

He looked at his hands, flexing his fingers as if testing their reality. His eyes met mine again.

Hun-Came materialized before us, no longer the resplendent god of the ballcourt but a more subdued figure, his headdress dimmed, his painted face thoughtful rather than triumphant.

"Clever, little vessel," he said, circling us slowly. "You understand the nature of souls better than I gave you credit for."

"His wahy belongs to Xibalba now," I replied, not moving from Zen's side. "But the rest of him does not."

The death god's lips curved into what might have been a smile or a snarl. "Indeed. The jaguar spirit will serve me well in the underworld. As for the rest..." He gestured dismissively. "A human soul diminished is of little interest to me."

Li Xul stepped forward, his face contorted with rage. "My Lord, surely you can see she has cheated—"

Hun-Came turned to face the shaman, his eyes flashing with annoyance. "You lost the sacred game, shaman. Your soul is forfeit to Xibalba." He flicked his wrist dismissively, as if swatting away an irritating insect.

Li Xul's body crumpled to the ground, empty, a discarded husk. Above him, a wisp of pale smoke hovered for a moment before being sucked downward, into the stone itself, gone forever.

Franco gasped and scuttled backward, his eyes fixed on Hun-Came in terror.

Ignoring Franco entirely, Hun-Came raised his head toward the shadows gathering at the edges of the cavern. "The game has ended."

The world around us began to blur at the edges, reality reasserting itself slowly, like waking from a vivid dream. The last thing I saw before the vision faded was Hun-Came's ancient eyes, no longer hungry but calculating, as if he were already planning his next move.

When the cavern solidified around us again, we were alone except for Franco, who huddled against the far wall, staring at the spot where Li Xul had fallen. The cenote still glowed with its eerie light, but the oppressive weight of the underworld's presence had lifted.

Zen inhaled deeply, I kept one hand on his arm for support. He was alive, breathing, warm to the touch—but I could feel the absence in him, the space where his jaguar spirit had once resided.

"The ritual," he said quietly. "We still need to complete it. To make sure Hun-Came can't return to the world above."

"Can you do it?" I asked. "Without your jaguar spirit?"

He considered this, his eyes gleaming fiercely. I saw not diminishment but a different kind of strength. "Yes."

CHAPTER THIRTY-TWO

"How?" Izzy asked, appearing at my side. "We saw him die."

I supported Zen's weight against me. "Part of him did die," I said quietly. "His wahy—his jaguar spirit—remains in Xibalba. Hun-Came took it as payment," I explained, eyeing the cenote still glowing faintly in the darkness of the cavern.

Turning my gaze back toward Zen, I smiled tenderly at him. "Li Xul is dead. Hun-Came has returned to Xilbaba."

Zen nodded weakly, pressing his hand to his chest.

"It's over?" Izzy asked hopefully.

"It's never that simple with gods," Aedan said grimly.

"So, what happens now?" Izzy asked, looking around the cavern warily.

"I'll tell you what happens now," Franco growled. "We get out of this fucking cave."

"Not a bad idea, mate." Aedan glanced at Zen. "What do you say? Can you walk?"

"Yes."

"That's grand." Aedan grinned. "Because I'm thinking that after coming back from the dead, a spot of sunlight and fresh air might do you a bit of good."

Ulices jutted a chin in the direction of the waterfall. "We do not have supplies. Our packs are at the bottom of the garganta."

"Fuck that." Franco shouldered his gun. "I say we get out of here before those things wake up." He swept his headlamp across the piles of bones lining the cavern's walls. "Or we end up like them," he said, pointing to where the bodies of Li Xul's men lay lifeless on the cave floor.

"I agree. This is Hun-Came's domain. He is closest to his source of power here. We should leave." I slowly pushed myself to my feet, my body feeling surprisingly heavy. "Vamanos, chicos."

We moved slowly to accommodate Zen's weakened state but even so, I found myself struggling to keep up with the others as Ulices led us out of the cave. My arms and legs moved as if they were encased in stone, and I struggled to fill my lungs with oxygen. Panting, my heartrate spiking as if I were sprinting instead of walking, I resorted to using the stone walls of the cave for support, propelling myself forward rather than walking.

"How much farther?" I gasped, my voice barely audible over the sound of our footsteps echoing through the passage.

Zen appeared at my side, his warm hand finding mine in the dim light. "Not much further. I can feel a breeze."

I nodded, but couldn't find the breath to respond. With each step away from the cenote, I felt a strange resistance, as if invisible cords were pulling me back toward the sacred water, toward Xibalba. My wahy felt stretched thin, part of it still tethered to Hun-Came's realm through the blood I'd offered.

"Something's wrong with her," Franco said, turning back to look at me.

Aedan's eyes widened. "Niki, your skin—"

I glanced down at my arms. In the beam of Ulices' headlamp, my veins stood out, dark blue against my pale skin, tracing patterns that looked almost like the glyphs.

"Her soul is becoming untethered," Izzy explained quietly.

Zen placed his arm around my waist steadying me. "Hun-Came hasn't released his claim on her. He's using the blood covenant that brought me back to bind her to the underworld."

"We need to get her outside," Aedan urged. "Sun, air—she needs to reconnect with this world. I can work a spell once we are free from Hun-Came's cave."

The journey through the final stretch of cave seemed endless. I drifted in and out of awareness, occasionally coming back to myself when I stumbled or when Zen spoke my name. Finally, I glimpsed a patch of brilliant light ahead—the exit.

When we emerged into the daylight, I gasped as the sensation of sunlight on my skin sent waves of euphoria through my body. The contrast between the oppressive darkness of the cave and the vibrant world outside was dizzying. The green of the trees, the blue of the sky, the sweet scent of tropical flowers—all of it felt heightened, almost painfully beautiful.

"We made it," Izzy breathed, her face tilted up to the sun.

My moment of euphoria was short-lived. Weakness overtook me, and my legs gave way. I slumped to the ground, the world spinning around me.

"Niki!" Zen knelt beside me, his face etched with concern.

"What's wrong with her?" Franco demanded, hovering nearby.

"She's paying the price of being Hun-Came's vessel," Izzy said, her tone cold and clinical. "Her connection to Hun-Came is corrupting her wahy, making it difficult for her to move in this world."

Zen's eyes met mine, and I knew he understood what I couldn't fully articulate. The boundaries between worlds had been breached. And both of us had been irrevocably transformed. "Rest," Zen told me, his voice gentle. "We'll figure this out."

I tried to nod, but even that small movement seemed to require more strength than I possessed. The world around me blurred, voices fading in and out.

I heard Ulices organizing the construction of a shelter, Franco volunteering to hunt for food. The familiar rhythms of survival provided a strange comfort as I drifted between consciousness and something else—not quite sleep, not quite a trance.

When I opened my eyes again, the sun had shifted in the sky. Aedan sat cross-legged beside me, his eyes closed in meditation, his hand resting lightly on my arm as he channeled energy from the earth through him to me. Nearby, Izzy and Zen were engaged in a heated discussion.

"The K'ex ritual won't work," Izzy insisted, her voice rising. "Soul substitution doesn't work if the soul is already tethered to Xibalba."

"What the hell are you two talking about?" Franco asked, returning from somewhere with a bundle of wood in his arms.

"K'ex," Zen explained. "It means to substitute or exchange for something else. Among the Maya, it's used in healing rituals. When someone's spiritual co-essence is stolen or damaged, an animal—usually a chicken—is sacrificed as a substitute."

"A chicken?" Franco dropped the wood with a clatter. "You saw what happened in there." He jutted his chin in the direction of the cave. "There's no way a chicken and some peasant brujeria is going to fix her."

"It's not witchcraft," Izzy snapped. "And that's my point. This isn't a simple spiritual injury. Hun-Came has claimed part of Niki's soul. He's merged with her in a way that goes beyond what the K'ex ritual is intended to cure. It won't be enough."

"It will work," Zen insisted, his voice calm but firm. "We just need to adapt it. My wahyob may be gone, but that gives me an advantage—I already have one foot in Xibalba."

Aedan opened his eyes. "In druidic traditions, we have something similar. When we need to expel malevolent spirits, we use a combination of ritual cleansing and what we call 'the binding of the four quarters."

"Hun-Came is not an evil spirit," Izzy reminded him. "He is a god."

"Yes," Zen agreed. "But maybe we can use druidic rituals and protection magic to confuse Hun-Came and strengthen our abilities."

I struggled to sit up. "What exactly are you proposing?"

Zen moved to help me, his hands gentle on my shoulders. "The Maya use K'ex to substitute part of another soul for yours. The plan was to lure Hun-Came to take up residence in another vessel."

Izzy's eyes shifted quickly from Zen to me, then back to Zen. "We shouldn't be talking about this in front of her."

"He's not listening," I told her.

"Gods are always listening," she snapped.

"If he knows what we're planning so much the better because we're going to entice him by offering him something he won't be able to pass up. Kuxa," Zen said.

"Kuxa?" Aedan asked, watching them with interest.

"Life force," Izzy explained. "The Maya give kuxa not only to awaken and feed spiritual entities but also to placate them and goad them into action."

A worry line creased Aedan's forehead. "Life force?"

"Blood," Ulices said suddenly from where he had been quietly listening. "It's what she did when she called him back from the dead." His eyes shifted between Zen and me. "That is what the ancient ones offered. Blood to feed the gods."

A heavy silence fell over the group.

"If you're going to rip someone's heart out of their chest," Franco growled menacingly. "It will not be mine or Izzy's."

"Not human sacrifice," Zen corrected. "A blood

offering."

"Whose blood?" Franco asked, an unspoken threat behind his words. "Whose blood will be the offering?"

Zen locked eyes with him, his gaze steady and determined. "Mine. My blood will be the kuxa."

"Don't be an idiot. You've lost your wahy in Xibalba," Izzy countered. "Part of your soul is missing. How can you possibly stand against Hun-Came?"

Zen turned to look at her. "That's exactly why I can. My jaguar spirit may be gone, but my connection to both realms makes me the perfect substitute."

"I agree with Izzy, mate. You just came back from the dead. I don't think offering your blood is a good idea." Aedan shook his head. "There must be another way. Didn't you tell us that the Hero Twins tricked the Lords of Death," he mused. "Could we do something similar?"

"Maybe," Izzy breathed. "The K'ex ritual isn't just about substitution. It's about balance. Light and shadow. Sun and moon. Life and death. That's what we're missing. We need to reinforce that cycle, reestablish the cosmic balance," Izzy said. "Not fight against it."

"Exactly. The ritual should focus on correcting an imbalance in the universe. Druidic rituals also focus on the eternal cycle," Aedan offered. "The wheel of the year, the cycle of seasons—death and rebirth. Perhaps we can use druid rituals to reinforce the natural cycle and establish balance between the underworld and this one."

I raised my head. "That's what I did. In the cave," I interjected weakly.

Everyone turned to stare at me.

"That could work." Zen nodded slowly. "We combine the K'ex ritual with a druidic circle of protection to bind Niki and myself to the physical realm."

"And we use an offering to entice Hun-Came," Izzy added. "But instead of offering blood to feed him, we offer it to strengthen the cycle he's trying to break."

"Then it's decided. I'll offer myself as the substitute,"

Zen said firmly. "Part of me is already in Xibalba. I can use that connection. Combined with my connection to Niki I can give Hun-Came what he wants—submission. Two souls for the price of one. He won't be able to resist."

"I don't understand."

Zen reached for my hand. "Aedan will bind us to this world while we negotiate with Hun-Came."

"No," I protested. "It's too dangerous. You don't understand how powerful he is. It won't work."

He entwined his fingers with mine, the simple touch sending warmth through my body. "Do you trust me?"

"Of course, I do."

"Then trust me on this." His gaze held mine, unwavering. His voice softened. "Our connection is stronger than Hun-Came's claim on either of us."

As I stared into his eyes, the rest of the world faded until there was only the two of us. "Okay," I said after a long moment. "But I need you to promise me something."

"Anything." He caught my hand and pressed a kiss to my palm, the gesture so tender it made my heart ache.

"Promise me that whatever happens with this ritual, whatever Hun-Came tries to do—he won't destroy us."

"No one, not even a god of death can break what exists between us," he whispered, leaning down until his forehead rested against mine.

I held on to him, to his promise, wanting to believe him, needing to believe him. "Soulmates," I breathed.

"Soulmates," he repeated, his fingers once again intertwining with mine.

Aedan cleared his throat loudly. "Sorry to interrupt," he said, his Irish lilt more pronounced than usual. "But as my Nan used to say: 'What's sealed in love must be protected in strength.' If you two are finished making eyes at each other, we should get started, we don't have much time."

CHAPTER THIRTY-THREE

Dusk settled over the jungle, transforming the lush green canopy into tangled shadows. Around our hastily built camp, the others argued about our next steps, their voices rising and falling like the sounds of the forest.

"The question," Zen said, his voice still hoarse from his near-death experience, "is where to perform the ritual once we have the supplies."

Izzy frowned, arranging and rearranging small stones in a pattern only she understood. "We should return to the cenote. The entrance to Xibalba is there. Liminal spaces make crossing between worlds easier."

"That's precisely why we shouldn't go back," Aedan countered. "If the boundaries are already thin there, Hun-Came's influence will be stronger."

"But the ritual requires—"

"Caves and cenotes are powerful places," Zen acknowledged. "But they're also dangerous. The physical and spiritual worlds overlap there, yes, but that means Hun-Came can reach Niki more easily."

"I vote for outside," Aedan said firmly. "Under the sky, surrounded by living trees and earth. That's where druids draw their power."

"The ritual is Mayan, not Celtic," Izzy protested.

"Aye, but we're combining traditions, aren't we?" Aedan pointed out. "Outside is where life thrives. Hun-Came is a Lord of Death—he is weakest where life is strongest."

"He's right," Zen said softly. "We need every advantage we can get."

"In the cenote, we'd be on his territory," Aedan added. "Out here, he's the visitor, not us. Out here, we can carve protective runes into the trees, create a circle of life energy to contain and direct the ritual."

"Good point. We can conduct the ritual out here, but we need the packs which are still at the bottom of the waterfall," Zen said, his amber eyes reflecting the last rays of sunlight. "Everything we need for the ritual—the copal, the obsidian mirrors, the ceremonial herbs—it's all down there."

Franco snorted, cleaning his gun with methodical precision. "And I suppose you want us to go back into that death trap to get them?"

"We can't conduct the ritual without them."

"I will go," Ulices replied.

Aedan, who had been whittling a piece of wood, pushed himself to his feet. "You'll need help. There are six packs." He looked over at Franco expectantly.

Franco's hands stilled. He stared at the guide for a long moment before cursing under his breath. "Fine. I will help. But we go now, and we don't linger."

I closed my eyes, the voices around me fading as a strange sensation washed over me. The world seemed to shift, colors becoming more vibrant even behind my closed lids, sounds growing more distant. When I opened my eyes again, I was no longer in the jungle clearing.

***

I stood in a place of mist and shadow, neither Xibalba nor the world of the living. The familiar pull of the night surrounded me, the whisper of the earth beneath my feet both comforting and unsettling. Moonlight filtered through the mist, casting an ethereal glow over everything. Here, I could feel the pulse of life in the soil and the slow breath of death in the air—balanced, as they should be.

"Your friends conspire against us."

The voice seeped into my bones resonating with ancient power. Hun-Came's presence coalesced from the mist, not fully corporeal but unmistakable—bones gleaming with an inner light, eyes burning like dying stars.

"No," I replied, surprised by the steadiness in my voice. "They search for a way to restore balance to the cosmos."

Hun-Came's laughter was like stones grinding against each other. "Balance? Is that what they told you? There is no balance, little vessel. There is only power and those too weak to seize it."

He circled me, a predator assessing its prey. "You have become such a disappointment. I ask only for freedom to travel in your world. In exchange, I offer you a taste of my power—power you cannot even fully comprehend."

His skeletal fingers brushed my cheek, leaving a trail of cold fire in their wake. "Yet, you refuse to accept. I know you taste it, hunger for it, yet you deny yourself. Deny what you can become. Deny what you are."

As he spoke, something changed in the air around us. A sweetness filled my nostrils—cloying, thick, intoxicating. The death of a thousand souls on my tongue, metallic and honeyed at once. My skin tingled as if a million tiny sparks danced across its surface.

"Feel it," Hun-Came whispered, his voice suddenly intimate. "Feel what could be yours."

Power flooded my veins like liquid fire, burning away the weakness that had plagued me since our escape from the cenote. I gasped, my back arching as the sensation intensified—as if I'd opened my veins and injected Hun-Came's power directly into my body, feeding on death itself. Every nerve ending sang with dark ecstasy, every cell in my body hummed with energy.

Gods, it felt good. Better than good—it felt right, as if a piece of me that had been sleeping was finally awakening. The world around me sharpened, colors more vivid, scents more powerful. I could sense the life force of every creature within miles—birds roosting in trees, jaguars prowling the underbrush, insects burrowing in the soil—all of them suddenly luminous to my enhanced senses.

And I could end them with a thought. Just reach out and pluck those fragile threads of existence, feel them snap between my fingers, absorb their essence into myself...

"Yes," Hun-Came purred, his voice silken with approval. "You feel it now. The truth of what you are."

My mouth watered, my body trembled with need. I couldn't deny it—I craved this power with an intensity that frightened me. It called to something primordial within me, something that had always been there, waiting.

"Take it," Hun-Came urged. "Embrace what you were born to be. Your sister understood—she was weak. But you..."

The mention of Nayla sent a jolt through me, like cold water on my overheated skin.

"What about my sister?" I demanded, the seductive fog of power receding just enough for me to think.

Hun-Came's skeletal grin widened. "Ah, she never told you? She was weak and foolish."

"You're lying," I whispered, but doubt crept in. Had Nayla faced this same temptation? Had she died because of it?

"Am I?" Hun-Came circled me again, his robes brushing against me like cobwebs.

The mist around us thickened, and Hun-Came's form began to fade. "Remember this feeling, little vessel. Remember what awaits you if you embrace your true nature. Because when your friends fail—and they will fail—this power will be the only thing standing between you and oblivion."

***

As suddenly as it had come, the vision dissolved. I found myself back in the jungle clearing, on my knees, gasping for breath. Zen knelt before me, his hands on my shoulders, his eyes wide with concern.

"Niki? Are you okay?"

I nodded, unable to find words. The phantom taste of death lingered on my tongue, the ghostly sensation of power still humming beneath my skin. Even as it faded, I mourned its loss.

And that terrified me more than Hun-Came himself. "Hun-Came knows about the ritual."

"What did he say?" Izzy asked, her voice tight with apprehension.

I looked up at the circle of worried faces surrounding me. How could I tell them that part of me wanted to accept his offer? That even now, a traitorous voice inside me whispered I was making a mistake?

"He..." I swallowed hard. "He knows what we're planning. And he mentioned Nayla. Said she faced him too, before she died."

Zen's grip on my shoulders tightened. "He's trying to manipulate you. To make you doubt yourself."

"It's working," I admitted, my voice barely audible.

Zen reached for my hands and pressed them against his chest as he crouched beside me, his eyes intense. "Listen to me, Niki. Death gods are masters of temptation."

"It felt so real," I whispered. "So right."

"Of course, it did," Zen said softly. "Power always does. That's why it corrupts so easily."

I looked into his eyes, searching for judgment but finding only understanding. "What if I'm not strong enough to resist him?"

"You won't have to be," he promised. "That's why we're doing the ritual. That's why we're here."

Franco and Ulices exchanged a look I couldn't interpret.

Franco adjusted his headlamp and jerked his head in the direction of the cave. "Let's get the fucking packs. The sooner we perform this ritual and get the hell out of here, the better."

Aedan and Ulices nodded. My eyes followed them as they disappeared into the cave entrance.

Zen stayed by my side, his presence a comforting

anchor. But even with him there, I couldn't shake the memory of how it had felt to taste Hun-Came's power—or the terrible fear that when the time came, I might not want to let it go.

I sat in the clearing, watching the entrance to the cave, waiting for the men to return with the packs. The jungle hummed with life around me, but I felt disconnected from it all—suspended between worlds. Zen's hand rested in mine, warm and solid, yet I couldn't shake the lingering cold fire of Hun-Came's touch.

Was it real? The power I'd felt in that vision—the intoxicating rush, the sense of rightness that had washed over me. Part of me hoped it was just an illusion, a trick played by a desperate god. But deep down, I knew better.

It had felt like coming home.

I closed my eyes briefly, ashamed of the thought. I could not allow myself to travel down that dangerous path.

My gaze drifted to Zen, who sat watching the stars appear one by one in the darkening sky. The thread connecting us seemed to pulse in time with our heartbeats. I loved him—had always loved him, even before I knew what that meant. But was love enough? Was it strong enough to counter the ancient power Hun-Came offered?

Nayla's face flashed in my mind. My sister—my twin—the other half of my soul. Even in memory, her radiance was almost painful to look at. She had always been the bright one, the daughter of the sun, and people had been drawn to her like moths to flame. I had loved her fiercely, had been so proud of her brilliance, her effortless charm, the way she could light up any room just by entering it.

But God, how it had hurt sometimes.

I had told myself I was content to exist in her shadow, to be the moon to her sun, reflecting her light but never generating my own. But late at night, in the quiet moments I'd never admitted to anyone, I had wondered what it would be like to be seen first, to be the one people remembered, to shine with my own light instead of always being "Nayla's sister."

The guilt of that jealousy still sat heavy in my chest. How could I have envied her when I loved her so much? How could both feelings exist in the same heart? But they had. They did. Even now, with her gone, I found myself caught between pride and envy, between grief and an awful, shameful relief that I no longer had to live in her shadow—followed immediately by crushing guilt for even thinking such a thing.

I missed her. I loved her. And I had resented her.

All of it was true. All of it hurt.

Hun-Came's words echoed in my mind: *"She was weak and foolish."* Had Nayla faced this same choice? Had she died because she turned away from what Hun-Came offered? Or because she embraced it?

I shivered, remembering how it had felt to sense the life force of every creature around me—to know I could extinguish those lights with a mere thought. The power had called to something deep within me, something that had always been there, waiting. Hija de la luna, the moon daughter. The child of night and shadow.

Hun-Came understood that part of me. He saw the darkness I'd always tried to hide—even from myself.

I looked again at Zen, at his familiar face now marked by his journey to Xibalba and back. He'd given part of himself to save me. He'd promised that nothing would destroy the connection between us, no matter what Hun-Came tried.

But what if I'm the one who severs the connection?

The thought terrified me. What if, when the moment came, I chose power over love? What if the darkness within me was stronger than my connection to Zen? What if my nature as the hija de la luna meant I had always been destined to be claimed by Hun-Came?

As twilight deepened into true night, I wondered if I was strong enough to resist becoming what Hun-Came wanted me to be—if what he said was true. Perhaps, this need for power was what I had always craved, and only now was I finally awakening to my true nature.

I closed my eyes and held onto the connection that bound Zen and me. I clung to it desperately, hoping it would be enough to lead me back from the edge when the time came. Hoping my love for him and my sister would be stronger than the seductive whisper of power that still echoed in my bones.

But in the silence of my heart, I wasn't sure. And that uncertainty terrified me more than Hun-Came himself.

CHAPTER THIRTY-FOUR

After Ulices, Aedan, and Franco returned with our packs, we set up the tents and rolled out the sleeping bags, but none of us slept. We sat in tense silence under a swollen moon, anticipation crackling between us like the wood burning in our fire.

I inhaled deeply, breathing in the scent of smoke, lush vegetation, and warm earth. I was grateful to be away from the cave and Hun-Came's sacred pool. Aedan had created a protective circle around our campsite, scratching runes and carving Ogham letters into whittled branches that he staked at each of the four quarters. Izzy had followed behind him with a compass, tying scraps of colored cloth—white, yellow, red, and black—to the stakes corresponding with the compass points north, south, east, and west. Druid and Mayan cosmology merging together.

But even surrounded by their protective magic, I could feel Hun-Came's presence coiling tighter around my soul like a serpent preparing to strike. Each breath felt stolen, each heartbeat a countdown to my surrender. The terror wasn't just that I might lose this battle—it was that part of me didn't want to win.

Aedan, Izzy and Zen had decided the ritual would take

place at dawn, the liminal space between night and day, the time of death and rebirth. Until then, we sat silent in the darkness, waiting. Even Hun-Came—who had returned to once again lay claim to my body as his physical vessel—was silent and watchful. His unease was both comforting and distressing.

I pressed my palms against my thighs to stop them from shaking. What if I couldn't resist him when the moment came? What if, when Hun-Came demanded I choose him over everything else—over Zen, over my own life—I said yes?

Izzy brought out the copal from her pack and tossed a handful of the resin onto the flames to purify our ritual space. As the fragrant tree sap perfumed the air with its sweet smoke, I closed my eyes and leaned against Zen, feeling the solid warmth of him at my back.

I now understood I was bound to Zen, much in the same way Hun-Came was bound to me. A connection in which the barrier between self and other was no longer distinct.

My intermingling with Zen completed me in a way I'd never before experienced with anyone. Like the Celtic double spiral, our joining created a perfect balance of opposites, a whole—separate yet inseparable—igniting a flame within me that was both physical and spiritual. When I was with Zen, I could almost forget the darkness clawing at my insides, almost believe I was still wholly myself.

But Hun-Came's pull was becoming impossible to ignore. Each time I surrendered to the death god, it ignited something within me that terrified me with its intensity. Giving in to Hun-Came was like opening a vein and allowing him to feast on me. It was sensual, dangerous, and intoxicating—and I was losing the will to fight it.

"Not much longer," Zen murmured against my ear, his voice tight with tension. His arms wrapped around me, and I could sense his desperate attempt to anchor me to him, to this world, to life itself.

My connection with Zen dimmed as Hun-Came's

encroaching shadow grew stronger.

"What if it's not enough? What if the ritual isn't enough?" I whispered, my voice breaking. "What if I can't—what if I choose him?"

Zen's grip tightened, his fingers digging into my arms as if he could physically hold my soul in place. "You won't. I won't let you."

But we both knew when the moment came, the choice would be mine alone.

Ulices was the first to notice. The full moon began to darken around the edges as if someone were slowly swallowing it. "A lunar eclipse," he hissed.

Hun-Came chuckled, the sound reverberating through my bones. *"I so enjoy playing with mortals. Did you think I would let you attempt this pitiful ritual without providing... atmosphere?"*

Terror crystallized in my chest. He had orchestrated this. The eclipse, the timing—all of it was his design.

Aedan and Izzy exchanged worried looks. Zen's arms tightened around me protectively, but I could feel his heart hammering against my back. "Is that bad?" I asked, though I already knew the answer.

"A lunar eclipse is... powerful," Aedan said, his face turned upward toward the slowly disappearing moon.

"Powerful in a good way or a bad way?" I asked anxiously.

Aedan looked over at me, and I saw my fear reflected in his eyes. "The earth's shadow is blocking the moon from the sun's light, allowing the boundaries between realms to thin, giving supernatural beings access to our world."

My chest constricted as if Hun-Came's fingers were closing around my heart. "So, not good."

"It can be dangerous but..." He paused, struggling to find hope in the situation. "Rituals of transformation and manifestation conducted during a Blood Moon are very potent. That works in our favor."

"Blood Moon?" I asked, though Hun-Came's satisfied purr told me everything I needed to know.

Across from me, Izzy poked the fire with a stick, sending a shower of sparks spiraling upward. "It's called a Blood Moon because the alignment of the Earth, sun, and moon causes the moon to turn a reddish color. The ancient Maya thought it was a sign of profound cosmic disruption, a message of warfare. During eclipses they conducted rituals of blood sacrifice to appease the gods."

Blood sacrifice. The words echoed in my mind as Hun-Came's presence swelled with anticipation.

"Which is why this is a perfect time for us to conduct the K'ex," Zen said, but I could hear the forced confidence in his voice. He was trying to convince himself as much as me.

"I suspect we'll find out," Izzy replied, her eyes resting on me with cold indifference. "One way or another."

Zen's lips brushed the tender flesh of my neck, and I shivered—part fear, part pleasure, part desperation. "Ignore her," Zen whispered, his breath warm on my skin. "You don't need to worry. The K'ex is going to work."

I wanted to believe him, but as I watched the earth's shadow slowly swallow the moon, I could feel Hun-Came's presence growing stronger with each passing moment. His voice slipped into my head, filled with eager anticipation. *"A blood sacrifice for a Blood Moon. How poetic. Soon, little vessel, you will give me what I desire most—not just your body, but your willing surrender."*

The worst part was that he was right. I could feel my resistance crumbling like sand against the tide. Each breath brought me closer to the moment when I would stop fighting and let him consume me entirely.

"Surrender to me," he whispered seductively. *"We will hunt together and feast on the blood of your friends."*

I squeezed my eyes shut, refusing to listen to him. Instead, I concentrated on the solid feel of Zen's hard body pressed against mine, the heaviness of the iron bangle encircling my wrist like a lifeline, the chirring of the cicadas, the sweet fragrance of copal-infused smoke. I fingered the smooth contours of the jade pendant I wore above my heart and stared into the dancing flames of our fire. Reaching deep into the earth's life-giving energies, I focused on rooting myself firmly in the world of the living.

But even as I fought to stay grounded, I could feel Hun-Came's tendrils wrapping around my soul like thorned vines, drawing tighter with each heartbeat. Voices of lost souls, their whispering growing louder in my ears, as the barrier between the living and the dead thinned.

"I am the daughter of the moon," I whispered. My connection to the moon came to me from my mother, something I knew I could use to counter Hun-Came but the eclipse was blocking my source of strength. The world blurred as I focused all my energy on the moon, on its pulse, its rhythm. I let it wrap around me like a cloak, silencing the voices of the dead by chanting my mother's words. "Teorainn idir dá shaol, críoch idir dá fhód..."

Boundary between two worlds, limit between two realms.

I continued chanting under my breath even as I watched the moon as it slowly traveled into the earth's shadow, darkness crept across the moon's face until it disappeared completely. leaving only the faintest hint of light encircling a black void in a starlit sky.

Minutes, hours, days—I had no idea how long it took, aware only of my mother's magic and the solid warmth of Zen at my back, anchoring me to this world as the earth and moon continued on their inexorable paths.

Blocked from the direct illumination of the sun, the moon could only reflect the earth's light. It hung above us like a wound in the sky, deep crimson and pulsing with otherworldly light. The very air thrummed with supernatural energy.

"It's time." Aedan's voice broke through my almost hypnotic trance.

Aedan handed each of us a dried twig of mistletoe. "Hold this in your hand and let it absorb your fears and doubts."

I offered a final supplication to the druid moon goddess. I called on Ix Chel, the Mayan goddess of the moon, weaver of fates and guardian of childbirth, to guide my path. I invoked Fire Jaguar, asking her to protect my shadow soul on its journey. Then I rose to my feet and accepted the mistletoe from Aedan's hand.

Franco refused to participate, positioning himself at the edge of our circle with his rifle ready, but the rest of us gathered around the fire. The gray smoke spiraled upward toward the red-tinged moon illuminating the predawn darkness. We tossed our mistletoe into the fire and repeated the phrase—Cast away whatever impedes the appearance of light.

But even as the words left my lips, I felt Hun-Came stirring within me, eager and arrogant. *"Cast away your doubts, yes. Accept what you truly are—mine."*

Izzy removed several obsidian mirrors from her pack and placed them around the fire, aligning them with the stakes marking the four directions of our protective circle. She tossed more copal onto the flames and the air shimmered with sacred smoke.

I stood barefoot in front of the fire and inhaled. The piney sweet scent filled my lungs, but even that couldn't wash away the taste of death that coated my tongue. Beside me, Zen pricked his palm with an obsidian blade, letting his blood drip into the flames. "K'u'x la'j—heart of the world, accept this flesh for flesh."

The fire hissed and flared, casting dancing shadows across the obsidian mirrors.

Our eyes met across the flames, and in that moment, I saw everything—his love, his terror of losing me, his willingness to sacrifice anything to save me. The gold in his eyes glowed like embers. His eyes blazed brighter, a desperate beacon in the encroaching darkness.

"I return what was never mine," I said, my voice shaking as I forced the words out. "Take this shadow, not my breath."

For a moment, I thought I saw Fire Jaguar's form outlined in the smoke. The Mayan god had disappeared from my life the moment Hun-Came had taken up residence in my soul. I took comfort in her appearance, clinging to the hope that if Fire Jaguar was here, maybe this ritual could work.

But Hun-Came's response shattered that fragile hope.

"You think to trick me with this pathetic display?" Hun-Came's voice thundered through me, his presence suddenly overwhelming. The fire roared higher, and the obsidian mirrors began to crack under the force of his rage. *"I am Death incarnate! I am the Lord of Xibalba! You cannot banish what you have already welcomed into your very soul!"*

The iron bangle around my wrist grew so hot it burned, but I didn't release it. Instead, I grasped Zen's hand, desperately seeking to share his strength as I fought against Hun-Came's hurricane force.

A slow pulsing sensation began behind my heart, and my skin grew hot like molten sugar dissolving into something scalding yet achingly sweet. This was it—the moment of choice. I could feel Hun-Came gathering his power, preparing to claim me completely.

"I do not welcome you," I said, surprising everyone including myself. The words tore from my throat like shards of glass. "You took what I did not give."

Hun-Came's laughter erupted from my throat, the sound like bones splintering under crushing weight followed by the discordant jangling of bells. *"Lies! You gave your life freely to me, spilling your blood and your life essence as an offering. You may not take back what was freely given. You are a child of the shadows and the night. You crave what I offer. Embrace your true nature. Submit to the dark! Submit to me!"*

The horrible truth was that part of me did want it. I could not deny the seductive pull of sinking into that dark embrace.

"I am no longer willing to be your vessel," I gasped, but

the words felt hollow even as I spoke them.

"*No?*" Hun-Came's voice swelled with arrogance, resonating through the clearing like temple bells. "*You do not choose, little vessel. I do. And I choose…Now.*"

The trees shook with the sounds of thousands of lost souls crying out in the darkness as the cord around my heart constricted, each beat of my pulse a desperate struggle against a crushing weight. My knees buckled as agony tore through my chest—not just pain, but the sensation of being hollowed out from within, my very essence being devoured piece by piece.

I could feel myself breaking apart, my soul fracturing like ice under pressure. The seductive whispers were gone, replaced by Hun-Came revealed in all his terrible glory— ancient, pitiless, hungry. The stench of rotting corpses flooded my nostrils, so overwhelming I retched, bile burning my throat. My vision darkened at the edges as something fundamental inside me began to die, my connection to the world of the living withering like flowers touched by frost.

Zen's anguished cry cut through the supernatural maelstrom. "Niki!"

But I was losing. I could feel my will crumbling, my sense of self dissolving into Hun-Came's overwhelming presence.

Trembling with the effort to remain on my feet, I turned toward Zen. His face was a mask of desperate love and terror, his amber eyes blazing with inner fire as he fought to reach me across the supernatural barrier Hun-Came had erected between us.

"I'm sorry," I whispered to Zen, my voice barely recognizable as my own. The words scraped my throat raw, each syllable a monumental effort as Hun-Came's presence expanded inside me like poison in my veins. My bones felt hollow, brittle as dried kindling. The warmth was leaching from my body, replaced by the infinite cold of the grave. "I can't… I'm not strong enough."

I collapsed against Zen as the fire suddenly burst into a column of shooting flame that reached toward the blood-red moon. The radiant light, hot and binding, shot from the flames like a comet just as the first rays of sunlight touched the dark sky.

A golden quetzal burst forth, its feathers trailing stardust, its cry piercing the night.

Nayla.

Effervescent in life, incandescent in death. My sister spiraled upward, leaving a trail of golden fire in her wake, more beautiful and terrible than I had ever seen her.

I felt Hun-Came's attention shift suddenly, his grip on me loosening as his interest was caught by this new presence. "*What is this?*" he hissed, but I could hear the greed in his voice. "*Two souls for the price of one—twin souls, bound by blood. Twin souls—dark and light, sun and moon, life and death.*" His avarice overrode his caution. "*Yes!*" Hun-Came sizzled with satisfaction. "*One wahy that has crossed death's realm and escaped my grasp—one still tethered to flesh.*"

Nayla's wahy spiraled higher, and Hun-Came's attention followed like a predator tracking prey. As his focus shifted away from me, I felt air rush back into my lungs, felt the crushing weight on my chest ease just enough for me to draw breath.

Hun-Came's grip on my wahy loosened as Nayla's radiant spirit soul called to him, offering herself as a prize. His arrogance and greed overcoming his caution as he reached for her.

But the moment he released my wahy to claim Nayla's, the trap was sprung. My sister had become something more than human in death, her wahy transformed by her passage through the underworld. She wasn't offering herself as a victim—she was offering herself as a prison. As Hun-Came's essence flowed into her spirit soul, she began to drag him deeper into Xibalba, away from the world of the living.

"Now!" Aedan shouted as the sun's rays began to lighten the sky.

The gold in Zen's eyes blazed like molten metal as he grabbed my hand. With one quick slice of his knife, he drew blood from both our palms, pressing them together with desperate strength.

Our blood mingled and the world exploded.

Lightning without thunder split the sky—not above us, but through us. I screamed as the flash tore through my body like a blade of pure light, every nerve ending set ablaze. The sensation of being split in half was literal—I felt my soul cleaving, Hun-Came's darkness on one side, something else entirely on the other.

The pain was exquisite, unbearable, transformative—like being reborn through agony itself. I could feel my wahy being pulled in two directions—part of it still trapped with Hun-Came, part of it fighting to return to my physical body.

Hun-Came's fury erupted as he realized what was happening. "*No!*" Hun-Came raged as he realized the deception. "*You will not bind me to death's realm! I will not be contained!*" His voice detonated from within me, my ribcage vibrating with the force of his rage.

But it was too late. Like a supernova, Nayla's wahy exploded into a violent ball of flame. Hun-Came's essence poured out of my shadow soul like black smoke, drawn inexorably toward the golden quetzal. My sister's luminous form began to sink rather than rise as a final gust of wind swept through the tree canopy, shaking leaves and silencing the cries of the dead.

"I don't understand," I whispered, tears streaming down my face as I watched my sister's shadow soul fade in the lightening sky.

"The Hero Twins of the Popol Vuh," Zen said, his voice hoarse with exhaustion and relief. "Hunahpu and Xblanque. They tricked the Lords of Death by substituting themselves for each other. This K'ex is a ritual of substitution—Nayla's wahy for yours. Hun-Came anchored himself to the living world through you, but Nayla's wahy belongs to the realm of the dead. As soon as he accepted her as his vessel, he lost his connection to this world."

I stared up at the rising sun feeling a complex swirl of emotions. Grief, because I was losing my sister all over again. Relief, because Hun-Came's stranglehold on my soul was finally broken. But also, something else—a strange, hollow ache where the shadow parts of myself used to be.

"Will I...?" I started to ask, then stopped. How do you ask if you'll still be yourself when part of your soul has been torn away? Though it wasn't my connection to Hun-Came, I was grieving. Rather it was the aching loss of my bond to Nayla—a connection forged since the moment of our birth, one that even her death hadn't severed.

Zen seemed to understand. He pulled me closer. "You're still you," he whispered against my hair.

As Nayla's form disappeared, taking Hun-Came's raging essence with her into whatever realm awaited them, I felt something I hadn't experienced in months: complete, undiluted peace. The weight on my chest lifted. For the first time since this nightmare began, I could breathe without feeling like I was drowning in shadows.

I clung to Zen in the aftermath, watching the moon slowly return to silver then white as the sun rose in the east. The power of the moon—not death, but transformation. Not ending, but change.

Death wasn't the opposite of life—it was part of its cycle. The moon didn't steal the sun's light—it borrowed it, transformed it, and gave it back when darkness fell. And the dead weren't gone—they lived on in the love they'd left behind.

LISA DIETRICH

EPILOGUE

Six Months Later

I rolled over in my bed and curled my body around the man sleeping next to me, enjoying the warmth of the California summer sun shining through the open window. The constant whisper of seductive darkness was gone. I had reached deep, past Hun-Came's seduction, past the intoxicating rush of stolen life, to the place where my true nature dwelled.

My place was in the light not the shadows, next to the man I loved.

Zen stirred beside me, his arm tightening around my waist as consciousness slowly returned. Even in sleep, he kept me anchored to the world of the living—though I no longer needed the lifeline.

"Morning," he murmured against my shoulder, his voice rough with sleep. The gold in his eyes caught the sunlight streaming through the curtains, warm and alive and completely mine.

"Good morning," I whispered back, marveling at how ordinary the words sounded. How beautifully, perfectly ordinary.

The nightmares had stopped after the first month. The phantom taste of grave dirt had faded. The iron bangle around my wrist—which I still wore, though more as a reminder than protection—no longer burned with supernatural heat. I was, for the first time, in longer than I cared to remember, completely and utterly myself.

Well, mostly myself.

I touched the jade pendant at my throat, feeling the familiar pang of loss that always accompanied thoughts of Nayla. Part of me would always ache for my twin sister, for the connection that had been severed when she dragged Hun-Came into the depths of Xibalba. But even that grief had transformed over time, becoming something I could carry rather than something that carried me away.

"You're thinking about Nayla," Zen said softly, reading the shift in my expression.

I nodded, not trusting my voice. Even after six months, talking about Nayla was difficult. But Zen had learned to navigate my grief with the same careful attention he'd used to help me resist Hun-Came's influence.

He pressed a gentle kiss to my temple.

Nayla had sacrificed herself not just for me, but for everyone. If Hun-Came had succeeded in fully possessing me, using my wahy as a permanent bridge between worlds, there was no telling how many lives would have been lost.

"I dream about her sometimes," I admitted, something I'd never told anyone before. "Not nightmares—good dreams. She's... happy. Free. I can feel it, even across whatever divide separates us now."

Zen's arms tightened around me. "And you? Are you happy?"

I turned in his arms, studying his face in the morning light. The sharp angles of his cheekbones, the way his dark hair fell across his forehead, the pattern of scars along his shoulder and chest. Every detail was precious to me now, no longer overshadowed by darkness or the threat of loss.

"Yes."

"What about you?" I asked. "Any regrets?"

His laugh was warm and genuine. "Never."

"I love you," I said simply, the words carrying all the weight of everything we'd survived together.

"And I love you," he replied, pressing his forehead against mine. "Every part of you. Light and shadow, past and present, exactly as you are."

LISA DIETRICH

A Note to My Readers,

Thank you for joining Niki on her journey through the Guatemalan jungle. When I first set out to write this story, I thought I was simply crafting a romantasy that would blend my love of fantasy and romance with my background in anthropology.

But somewhere along the way, this book surprised me. What emerged wasn't just a story about ancient gods and dangerous love—it became a story about sisters. About the bonds that transcend logic, the fierce protectiveness that drives us into dark jungles both literal and metaphorical, and the lengths we'll go to for the people we love most.

I wrote much of this book thinking about my own sister, who had a wicked sense of humor and would have absolutely roasted me for some of the steamier scenes while secretly loving every page. She won't be able to read this story—cancer took her from us before I could finish it— but I like to think she would have gotten a kick out of seeing our shared love of sarcasm and stubborn determination reflected in these characters.

If this story moved you, made you laugh, or kept you turning pages late into the night, I would be incredibly grateful if you could take a moment to leave a review. Reviews help other readers discover books, and they mean the world to authors like me who are still pinching themselves that people actually want to read the stories we've dreamed up.

Thank you for reading, for believing in the magic of a good story, and for understanding that sometimes the most powerful forces in any world—supernatural or otherwise— are the bonds between the people we love.

With all my gratitude,
Lisa Dietrich

LISA DIETRICH

ACKNOWLEDGEMENTS

Writing a book involves many lonely hours of researching, writing and revising, but it is never a solitary endeavor. I am deeply indebted to my stalwart sisters in literature, Amy Strommer and Kathy Burke whose insight and encouragement shaped this book from its earliest drafts—including that crucial opening line. To Sue Armstrong and her discerning eye, thank you for your unwavering support, friendship, and superior knowledge of grammar. To Mike McDermott who also appreciates a well-turned phrase and good grammar, thank you for reading this one.

A very special shout-out to Amelia Merryman who helped me choose the perfect name for Aedan and to Charlotte Merryman for introducing me to the genre of Romantasy. To Kris Palouda and the Barbie Book Club, thank you for championing this new author.

Emily's World of Design transformed my vision into the stunning cover art gracing this book. Toni Kelly polished my prose with her skilled editing. Melissa Keir has been supportive and encouraging. Working with InkSpell Publishing has been an absolute joy.

Finally, to my husband John, my companion through every adventure—none of this would be possible without you.

LISA DIETRICH

Don't Miss Out on the First Book!!

In the Silence of Darkenss

Some bloodlines can't be outrun.

Niki Balam traded her Mayan father's ancient stories for law books and logic—until terrifying nightmares about her twin sister force her into the depths of the Guatemalan jungle.

At the remote archaeological site of Choja q'eq, her sister Nayla has disappeared, leaving behind only questions and the unsettling presence of Zen Cazares. Golden-eyed and dangerous, Zen is everything Niki's ordered world has taught her to avoid—wild, untamed, and carrying secrets that could unravel everything she believes about reality.

But when supernatural forces begin hunting them through the jungle and a malevolent shaman rises to claim an ancient power, Niki realizes Zen might be the only one who can help her navigate a world where ancient Mayan gods still demand blood and sacrifice.

The Mayan god of death Hun-Came is stirring, and his hunger—for power, for blood—will not be denied.

Join author Lisa Dietrich as she weaves a tale of danger, hungry gods, and death magic, that draw the reader through the jungles of Guatemala and into the underworld. Fans of Sarah Maas'-"Court of Throne and Roses" series and Jennifer L. Armentrout's - "From Blood and Ash" series will love Ms. Dietrich's new supernatural series.

EXCERPT

"Keep moving," Zen said softly as the sound of rustling leaves grew louder and more aggressive, the monkeys turning to face us as we passed like tracking sensors. "We'll head that way," he indicated the direction by shifting his eyes to the left. "Don't stop," Zen cautioned. "Just keep moving."

A large red howler monkey suddenly leaped from his perch to another tree directly in front of me—but the movement wasn't quite right. It didn't arc naturally but jerked through the air as if pulled by invisible strings. I clutched my machete with sweaty palms and locked eyes with him. In their depths, I saw something else looking back—something ancient and hungry.

The monkey rocked back and forth in agitation, its movements mechanical, puppeted. It let out a short warning bark that sounded more like the blare of a foghorn than a monkey.

The low guttural roar sent shivers up my spine, ice spreading through my veins despite the tropical heat. "Zen?" My voice shook, barely audible even to myself.

The red howler thrust out his thick neck and bellowed a second warning, setting off a chain reaction among the monkeys until the jungle was filled with the harsh grating bellows, pummeling us with noise—but beneath that sound, I heard words: "Death walks."

My eyes darted back and forth as I warily watched the agitated monkeys, now certain they were vessels for something else—Hun-Came's eyes in the jungle, his voice in their unnatural calls.

The loud roaring reached a crescendo as the emboldened animals began to drop from the trees onto the ground surrounding us. Their fur rippled like liquid, bodies reforming as they landed—larger, more dangerous, less monkey and more nightmare.

Zen whirled around to face me, his face pale beneath his tan. "Run!"

ABOUT THE AUTHOR

Lisa Dietrich holds a Ph.D. in Anthropology, which means she's professionally qualified to explain why ancient civilizations are infinitely more interesting than whatever is currently trending on social media. When she's not busy debating the finer points of Pre-Columbian mythology with her extremely patient husband, she writes steamy romance novels.

www.ingramcontent.com/pod-product-compliance
Lightning Source LLC
Chambersburg PA
CBHW052019240626
47153CB00006B/1881